TENDING TYLER

LONE STAR SERIES
BOOK 1

JODI PAYNE

BA TORTUGA

Tending Tyler

Edited by LC Hinson

Cover illustration by AJ Corza
http://www.seeingstatic.com/
Cover content is for illustrative purposes only and any person depicted on the cover is a model.

ISBN: 978-1-951011-47-5

Published by Tygerseye Publishing, LLC, May, 2021
Printed in the USA

Tending Tyler

Lone Star Series, Book 1

by Jodi Payne and BA Tortuga

Bartender Tyler McKeehan feels like his whole life is on hold. All he does is work and sleep because he doesn't know how to move on with his day to day after the shocking loss of his best friend. When he meets Matt at the bar where he works in New York though, he thinks he might have found someone who can nudge him out of his rut. The cowboy seems to live on fast forward, but at the same time this kind, generous man makes Tyler feel wanted and safe.

Ranch owner Matthew Whitehead is just in New York for a visit. But when he runs into Tyler at Les's Bar, he knows right away that Tyler is special. Matt's family thinks he makes snap decisions, and they worry about him, but he knows what he wants, and even after just a few days he's willing to fight to keep Tyler in his life. When Matt has to head back to Texas, he asks Tyler to come visit him and meet his kids. Soon.

Tyler doesn't know if he can pick up and go to Texas, but he misses Matt's affection and calming presence, so when life gets overwhelming, he makes the call. Between Matt's huge, boisterous family, his children, his busy ranch, and the vast differences between New York City and Texas, Tyler wonders every day if he should go back to his old life. Matt is determined to keep Tyler right where he is, but can they overcome the odds against them and make a new life together?

The books in this duet are stand-alones and can be read in any order.

THE ON THE RANCH SERIES

Tending Tyler

Roped In

Diamonds in the Rough

Outfoxed

These are all stand-alone novels
and can be read in any order.

To our wives.

1

Four to closing was a long shift at the bar, especially on a weekend, but Tyler didn't mind it. He was busy all night long, and he usually went home with good tip money in his pocket and just exhausted enough that he could actually sleep. Sometimes he slept so long he'd get up, shower, and go right back to the bar for his next shift.

Busy was good. The busier the better.

He was on with Peter tonight, and they had it handled. They'd been working together so long they didn't have to think, so they moved around each other easily and got the job done.

"Need ice!" Peter called out before disappearing through the swinging door next to the bar.

He gave Peter a nod and kept making drinks like it was the only thing left in the world. Which it kind of was.

Margarita. Bloody Mary. Cosmo. Three daiquiris—peach, strawberry mango. Five beers.

He caught sight of a cowboy hat and pulled Dex a Coke. Dex was the boss's best friend's guy, and the man tipped like a dream. It served him well to keep the guy happy.

Tyler ran it over, shocked as hell to come face-to-face with a silver fox that was, unquestioningly Not Dex.

It threw him, and it took him a second to snap out of it. He set the Coke down on the bar, blinking at the stranger. "Hey." Friend of Dex's maybe? Not too many cowboy hats walked in here. "Sorry. What can I get you?"

"Coors and a shot of Cuervo, please, sir." The voice was low, gravelly, and pure southern. God, that was strangely ominous.

"Gold or Silver?"

"Silver, please." He got a smile, a nod, the man holding his gaze.

"You got it." Ominous, but polite. Kind smile. Taller than Dex.

Tyler danced around Peter who was dumping ice from two big buckets into the freezer. Coors was on tap, and he got that started, then reached for the Cuervo. They were going through the tequila tonight for sure. Probably the warm weather.

Well, not this guy. This guy just looked like a tequila guy. He poured the shot generously.

"Coors and Cuervo." He set them down on the bar. "Running a tab?"

"Yessir." A card was handed over, easy as you please. "Y'all are busy as a one-legged man at a butt-kicking competition."

That made him grin. "I like that. Yes, we are. Fridays are our busiest night usually." He glanced at the card out of habit, clipped it to a bill and wrote 'Coors/Cuervo (Sil)' on it. "Where are you from?" *Matthew*. The card said the man's name was Matthew. Could be Matt or Matty, maybe.

"Central Texas—between Austin and Houston. I got me

a ranch there." One huge, square hand was offered to him. "Matthew Whitehead. Pleased."

"Tyler McKeehan. Also pleased." He shook, the hand solid and strong in his. "Welcome to New York."

"Can we get—" The guy sitting next to Matthew tapped his glass.

"Sure, no problem." He poured a couple of refills. He was about to ask Matthew what brought him to the city, typical bartender small-talk type stuff, when one of them stopped him.

"Aren't you Tyler?"

"I...yes?" He thought they looked familiar too, but he couldn't remember where he'd met them.

"We thought so, we kept saying we thought you were... Uh. Yeah. Sorry about Will. We were so shocked."

Will.

Tyler's stomach twisted, and his heart started to pound. He tried to put their drinks down on the bar with shaking hands and missed, one of them dumping back toward him, but the other tipped toward Matthew.

Matthew caught it, but the glass stem shattered in the man's big hand. He handed Tyler the top part of the glass with blood already starting to drip. "Point me toward the washroom, if you would."

"Shit. Shit, I'm sorry. Fuck." He stared at the broken glass and then at the blood in Matthew's hand. God. Not more blood.

"Whoa. Ty?" Peter stepped around him with a towel and handed it to Matthew. "You okay, sir? How bad is it?"

"It's fine, y'all. No worries. I'll wash it off, and we'll be good as gold." Dark gray eyes landed on him, so quiet, so calm. "You okay, honey?"

"Yeah." *No*. He looked away; those eyes were strangely

comforting but they also wanted honesty. "All good. I'm so sorry."

"Men's room is around to the left." Peter pointed in that direction and cleaned up the bar.

"Sorry. I'll get you guys new drinks. I'm sorry."

Peter stopped him. "It's okay. I've got it, Ty."

"Oh. Yeah, okay." He stood there for a second, dumbly, not sure what to do with himself.

"Go make sure the cowboy is okay, man. Antibiotic cream, bandage." Peter offered him a super quick hug. "Breathe. Go."

"Right. I'm good. Got it." Because that wasn't embarrassing or anything. He stopped by the office First Aid kit and pulled out a couple of Band-Aids, some gauze, and a tube of Neosporin, then headed for the men's room.

Matthew was in there, a chunk of glass on the counter, paper towels jammed in his palm. He looked up as Tyler walked in. "Hey, there. I don't suppose y'all have a tube of superglue?"

"Superglue." Tyler dropped everything he'd brought on the counter and blinked at Matthew again. Did he hear that right? "Superglue? I don't know. I can check the office. Do you need stitches? I can call..."

"I don't, no. I just need a little glue, honey, to push the edges together, and I'll be right as rain."

"Okay... I'll be right back." Superglue. Seriously? Tyler jogged to the office and dug through the boss's desk. Les's drawers were neatly organized and he was making a mess—he'd apologize later—but he found a brand-new tube in a little cubby in the top drawer.

Wow. Right on. He rushed back to the men's room with it. "Superglue. I can't believe it."

"Good deal. I got my smart hand, so I'll need you to open the glue for me, okay?"

"Oh. Sorry. Sure." *Wake up, Ty, the man needs some help here.* He used the little tricky cap to open the tube. "You got this?" His hands had stopped shaking, but he wasn't sure anybody should be trusting him with anything right now.

"I got this, thank you, sir." Matthew gave him a grin. "Don't beat yourself up, huh? It was my bad."

"No. No, that was definitely my fault." He covered the bloody shard of glass with a paper towel and threw it out, willing his hands not to start shaking again, then cleaned up the counter. "Shaky hands. Totally on me." He just hadn't heard Will's name in a while. Every time he thought he'd put that awful image out of his mind, someone would say something, remind him, and he was staring at a bloody bathtub again.

"Sounds like someone gave you a fright." Matthew cleaned the blood off and dripped the glue into the meat of his hand then pushed the flap down. Sweat popped out on the man's cheeks, and a low sound escaped.

"Sort of." Matthew had obviously done this a few times, but that glue had to burn. "How about I get you another shot?"

"I think that would be a fine idea, yes. If you don't mind." He got another of those strange, wonderful smiles.

"I'm on it." He dashed out of the bathroom, but stopped and ducked his head back in. "Anyone ever tell you that you have a great smile?"

It wasn't until he'd left again that he realized Matthew might think he was flirting, and that just made this whole evening even more fucking awkward.

"Is he okay?" Peter asked as Tyler pulled the tequila off the shelf. "Are you?"

"He superglued his hand. Superglue. He glued the cut together." Tyler shook his head. "Craziest thing ever." He avoided the question about himself, he just didn't know. He still felt anxious.

"Is that for him?"

"Yeah, on me." The whole night would be on him.

"Good man. Here he comes. Breathe."

Matthew seemed to take up the entire room, somehow, sucking the air out of it. Jeans, a white button-down, huge silver buckle. And that hat. It was like a costume, except you could tell it wasn't.

How was he supposed to breathe?

"I made it a double." He sat the glass down on the bar carefully, sliding it toward the cowboy.

"Thank you, sir." Matthew lifted his shot in salute, then knocked it back, humming deep in his chest.

"Not one of my better nights. I'm sure that's not the kind of souvenir you wanted to bring back from New York."

The couple that had asked about Will was gone...could this night get any worse? Les would probably hear about that.

Matthew winked at him, and he got to see that smile again. "No worries, honey. Seriously. It's a little cut. I don't suppose I could get me a Coke? If I don't slow down, y'all will have to roll me out of here at last call."

Matthew kept calling him "honey". And it didn't feel weird. Which was...well, weird.

"You mean a Coke-Coke or like a Dr Pepper or something-Coke?" Thank you, Dex. That little bit of regional knowledge had upped his bartender game with some out-of-towners.

Jesus, that smile just got warmer. "Y'all have Dr Pepper? Because I'd love that."

That felt good, it made up for ruining the guy's night a little. "We do. Sit tight." They kept it in cans because it wasn't hugely popular, but Dex drank it like it was going out of style so there was always some cold in the fridge.

He grabbed a can, having a look around the bar to see if Peter needed help. It must be late because it had cleared out some and there were a number of empty seats at the bar. Peter was actually doing some restocking.

"One Dr Pepper." He opened it for Matthew and poured it over a few ice cubes in a tall glass. He seemed to have relaxed enough not to spill this too.

"You rock. Thank you. I need to be able to find my hotel room again, so I have to pace myself some."

"Oh, we're experts around here at getting people rides back to their hotels. No worries." He winked at Matthew. "So what brings you here? Not here, like the bar...men don't usually wander into the bar for no reason...but here. To the city."

Well, that was articulate. Jesus, maybe he needed a drink. He glanced at the clock. Nope, not close enough to closing yet.

"You got to promise not to laugh."

Oh, that was intriguing.

"I'll guess. You do a drag show in Daisy Dukes." Tyler grinned and leaned on the bar. "No?"

"I am not the drag type, unfortunately. It stains the beard. I have been made up, but it's not why I'm here." Matthew chuckled softly, and he thought that was a blush. "I am a big reader, believe it or not, and I came to BookExpo America. It's what I do for vacation every year. I get enough books for me, my girls, and the little library van that goes from ranch to ranch."

Oh, wow. That was so...sweet. And kind. And it was so

wholesome it hurt. "Books. I was definitely not expecting that." He wasn't expecting the blush either. He smiled back. "Not exactly the rough and tumble cowboy image."

"No, I know, right? Still, it is what it is, and I shipped my first two boxes this afternoon." Matthew sipped his drink, licked his mustache. "So, are you a reader?"

"Well, I read. I don't know what makes a reader."

"I guess if you like it? I mean, I know lots of folks that never read a book." Matthew chuckled softly, the look suddenly wicked. "I'm not sure my brother knows how to read."

Tyler laughed. "I like to read. I'm slow. I tend to read in chunks, but I read. I like those detective books about serial killers, and mysteries. And I like books about people and how they...get through things. Like rowers at the World War Two Olympics. Stuff like that."

"I get that. I love thrillers, histories, spy novels, westerns—hell, I like a good racy romance, too. I live on three thousand acres, so I read at night a lot, while the TV is on." He got a wink. "My daddy tried to convince me to whittle instead, but I never could make anything fancier than a square."

"Three thousand acres? I don't even have three thousand feet." He laughed. "I'm not sure I have three hundred. Wow."

"Yeah, I have a decent-sized ranch—I raise Beefmasters and Herefords, along with cutting horses. We got goats and chickens too, but they're not money-makers."

"We...?" Tyler was a bartender; he paid attention. Matthew wasn't wearing a ring. "Oh, you said you had girls, right?"

"I do. I have two—eight and ten. My wife died six years ago." Matthew didn't look away from him, at all. "And yeah. I know this is a gay bar. I swing both ways."

He nodded, returning the look. "I'm sorry about your wife. Technically I swing too, but my pendulum's been stuck on one side for the last few years." Six years ago. Damn. Those girls had been little.

"I understand that. I dated Deb in high school, a glorious young man in college, and then when I went home to work the ranch, Deb was there." Matthew chuckled softly. "And before the end of the summer, she'd caught pregnant, so..."

"Women have a way of doing that if you're not careful." He nodded sagely. He wasn't going to ask what happened to her, he'd learned the hard way how difficult that question could be to answer. "If you're looking for company, most people have good luck on our dance floor."

"I found someone friendly to chat with, honey. That's way more important than a hookup."

"A friendly klutz." He smiled though; something about Matthew soothed him deep down and let him hang out in the moment for the first time in a while. "That's supposed to be working." Though Peter wasn't busy and hadn't even given him a look yet.

"I can wait if you have to wander. I don't mind."

"Thanks. I'll have to at some point, but it's slow right now." He did take the time to start cleaning up, staying where he could still talk. "Tell me about your girls. Who's with them while you're here?"

"They're at my folks'. They have a place down the road and a new in-ground swimming pool. My girls were so ready for a week in the water. I'm going to have to consider getting one too, now that they're old enough to not worry so much."

"That's a chunk of change from what I've heard."

Matthew nodded. "I know a few guys who I can trade straws for it. My bulls go for fifteen a straw."

A straw? Dex did this occasionally too, said something that only someone who had reason to know would know. "I have no idea what a straw is. I'm sorry."

"It's a glass straw of bull semen. That's where my money is."

He blinked at Matthew again, who at this point must think he didn't have a brain cell in his head. But that was the second time tonight that Matthew had said something he was not expecting. "I...had no idea." He chuckled, grinning, embarrassed.

"That you got bulls' spunk in glass straws or that you could sell it?" There didn't seem to be any evil in Matthew, just this easiness, this warmth.

"Well, I guess I'm trying to imagine how you get semen into a straw...and I have a really bad imagination." He bit his lip to keep from laughing, but it only kind of worked.

"Believe it or not, I have artificial vaginas and a set of cowboys whose entire jobs are to get the bull's cock into the AV. That flows into a vial and then it's tested and frozen in glass straws." Did Matthew just say all that with a straight face?

"I am not drunk enough for this conversation." Not even close. He tried to picture that whole operation in his head. "Artificial vaginas. I've heard some stories but that's...wow." He looked at Matthew seriously. "I mean, I'm not making fun I just...said like that it sounds so absurd." And it was hard to believe that made Matthew swimming pool type money.

"Right? I grew up doing it—not at the level I am now. I lucked out, bred a couple of amazing buckers and three or four big show bulls, but it's a going operation. Hell, I just had to fire this one son of a bitch for trying to steal bull spunk. No shit."

"That's cool. Totally out of my range of experience, but very cool."

"Yes, well, I am on my sixth year of coming up, and I only learned how to use the subway last year."

Tyler laughed. "Oh, the subway is probably way scarier than a bull."

"Absolutely. You got to remember, my closest town has ninety folks in it."

"God, that sounds nice. Quiet. It's...not quiet here." Tyler was tired. He didn't sleep much, but that had nothing to do with the noise.

"No. No, it's not. It's neat, but quiet? No." Matthew sounded like he knew, like he understood somehow, but how could he? "Are you from here?"

He nodded. "Yeah. I was born here. Went to city schools. I was taking the subway to school with my friends by third grade. I had a lot more than ninety people around me."

"That's fascinating. Do you like it?" No one looked at him like that, like he was fascinating.

Did he *like* it? It was home, it was all he knew. He'd never thought about whether he liked it. "I guess?" There was nothing fascinating about trying to make a living in New York.

"I swore when I headed to Austin for my degree that I was moving away, but that didn't happen. By the time I graduated, I was building the house on the weekends and aching to get home."

Tourists thought it had to be cool to live in the city. "I really don't know where else I'd go. I don't have any reason to move. I've never really been anywhere." Not anywhere he'd live. He used to do a winter vacation somewhere warm with friends before—he hadn't gone this past winter.

"I get that. I mean, I like to go. I run down to the beach a couple times a year, out to Angel Fire to ski, here, but I'm always ready to go home."

He shrugged, uncomfortable with the conversation, and took a beer order from a couple of newcomers. "I guess I'd have to get away for a while to figure out if I'd miss it. Excuse me a second?"

He made his way down the bar to pull the two beers and put in an order for nachos.

Matthew nursed his Dr Pepper, eyes on his phone, the light casting amazing shadows on the strong features.

"Flirting with the cowboy?" Peter got him with an elbow.

"No. He's freaking me out a little actually, the way he looks at me...like he knows me. Nice guy though. Kind, Friendly."

Peter nodded. "Ah. But you're not interested."

"Shut up." Did it matter? The guy was from *Texas*.

"Okay. Okay, sure. You want me to wait on him? I will, tell him you're busy."

"No. No, did I say that? I got it." He picked up the beers. "Yell if you need help."

He could almost hear Peter shaking his head behind him.

Tyler handed off the beers and took a card for a tab from the new guys, then stepped back over to Matthew. "You need a refill?"

"Please, thank you." Matthew met his eyes, smiled, but he thought the look was a little sad. "I didn't mean to disturb you. My apologies."

He held Matthew's eyes for a second. That wasn't fair; the cowboy wasn't being anything but nice. "It's not...it's just been a while since I had a real conversation with anyone. So...maybe I needed a little disturbing. I like talking to you, you've been—You're very warm. And I'm kind of in a cold place."

Jesus. Maybe he needed that therapist Les offered him after all.

"Well, I'm enjoying chatting with you. I like to talk—I'm sure you've noticed, so if you want to conversate, I'm willing."

Conversate.

"I'm in. Let me get you that refill. Oh...on the Cuervo, the Dr Pepper, or both?"

"Just the Dr Pepper. I don't need to be liquored up to chat with you."

Damn, if he did want to flirt, this would be the guy to do it with. Matthew was saying all the right things.

Oh. Oh shit, was Matthew flirting? Saying all the right things was flirting, right? Oh. Shit.

He grabbed another can of Dr Pepper and a new glass of ice and poured out the can into the glass. "How long are you in town? Is the convention all weekend?" He'd never heard of Book-thing. World? Expo? Something.

"I am. I'm here until Tuesday. The Expo is over Saturday, but I like a day to explore and a day to just chill out."

"Nice. What have you planned to see?" Because he was an excellent tour guide. Not that he had any time off. Well, he was technically off Monday, but he usually came in to help with inventory.

"I haven't! Like I said, up until last year? I just stayed close, took the Expo transportation. Then I decided to be brave. I picked a hotel that looked amazing and fun. There was an advertisement in the lobby for this place." Matthew's eyes lit up. "So I've got the Expo tomorrow to get some books, then I'm golden. Would it be creepy if I came back in to talk to you again? Maybe invite you to a meal?"

"Creepy? No. Everybody's gotta eat, right?" He smiled despite shocking himself by so easily agreeing to a...to a what? A meal? A date? Brunch or something. "That sounds great."

"Excellent. You let me know when is good for you, and I'll be there with bells on."

"Well, I'm on shift here at four tomorrow and Sunday, and I'm off on Monday."

Whoa.

He just handed out his schedule.

How long had it been? He barely remembered the part of him that was interested in anything at all much less... whatever this was. He felt like he should be more freaked out than he was.

"How about noon tomorrow? We could have a lazy lunch before you work?"

He nodded before he could chicken out. "Sure. Just tell me...oh, or maybe I should tell you where." Tyler laughed.

"I'll meet you wherever. Let me give you my number, and you can text me." Matthew chuckled softly, the sound sliding over his nerves and soothing them. "And we can both try to figure out whether we're brave or a little crazy."

"It's lunch." They didn't have to be brave or crazy to have lunch. He put Matthew's digits into his phone, and then texted the number so Matthew had his. It was *just* lunch.

"It is. No stress, no strings." Matthew took a long swig of his drink. "I appreciate you letting me visit with you, man. I spend all day talking to someone—kids, cowboys, family. I was beginning to worry that people were going to think I was a nutjob, muttering to myself."

"Oh, no. That's totally common here. I bet you wouldn't

even get a second look. Someone might hand you a sandwich though." Tyler laughed. That sounded like Matthew was heading out. He reached for the card Matthew had given him, handed it back, and tore up the bill. "I'm really sorry about your hand."

"Oh, wow. Are you sure, honey? I'll pay for my drinks." Matthew stood, and it happened again. It was like Matthew filled the space.

This time, though, he managed a breath and stuck his hand out first. "The least I can do is buy your drinks. It was nice to meet you."

Matthew took his hand, and he swore electricity shot up his arm. "It was my pleasure. You let me know where to meet you tomorrow, okay?"

"I...yeah." He smiled, bewildered. "Yes. I'll text you. Take care of that hand."

"I will." Matthew stroked his wrist before letting him go to put two twenties in the tip jar. "Y'all have a good one."

Tyler watched Matthew go, eyes following until the door closed behind him. Then he looked down and ran his fingers over that spot on his wrist. He didn't know what he was doing, and he didn't know why either. But something in him that had been sleeping seemed to be waking up.

There was just something strange and wondrous about that cowboy.

2

"I know, Jonas. I know. It's just lunch. I'm allowed to have lunch with a nice young man."

"Uh-huh. Matty, you have to be careful. You're vulnerable. You trust people. That's why you don't get to run the corporation." His brother—older by fifteen months, dammit—was a shark. Him? He just wanted to be a cowboy.

Matthew grunted noncommittally. Whatever. He was still going.

"Are you listening to me, Bubba?"

"Yes, sir." Nope. Not even a bit.

There had been something about Tyler that called to him. Something quiet and sad. Something that needed care and touch and a little peace. He wasn't looking for a love affair, but he could be a friend, couldn't he?

"Matthew Efraim Whitehead!"

He looked out the window of the Uber car. "There's sure lots of traffic out here."

"Dammit, Matty. Have you ever had a one-nighter? Everything is all or nothing with you. Don't take this joker back to your hotel. You hear me?"

"It's not like that! I'm not...it's lunch!" And there was something special about Tyler. Something dear.

"Fine. Lunch. Keep it at that. Have you talked to Momma? She told me Emma lost a tooth this morning."

"What? No! When? Goddammit! I have to let you go. Love you. Bye." He hated missing things. Hated it. But this was...well, it was important. He'd told Momma not to let anyone do anything cool!

At least he could count on the Tooth Fairy showing up. Momma had done that a couple three times. He and Jonas had practically made losing teeth a competition.

He dialed Momma's phone, tapping his toes until she answered. "What happened? She lost a tooth? Anything else? Lord, I'm gone a handful of days, and my girls grow up on me."

"Oh, I'm fine, thank you for asking." He could almost hear Momma rolling her eyes. "A phone conversation usually begins with a polite 'hello', son."

"Hello, son. Your daughter lost a tooth and I immediately called you." Evil, wonderful old woman.

"Oh, you're a smart one, aren't you? You get that from me." Momma laughed, the sound light and happy. "She bit into a waffle this morning and it got stuck and she swallowed it. Not to worry, she was so tickled she giggled all morning over it. You remember when Soph did the same thing and she was in hysterical tears all day?"

"God, yes. That damn hot dog. I thought she'd never stop sighing and sobbing. I swear to God, Momma, I had nightmares of her sorting through her own poo to make sure it didn't get stuck."

"Oh, you did not." Momma snorted. "She's sound asleep, and the Tooth Fairy has come and gone, or I'd let you say hello. You'll call her in the morning, all right? I'll tell her."

"You mean she didn't finagle you into staying up late-late? I'm shocked." He shook his head and grinned. "I got y'all a ton of books. I mailed eighteen boxes home."

"She and her sister swam all day long and wore themselves out. She tried, but she climbed up into Papaw's lap after dinner and laid her little head on his shoulder and that was all she wrote. Eighteen boxes? I guess I have my work cut out for me this summer."

"Yes, ma'am. I met a guy, Momma. A bartender. We're going to lunch together."

"Well, you enjoy your lunch, son. But you don't need to bring home a Yankee, I told you Annabelle has a nice young man to introduce you to. And he doesn't work behind a bar."

"Momma! I'm not looking for a lover. Just a friend."

"You don't have enough friends?"

He rubbed his forehead. "Momma..."

"You don't tell your mother that you 'met a guy' if he's not someone you think might become more than a friend. I wasn't born yesterday, son, and I do know men."

"Yes, ma'am. I got to go. I love you. Kiss the babies for me." Everyone was always so damn worried.

He wasn't worried. Tyler was interesting, dear, and Matthew wanted to wrap him in cotton and keep him safe.

Was that weird? It was probably weird.

"Be safe and don't forget to call Emma in the morning. I love you."

"I love you. Night, Momma." They pulled up to the hotel, and he thanked the driver and headed in. Lord have mercy, he was... So he met a guy. So he liked him. So what?

He wasn't a horndog. Or a freak. He just...could tell when things felt good.

His phone rang, his sister's face popping up. "Hey, Rache."

Goddamn. Who'd called her—Jonas or Momma?

"Hey, baby brother. You sound happy. How's New York? Meet anyone wonderful? If you did, I know nothing about it."

"Who didn't tell you?" He cracked up, heading upstairs and letting himself in his room. "How are my gorgeous nephews?"

"Jonas called, of course. Your self-appointed moral compass." Rachel laughed. "Elias is fine. He got his straight As, and he's fixin' to start his summer job. But don't get me started on Noah." She sighed. "All he cares about is his car and his girlfriend." They were both good boys, they were just as different as he and Jonas were.

"God, has Alan given him the condom talk yet? You're too young for grandbabies." He was going to tie his girls' knees together and just shoot any boys that came around for...forty years, at least.

"It probably went, 'Don't make me kick your ass'. You keep those girls on the ranch. Teenage boys are no joke." Rachel sounded so much like Momma. "Tell me about New York."

"It's big, busy, loud. I found a little local-ish bar. I found tons of books." *I found me a pretty little bartender that needs a hug.* Christ on a cracker, he was a dork.

"Elias seemed excited about whatever he asked you to find him. And the local bar has a particularly interesting bartender, I hear?"

"We're going for lunch tomorrow. He's just—he seemed like he could use a friend, Sister. Someone to talk to."

"You could use a friend too, Matty. I don't know if you need one in New York, but if someone put him in your way, I'm sure there's a reason. You understand what Jonas is worried about, right?"

"Yes, ma'am." They always worried about the money thing, both of them. They worried about the fact that he didn't worry about it. To them, Matthew was still the baby. He guessed he always would be.

"Okay, then." Having done her job, Rachel's tone changed completely. "Is he hot? When is lunch? Will you call me after?"

"Noon, and of course I'll call. He's pretty, and I want to wrap him up and hold him, and that's weird, right? I'm weird?" It didn't feel weird. It felt as easy as pie and right.

"No, honey. That's what you do. You take care of people. That's why your girls are the luckiest girls in the world."

"Did you hear that Emma lost a tooth, and Momma didn't even call?" He was still a little horrified.

"I knew she lost a tooth. I didn't know that you didn't know. Maybe Momma thought calling you would just make Em miss you. I heard they've been in the pool nonstop since you left."

"Yeah, I've already got a phone call in with Jeremy. He's going to start digging next week." His girls could spend all the rest of the summer and most of the fall in the water, spending energy. "Did I tell you we got six more calves today? Ben and Little Tim sent video."

"My goodness, Matty. You're still the baby whisperer." Rachel had been calling him that, teasing him ever since he got Deb pregnant with Sophia.

"Always." He liked being on the ranch, growing beans and raising cattle and running horses. He was happy there.

"All right, I have to report back to Jonas that you're a responsible adult. I love you, baby brother. You be good in big, bad New York."

"I promise. Love you, Sister." He hung up and stripped

down to his skivvies, then ordered himself another Coke and a burger and fries.

He couldn't wait for tomorrow—books, lunch, a new friend. It sounded like magic. All it was missing was his babies.

3

Jesus, Matthew was tired. He'd got himself up and dressed, bought a copy of every book on earth, and then headed to an address that meant as much to him as if it was on the moon.

Good thing he was smart and had a phone and the ability to google.

He ended up at a corner, not sure where he was, but he was early, dressed like a gentleman, and not at all stressed about being somewhere new, because this was his idea. Dammit.

It was an absolutely beautiful day, sunny with a little breeze, and he watched all kinds of people walk by—all ages, some with dogs, even one or two with kids in strollers. It was definitely a busy city block, but the street had trees lining it, and it had a quiet neighborhood feel.

He squinted down the block, pretty sure his lunch date was headed his way. Blue jeans, T-shirt, and much the same Tyler he'd met last night, only with sunglasses and without the bar towels.

There was no question that he stuck out, with his hat and his button-down, but Matthew reckoned that was good.

Tyler waved when he was still too far away to say hello, but his smile was bright enough to see from blocks away. The light turned and Tyler was stuck on the other side of the intersection as the cars rushed by, and he stuffed his hands in his pockets while he waited, everything about the man looking just like he belonged here.

That smile buoyed his heart, and Matthew waited patiently. He couldn't imagine living with this much traffic —it was like Houston and Dallas smooshed together.

When Tyler could he jogged across the street instead of walking. "Hey. Did I keep you waiting? Am I late? The subway was so crowded."

"I'm early. No worries. It's good to see you, honey. How's your day been?" *Aren't you the prettiest thing?*

"So far so good. I only got out of bed an hour ago. Are you hungry? You want to go in?" Tyler pointed over his shoulder.

"Absolutely. My cup of coffee was a long time ago. I was up and out and about early." He was used to being up at six, every morning, rain or shine.

Tyler opened the unassuming front door and led him in. "The bar closes at two, and on Fridays there's still clean up to do. I'm usually toast by the time I get home." Inside the place looked like a cross between someone's living room and a library. Small tables, a couple of couches, bookshelves on the walls, and a spiral staircase that led up to a second level.

"Oh, now look at this! I ought to do this in my office!" He loved that and the girls were old enough that a spiral staircase wasn't dangerous anymore.

"Isn't it cool? I thought you'd like the reading room feel."

A young hostess seated them right away at a table near

the front where lots of light was coming in through filtered glass.

"Oh, I picked you up a signed book this morning—it's a thriller with a great hook." He handed the book over, the cover lurid and wonderful. He figured it was a decent gift, but nothing that would be weird.

Tyler reached for it tentatively, like Matthew might change his mind and take it back. "You got me a book?"

"I did. I thought you'd enjoy it." He left it on the table and picked up the menu. "Have you eaten here before?"

"Yeah, a couple of times." Tyler pulled the book toward him, picked it up, and looked it over, flipping it over to read the back. "It sounds really good."

"Good deal. I thought it looked fascinating. I liked the idea of a blind killer. It sounded wild. I mean—how does he manage it?" Matthew chuckled and his cheeks heated. God, he was a dork. "I guess that's the reason to read it, huh?"

"I'm looking forward to it. Thank you. And it's signed, how cool. It's my first autographed book." Tyler set the book down, that sunny smile sweet, but softer this time. "Thank you."

"You're more than welcome." His phone buzzed with "Troubador", and he picked it up, curious as to what Daddy wanted.

The text was a picture of his girls in the pool with their cousins playing chicken, Emma and Sophia on the boys' shoulders. "Oh, look. These are my babies."

He showed Tyler the phone.

"Wow, look at them. How much fun are they having? That's awesome. Who are the boys?"

"My sister's boys—Elias and Noah. They're eighteen and just turned sixteen."

"That's cool. I'm a little jealous, I love to swim." Tyler handed him back his phone and picked up a menu.

"I'm going to put one in. I decided for sure. The girls are having a blast at my folks'." He spoiled those babies, but that was what having money was for.

"They're lucky to have such a great dad. They're readers too, I guess?"

"Sophia more than Emma. Emma is very visual—she loves to draw and paint and make things with clay." Both of his girls were happy to be around the ranch, to ride and show their critters.

"They sound like fun. I bet you miss them."

"Are you guys ready to order?" The server put waters down for them.

Tyler glanced at him. "I'm thinking about the fancy three-cheese grilled cheese and tomato soup."

He checked the menu real quick. "BLT for me. Do y'all have onion rings?"

He was a sucker for deep fat fried battered anything.

"We do, they're *so* good."

"I'm stealing one." Tyler grinned, handing the menus back to her. "Can we get a Dr Pepper and a ginger ale too, please?"

"You got it. Thanks guys."

"This is a sweet place." He loved a little hole in the wall. This was fancier than that, but the idea was the same. "So, tell me about you. What's your favorite movie?"

"My favorite what kind of movie? I love movies. Favorite funny movie? It's so wrong, but *Blazing Saddles*. Favorite SciFi? *Alien*. Favorite superhero? *Iron Man*...what else?"

Oh, Tyler was an old soul. He approved. "Do you watch any animated movies? I have seen *Frozen* and *Despicable Me* approximately eighty thousand times."

"*Despicable Me* is way up there, also, all the *Toy Story* movies. *Megamind.* And...okay don't judge me. *Beauty and the Beast.* I used to get such shit about that from—" Tyler's brow furrowed for a second and then it was gone. "I used to get a lot of shit about it."

"I love that one, but my favorite will always be *The Lion King.*" Oh, that was a sad look. Bad break up? That was his guess.

"I read somewhere that the whole opening lyrics basically translate to, 'dude, here comes a lion' over and over." Tyler giggled—yeah, that was a giggle—and sipped his water.

"No shit?" Oh, he loved that. He seriously did. "Have you seen the musical? I took my girls to Austin to see it. Sophia loved it. Emma was a little scared—it was too big."

"No, not the show. Which is funny because I live here, right? But I don't see as much theater as you'd think. So you've seen the animated movies because you have kids... what do you watch just for you?"

"Lord, that's a hard one." He thought about what he had on his nonparent-controlled account in the bedroom. "My favorites are the *Lord of the Rings* movies, but I'll watch anything with Johnny Depp and Leonardo DiCaprio. Oh, and monster movies. I love those."

"*Wolf of Wall Street* with Leo? I loved that one. I forgot about the *Lord of the Rings.* I liked those too. Have you read the books a hundred times?" Tyler seemed genuinely interested, not just making small talk. His eyes were pinned on Matthew. Baby blue. Pretty.

"I've read them a few times. When I was a teenager, I was obsessed. I wanted to be a ranger, you know? I even spent a summer apprenticing with a swordsmith." He'd felt like the world's biggest stud.

"You can swing a sword? That's nuts."

"I can make them. I have a forge on the property. I don't get to go play as often as I'd like, but it's there." He chuckled. "I have a lot of interests, I guess."

"Wait." Tyler stared at him, wide-eyed. "You have a forge at your house? Like an actual, real, forge? Are you kidding?"

"Not at all. Would you like to see?" He grabbed his phone and started flipping through pictures. Most of them were kids and livestock and dogs. "Okay, this is the house. It was my grandparents until I bought it and built on the second floor and added another two thousand square feet to the ground floor. The roses in the front were planted by my granny in the seventies. Then this is the garage, the workshop, and the forge. You can just see the horse barns from there."

"Oh my God. Matthew. This is incredible." Tyler flipped from picture to picture and back again. "Your place is beautiful. And big. Like, really big. Wow."

"Thank you. I've been super lucky." He'd been born into a good situation, and he loved what he did and made money with it. "I'm very blessed."

Tyler nodded. "And rich. Like whoa. I mean, I don't mean to be rude. That's a beautiful house. I've just never seen anything like it."

"Like I said, I'm lucky." He wasn't going to be ashamed. It wouldn't change the fact that he was on the cushy side comfortable.

"So...school is out for the summer there?" He'd have sworn Tyler's fingers brushed his on purpose as he took his phone back.

"They got out a couple of weeks ago, yeah. They're so excited about summer. It's all horses and swimming and sleeping in for three months." In fact, he needed to find someone to help out around the house too. Little Stephanie had finally graduated from Rice and had her an internship for the summer. They had a cleaning lady that they all shared between them—Aunt Kathy on Monday, Momma's on Tuesday, Jonas on Wednesday, Sister's on Thursday, and he was Friday—but Vera was not interested in wrangling kids.

"Living the dream, huh? I'd like to be a kid again. Well, maybe not a New York kid again. I did that. But a Texas ranch kid? Sounds like fun."

Their food arrived, and the server set down a huge plate of onion rings between them.

"Any time you want to come out, holler. I got a guest suite, and there's always stuff to do. Damn, that looks good. I do love an onion ring." He looked at his sandwich and tried to decide how to attack it.

Tyler laughed. "I wasn't looking for an invitation. I don't even remember your last name, Matthew. You can't just invite random strangers from New York home with you. I might be a serial killer or something. You have girls, man."

"I do. And both of them can fire a gun, believe it or not." Girls, cowboys, his folks, his sibs, and the fact that Westley and Buttercup, the lead stud and bitch of his Lacys would tear a bad guy's throat out if they hurt the girls—he felt pretty confident. "It's Whitehead, by the way. Matthew Whitehead."

Tyler blinked, then nodded. "Right. Sorry. Onion rings are good?" Tyler picked one up.

"They look damn good. So tell me about you. Do you like tending bar? It seems like a hell of a lot to remember."

"I do. Or, well, I did. I'm good at it, it pays the rent, I work with great people." Tyler shrugged. "It's good. It's fine." Tyler took a big bite of an onion ring. "I've thought about other things but... I don't know. I'm tired, you know? I'm babbling."

"So what happened that changed everything?" It wasn't like the kid hadn't given him a bunch of clues that shit had gone on, and he wasn't anyone, just a stranger. It was easy to talk to them.

"Will died." Tyler put his sandwich down and studied his fingers. "Will...my best friend. I'd known him since we were kids. He...he had problems. Depression. Drugs. He took his own life."

"Oh damn. I'm sorry. Depression is a vicious whore." He reached out and took Tyler's hand. "My sister, her first husband had that happen to him. He tried hard to heal, but —it sucks, man. Deep down. I'm real sorry. Has it been long?"

"Six months. It feels like six days. I'm sorry for your sister, it does suck. It..." Tyler cleared his throat and took a big sip of his water. "It's changed everything. He was my whole family. I don't have a reason anymore, you know? I'm just kind of...doing things. I can't sleep. I—"

Tyler looked up at him with a horrified look in his eyes and pulled his hand back. "Oh, God. I'm sorry."

"For what? I asked." Matthew got this. Less well than some, better than others. No one really expected someone to give up on living, and then you got the guilt for being mad because they did, the shame of admitting it to other people, and then the bone-deep missing part. "Grief is a real thing. It's not shameful."

Tyler leaned back in his chair. "It's a little heavy for lunch. I really wanted to be...flirty, funny, interesting. That guy. Not this...disaster."

"I get that." When Tyler blinked at him, he held his hands open. "I want to seem amazing and fascinating and studly, and I'm just a cowboy and a dad and a guy who flies to New York City to come to a book convention."

Tyler gave him a gentle smile. "I think you're doing pretty well, actually."

"Thank you. I think you are too. I am glad to be lunching with you." He picked up his sandwich and tried to make it smaller. "How do you reckon I bite into this?"

That got him a slow but much brighter smile. "Um... squish it? And then be studly and take a cowboy bite."

"No princess bites?" he teased. "Right on."

He squished, leaned forward, and took a bite. Oh. Crunchy. Bright. Creamy. Best of all? Bacontastic.

"Oh. There you go. You look like you're in bacon heaven." Tyler picked his sandwich back up and dipped a corner into his tomato soup.

"Bacon heaven is a damn fine place. It's next door to taco heaven and across the street from brisket heaven."

"And kitty-corner to pizza heaven." And look at that, he got Tyler laughing.

"I think that I might need an ice cream heaven too. Homemade ice cream is something special, don't you think?" Peach. Peach was his favorite.

"Homemade like in your own kitchen? You can do that? There are some great ice cream places around the city."

"I have two different ice cream makers: one fancy nice one and one old wooden one that I use to torture my children. Have you never made it homemade? I make it a lot, especially during peach season." He tried an onion ring. Oh damn. Yummy.

"Never. It sounds fun. Is the old one slower or something? Why does it torture your kids?"

"It's an old crank. I put the ice and the salt in and set the kids to churning. It can take most of an afternoon." He grinned, knowing it was wicked.

"That'll wear them out." Tyler swallowed the bite he was chewing. "I grew up in the city. Mom worked a lot, I went to school and worked after school, so we didn't really have time to do things like make ice cream. We went to the movies on hot days in the summer, and we'd sleep a lot in the winter. Mom liked to read. I listened to music. That's what we did."

"I was always, always busy. Muck out the stalls. Go find your brother. Wash the dogs. Go pick beans. And then we rode horses and fished and jumped on the trampoline and caught crawdaddies." He'd been a busy kid. He was a busy adult.

Damn he did have fun though.

"Sounds different. I had a little more fun when Will and I hit high school and had more freedom. We'd play basketball and smoke and watch girls—and guys—and we'd stay up stupid late sitting on the fire escape and talking about where we'd go when we graduated. He grew up in the apartment right below mine."

"That's cool. I've never seen a fire escape up close. Hell, I've never lived in an apartment. Even in college, about thirty of us rented a big house." He shuddered as he remembered. "God, the smell in there...whoa."

"Oh gross. Where did you go to college?"

"University of Texas at Austin. I have a degree in environmental science." He knew. Boring. But it had helped convince Momma and Daddy that he wanted to work the ranch.

"Oh nice." Tyler reached over the table and rested warm fingers on his forearm, just for a moment before taking them back again. "This is the first time I've been out to do anything since Will died. Anything at all."

"I'm glad you picked me." He wasn't bullshitting. It was an honor, and he was tickled as a pig in shit.

"I think you picked me. Our friends haven't really asked. I don't think they know what to say. They're processing too I guess, and it's awkward. I think maybe they thought we were sleeping together? We weren't."

"What did he do for a living?" Part of him figured Tyler just needed an ear, just needed to talk.

"He was a dancer. Well, he waited tables for a living I guess, but he was a dancer. He was really good. It's a competitive thing here. Hard to get a job."

"Wow. Like a ballet dancer, contemporary, jazz?" Emma and Sophia both took dance, every year, so he knew from dance styles.

"Whoa. Contemporary. He had a ballet background, but he danced contemporary. Wait..." Tyler leaned forward. "Do the girls dance?"

"Are you suggesting I haven't seen every single season of *So You Think You Can Dance*?" He managed a straight face for, oh, about eight seconds. "God, yes. Since they were three. Sophia is already planning on her attack to get into the high school drill team in five years."

"So you *have* seen every season of *So You Think You Can Dance*..." Tyler winked. "Me too. That sounds fun. Little girl recitals. Oh boy."

"Every season. Every. One. And four costumes, times two girls, twice a year. You know how many sequins that is? You know how many times a year I'm in the barns yelling, 'Don't let that horse eat your dress! He'll poop rainbows!'?"

"Oh my God." Tyler laughed hard enough he bent over. "Who makes the dresses? Your mom?"

"Momma volunteered. Once. Then Miss Vicki, the dance teacher, criticized her ruffles." He pursed his lips. "She told Miss Vicki to shove the fabric down her throat, and she could pull ruffles out her twat and see if they smelled like roses. It was...memorable."

Sophia had damn near died. Deb had gone to the dance class in her all her fired-up rage and explained how the cow ate the cabbage. Miss Vicki had decided both Sophia and Momma could come to the recital. No worries.

"Holy shit." Tyler stared at him. "Holy shit, that's crazy! I'd like to have some tea with your mom one day." Tyler was laughing so hard now he damn near fell off his chair. "Holy shit."

"She is a hoot and a half. My daddy? He's a gentle giant. Momma is a spitfire and keeps him busy."

"Never a dull moment, I bet." Tyler took another onion ring. "These alone were worth the trip."

"Yes. I do love crunchy things." He grabbed one of his own, wishing he had some jalapeno ranch to dip. "What's your favorite food? Pizza heaven, I know you mentioned."

"Mac and Cheese. My mom's recipe. Or pizza. Pizza is up there. Grilled cheese sandwiches. Maybe anything with cheese involved." Tyler took a bite of his sandwich and grinned at him.

"You and Emma. She's my cheese eater. She loves her macaroni and cheese."

"So what's next for you? You have more convention today? Tomorrow?"

"No. No, it's all free time for me until I fly home on noon Tuesday." He had two and a half days, and he hoped to spend some of it with Tyler.

Shit, he was a moron.

That hadn't ever stopped him, but...

"Nice. I could show you around on Monday if you want. I'm off work. And you know where to find me tonight if you're thirsty." Tyler waggled his eyebrows. "Or just feel like showing off your dance moves."

"Yeah, save me a bar stool. I'll wiggle on that." Okay. Okay, cool. He could handle that. "I'd love to go see things with you on Monday. Please."

"You do the easy stuff on your own then...museums and things. And I'll take you to the stuff it's easier to get lost doing on Monday. Is that good?" Tyler's voice was...enthusiastic. Cool.

"Sounds perfect, yes. I love the idea of discovering new things." He loved to bring stories home to his girls.

The server wandered over as Tyler pushed the last onion ring in his direction. "Can I get you guys anything else?"

"Tyler?" He intended to get him some ice cream; maybe Tyler had time to come with him. Hell, if he could watch Tyler lap at an ice cream cone, he could fantasize for weeks.

"I'm good. Thank you." Tyler pulled a wallet from his back pocket.

"Hey, I invited, it's my treat." He handed her his card. He was more than capable, and this sweet man was struggling. "Would you like to take a walk, go have an ice cream, or do you need to go?"

Tyler blushed, but didn't look embarrassed, just touched. He looked at his watch. "We could walk toward work. Then I'd have time for an ice cream."

"Perfect. Are y'all usually swamped on Saturdays? It seems like a place for regulars, you know?" He had a honkytonk that he went to, but not often. Usually he went to Maria's at just after six for breakfast.

"Not swamped. We get nuts almost every Friday night. Saturdays are super busy but not like Friday. The rest of the week it's just a neighborhood place, a very welcoming one. There's always room at the bar for everyone." Tyler stood, tucked his book under one arm, and added a couple of bucks to the tip. "Not because you didn't put enough. I just always do that. Tips are a thank you."

"Fair enough. Deb waited tables all through high school and college. It's important. She was very, very clear about that." He had always worked. Always. But it had usually been for himself. Or his daddy. Or gramps.

"So do the girls look like her?" Tyler stepped past him as he held the door. "Or more like you?"

"Soph looks like her—blonde and blue eyes. Emma is all black hair and gray eyes like me. Both of them are tall, where Deb was short and curvy. In that, they look like my sister, Rachel."

Tyler nodded. "Did Rachel remarry?"

"Yeah, nine years ago? The boys were just kids, and it was tough for a bit, but he wooed her. He was her personal assistant, believe it or not." And Alan had made it to where she didn't want to say no.

Tyler led them across the street. "That's good. That's good for her. I'm glad she's okay. And you're okay."

"I hope you'll be okay too. I imagine it's early days for that, but a man can hope." He knew that Tyler said they weren't lovers, but there had been love there, and it was lost now. "It took a long, long time before I could even...pretend to be alive for anything but my girls and my ranch." Those two things didn't care if he hurt.

"Time. That's what they say, I know. I just have to figure it out. I'm keeping really busy, so that helps a lot. Do you like soft ice cream or hard?"

"I like ice cream. All of it." He glanced at Tyler. "Busy

helps. I swear, between the girls and the critters and the drovers—they were the reason I got up of a morning."

"I'm at the bar. If I wasn't taking you around on Monday I'd be there helping with inventory, even though I'm off. I don't like just rattling around our—my—*the* apartment."

"I hear that. I have ten thousand things that need doing. I'll hit the ground in Houston around five Tuesday, pick up the girls around seven, and listen to cowboys and little ones for the next few hours." He grinned and shook his head. "Then I have to hire someone to watch girls and house for a few hours a day, check my calves, and take a ton of laundry to the cleaners."

"Work is never done? Sounds like you're a kick-ass dad though." Tyler pointed. "Ice cream."

"I try, and God no. Work is eternal. Good thing I like it." He thought it was a good place, a healing place.

"Damn good thing." They went inside and Tyler ordered himself a strawberry cone. "Sugar cones are the best."

He tipped his hat. "I'll have the same, please, ma'am, and a bottle of water. Ice cream makes me thirsty."

"Strawberry. Also the best." Tyler smiled, looking so much younger when he was relaxed. "This is on me."

"Well, thank you, sir. I appreciate it." He took the water, the cold water good on the cut on his hand. He hadn't even thought about it, all afternoon.

Tyler took his cone and held it out to him. "For you."

He bowed and took it, tongue dragging along the sweet cream. "Uhn..."

Oh, that was yummy.

Tyler's head tilted slightly. "Looks good."

"Yours, sir."

"Oh. Uh, yeah. Thanks." Tyler took his and licked around the bottom scoop.

Oh, that was pretty as all get out. Yeah, he could watch that for hours.

"Ice cream was a good idea." Tyler's eyes were tracking him as they left the shop. "It's been a while."

"It's delicious. Thank you very much. My first New York City ice cream." He knew he was blushing, but he couldn't help it. He was into Tyler, in a basic balls going heavy kind of way.

"Really? All these years coming here and you...right. This is your first year venturing out. You're a tourist virgin." Tyler's tongue swirled around the cone. "Mmm."

"Second, and it took me a ton of time last year to figure out the subway." That did not work for him. At all. Matthew didn't hold much with enclosed spaces.

"I'm always surprised that the subway is complicated to people because it's such a regular thing for me. It's good to use it though. It's faster and cheaper than taxis and services." Tyler turned up an avenue and he followed, bright sun catching him in the eyes.

"Oh, I'm sure. You got to remember that I'd never even been on public transportation until I went to college in Austin." And he hadn't used it much. He'd paid to park his pickup.

Tyler grinned. "Do you drive a pickup, Mister Cowboy?"

"Does a bear shit in the woods? I have three right now, plus a Harley, and I have this beat-up 1971 Mustang that I swear I'll restore one day." He wasn't sure that was ever going to happen. He did like to talk about it with Jonas though, yessir.

"Oh, the Mustang sounds like fun. I've never driven. I don't even have a license."

The neighborhood started looking familiar. He must have walked by here last night.

"No? I love to get in the truck and drive. I have a bunch of four-wheelers too, and those are fun to take out." He had a little boat for the pond, a bigger boat for the lake, some Ski-Doos. He guessed he liked his things with motors.

Tyler laughed, stopping outside the bar. "Your ranch is starting to sound like Disney World to me."

"It's got more cow poop and baby goats, but there are absolutely two princesses."

"Cute." Tyler inhaled the last two bites of his cone, making goofy faces as he chewed and swallowed it. "Okay. This is me. Where are you headed? If you come back for dinner, I can comp you."

"I'm going to find a bookstore and some fun geegaws for my people. I will definitely come and warm the barstool tonight." He was...hell, he didn't know, some mix of stupid and lonely and intrigued. He *liked* Tyler.

"Souvenirs are everywhere." Tyler smiled warmly. "So... I'll see you later then. Thank you for the book, and for lunch."

"Thank you for showing up. I had a ball. I'll see you in a bit. Save me a stool." Damn, Tyler had pretty eyes.

"I will." Tyler hovered by the door. "Okay, one of us has to walk away first. I guess I'll do it. Bye." He got a wink and Tyler disappeared into the bar.

Matthew chuckled and shook his head. "Damn, you got it bad, buddy. You'd best call Sister. You know she's waiting on you."

First though...

"Siri, find me a bookstore."

4

Tyler hurried to the back and pulled on his apron. He was almost late. Almost but not quite, and it was the strangest feeling because he'd been very early for the last few months. Sometimes hours early. It was also the first time in months that he thought he might like to be somewhere other than work.

"Gee. You're on time. I was starting to get worried." Peter rolled his eyes, the sarcasm dripping from his words.

"I slept in," he lied.

"Oh, bullshit."

Tyler glanced at Peter, unable to completely hide his grin. "What are you low on?"

Peter leaned on the bar. "Information."

"So...triple sec?"

Peter grabbed the nearly full bottle and jiggled it. "You're seriously not going to tell me? Come *on*!"

"We had lunch. He had onion rings and a BLT as big as his head. He's...nice. Friendly. Kind. Handsome." He took a mental inventory as he talked, not sure how to have a real conversation about Matthew yet.

"He's a silver fox. How old is he? Fifty?"

Huh. "I didn't ask." It didn't matter, he was too busy enjoying Matthew's company. "He's got two girls and a ranch. He lost his wife a few years ago. So he's older I guess, but fifty sounds steep." Even forty sounded steep. Maybe Matthew went gray early. Or maybe he just looked amazing for fifty.

No, no way. He'd said his wife had gotten pregnant right out of college. That put him mid-thirties at best. That felt more like it.

Hell, he didn't care one way or another. Matthew looked —just right.

"How's his hand?"

"Oh, shit. I didn't ask. He didn't even say anything." Jesus. "I'm an asshole. I can't believe I forgot to ask."

"It must be okay, then, right? If he didn't say anything." Peter started slicing lemons. "You seeing him again?"

Tyler tried to play it cool. This was sounding way too much like Peter thought it was a thing. Which it wasn't. It was just a...a...okay. Maybe it was some kind of thing. A fun weekend thing.

A fun weekend thing with a handsome cowboy who he liked a lot, and who was obviously into him.

Sure. Super casual.

"Well, he knows I'm here. He might stop by later."

"Yeah? Cool. He seemed decent. Just be careful. If you take him home, text me."

"Thank you. But I'm not taking anyone home." He could flirt. But you didn't take home a man that had children and a house back in Texas. He couldn't risk it being wonderful. Texas was a thousand miles and a time zone away.

It might as well be in another country.

"Bummer. You could use a good orgasm or twelve."

Tyler snorted, catching on. "Ah. You're in that cock cage again aren't you? Were you a bad boy?"

"Shut. Up." Peter actually stamped his foot, and wasn't that adorable? "I'll have you know I was brilliant. Dammit."

"I don't doubt it." He laughed and went to help a young lady in leather with a beer. Ah, Saturdays.

About three hours into his shift, Matthew came walking in, looking tanned and fine in a white button-down shirt, open at the throat, hat on, those gray eyes twinkling.

He found a stool at the bar and settled like he belonged there.

Tyler kept busy and pretended like he hadn't seen the cowboy for a few minutes just so he could steal some glances. The trim beard, crisp shirt, and easy smile... Matthew looked like nothing he'd ever seen and everything he never knew he wanted.

Matthew on the other hand, wasn't pretending why he was here. Those eyes watched him, but Matthew never seemed impatient, fully intending to wait until Tyler had time.

Peter gave him a nod, so he made sure everyone was settled and went down the bar to say hello, grabbing the Cuervo on the way.

"Howdy, stranger. You look amazing. Did you have a good day?"

"I did. I found a bookstore, had a fancy coffee, and found a goofy tchotchke store to get presents for home." Matthew held up his phone, showing off a picture of funny, silly things, from shirts to bobbing head dolls.

"What did you end up buying? More books?" He leaned on the bar and Matthew flipped through the pictures. "Because you definitely needed those."

"I got a couple of New York specific ones, yeah—I got

one about famous ghosts here—and I grabbed a signed Stephen King for my collection."

"Man, I can't even tease you about buying more books." He shook his head. Matthew meant business. "You're just... 'yeah, I totally did.'"

"Books. Cows. Goats. Some things you just have to buy when they come around." Matthew winked at him, teasing madly. "Could be worse. My brother? He's into art. It's everywhere. Stacked everywhere. You cain't even see most of it. My sister has at least ten zillion purses and a whole closet of shoes."

"Wow. I guess that's what you do with money, huh? Collect things? Do you have a huge library on your ranch too? I mean for your own books?" He set a shot in front of Matthew and a Dr Pepper.

Matthew winced, but he nodded. "I have some. I donate most of them to the library in town. Thank you, sir." Matthew handed over his card. "For my tab."

He caught Matthew's eyes and held them, then took the card and nodded, making sure their fingers touched. "Okay."

Matthew winked at him, thumb brushing his hand. "Having a good night?"

"It's a busy night." He clipped Matthew's card to a bill, but left it blank. First round was on him. "But it got better when this handsome cowboy walked through the door."

"That's fine to hear, Mr. McKeehan."

Wow. Matthew remembered his last name.

Oh! Speaking of remembering. "How's your hand? I can't believe I forgot to ask you at lunch. I can be such an idiot, I'm sorry."

"It's fine." Matthew held his hand out, palm up. There was a bandage across, hiding any grossness. "See?"

He snorted. "No, I can't see anything, cowboy. Does it hurt?"

"I don't want to poke it with a stick, but I'm not thinking about it." Matthew leaned in. "One day we'll compare scars. I have lots."

"One day, huh? You're a fast-moving cowboy." He could see it though. One day. Which made no sense.

"Just patient. No pressure." The neat part was that Matthew seemed to mean it.

"I have a few good ones. I was always getting into shit as a kid." But it would be a while before Matthew saw the one on his hip.

"What's your best story—mine is from a scar that's not for public consumption, unfortunately."

Tyler laughed. "Mine too!" He stepped back from the bar and tucked his hand along the front inside of his thigh. "Right there. I got mugged, and the guy had a knife. I was seventeen and decided not to give him my wallet. The knife was headed for my gut, but I caught his arm and almost took off my dick instead." He stepped back up to the bar, grinning. "Just give up your wallet. It's so not worth it."

"Jesus Christ! That's pure evil." Matthew actually looked...affronted. Utterly shocked that someone would do that.

"Nah. That's just a sketchy neighborhood in New York at an hour I shouldn't have been out anyway." He'd learned a lot of lessons the hard way around seventeen. "Where's yours?"

"On my left butt cheek." Matthew's lips twisted. "Nowhere near as dramatic as yours, though. Jonas and I were playing with Mitch and Damien, my cousins, when we were kids. Mitch was playing with my daddy's branding iron, and he didn't know it was on. Branded me right on my butt. The guys all went one way. Sister ran to tell. I screamed like a banshee and ran to the bathroom, locked myself in, and wouldn't come out. Uncle Coot went and got the boys. My momma had Daddy take the bathroom door off the hinges, and Dr. Fry was there to look at the infection and pull melted bits of my shorts out of it. I spent a week on my belly with my bare butt in the air."

"Oh my God." He laughed, but he was horrified at the very idea. "A branding iron. Are you serious? Holy shit, I bet that was a sight. That had to hurt like hell too. God."

"It was the smell. Gag. But yeah, I'm officially branded as belonging to the Flying W ranch, for eternity."

"Kinky." Tyler winked. "Does this come up often? It sounds like great Thanksgiving conversation."

Matthew rolled his eyes and laughed, the sound booming out and drawing everyone's attention. "You have no idea. Every goddamn year. However, I'm not the only crazy asshole with stories of setting something on fire or falling off a horse or sticking a bean up her nose and being scared to tell. So I'm just one in a line of stories."

"Yeah but you're the only one with a W on your ass to show for it." He giggled like he was the one who was drinking. "Oh, man."

"A *flying* W, thank you very much." And they were off again, cackling madly, Matthew slapping the bar with his big ham hand.

"Oh...my sides hurt." He poured Matthew another shot.

"Hey, Ty?" That was Peter.

Tyler looked down the bar. "Oh. Peter needs a hand. Sorry." He tapped the bar and gave Matthew a smile. "Back in a minute."

He wasn't though, he got a second to take Matthew's dinner order and another here and there, but it was late before the bar quieted down enough for him to try to have a real conversation again.

"Hey. Are you doing okay?" He poured himself a Coke and leaned on the bar. "Sorry it's so busy."

"You're working, honey. I'm not stressed. It means good tips." In fact, Matthew was damn near through a novel that was sitting next to him, a beer mat keeping his place.

"Never lonely?" He pointed to the book. "Is it good?"

"Not bad. I care about the hero. I want the bad guy to lose. Those are both good signs, right?"

"Sounds like it. I was going to grab some fries and take a break. You want to snag a table?" It was quiet now; he'd trade off with Peter.

"I would love that. Yes." Matthew stood, lifted book and Coke, and headed back to one of the tables along the wall.

He picked up his own Coke, ducked into the kitchen for his fries, and then found Matthew, looking comfortable and watching him cross the room. "I'm hungry."

"You've been working your heinie off." Matthew stood and pulled out his chair for him.

That made him feel important. "Thank you." He kept his eyes on Matthew as the cowboy sat down again. "How was your dinner?"

"It was good. I like a steak sandwich, and your cook makes good fries. I like when they're crispy. I can't ever make them like that." Matthew's eyes searched his face. "Do you cook?"

"A little. I make a few things. Nothing fancy. My kitchen is really tiny. But I enjoy trying. You?"

"Same here. I can make basic food, for the most part." Matthew chuckled softly. "I do better with the grill and eggs and stuff. And I can make oatmeal like a champion."

"Don't laugh. I make really good salads. I love salad. And

I do make mac and cheese. Some chicken dishes. Cooking for one isn't much fun."

"Are you sure you don't want to come visit the ranch? My baby girl is a fiend for mac and cheese."

Visit? Matthew was so sweet but... "If I were to visit anyone after knowing them for twenty-four hours it would be you." He smiled and rested his fingers on Matthew's. "I am touched that you trust me, that you'd trust me around your kids. I am. But you move fast, cowboy."

"I do. I've been told that before. I listen to my gut a lot." Matthew turned his fingers over, gave them a quick squeeze.

"I do too, and it's telling me you're a good man. Everything else it's telling me is about me, not you." His heart was in self-defense mode, and he knew it.

"You've had a hard row to hoe for a bit. I'm sorry." Matthew held his gaze, and he could drown in that gray. It was like clouds.

He hadn't pulled his hand away, he just let it rest in Matthew's, and didn't shy away from that gaze either. "You're the first person I've been able to have a conversation about Will with. That counts for something."

"It means a lot. I appreciate your trust, honey." Matthew took a deep breath. "You're the first person I've felt a connection to in a long time."

If there was something real here, what was the rush? "Where did you get your beautiful eyes from? Your mother or your father?"

"I am the spitting image of my daddy and granddaddy. Very, very much. Premature gray and everything. I started going gray at seventeen."

"I was going to ask. About the hair, I mean. Peter asked me if you were a lot older. It doesn't matter to me at all, so I didn't even think about it, but I told him I didn't think you were even forty yet."

"I turned thirty-three in December, so closer to thirty than forty." Matthew actually pinked, and that was adorable. "Jonas says I need to dye it, but... I have to admit, I like how it feels, and I'm used to it."

"No, no. Don't." He took Matthew's hand more firmly. "I like it. It's handsome. It's...you."

"Thank you." That blush deepened, and Matthew beamed at him, so obviously pleased.

He smiled at Matthew quietly for a second to let them both enjoy that moment, but curiosity got the better of him. "Are you a Christmas baby?"

"New Year's Eve. Born at 11:50 p.m. My folks were tickled pink because they got to count three kids on their taxes." Matthew winked at him. "What about you? When's your birthday?"

"Christmas Eve eve. Early in the morning. Between the two of us, we'll ruin the holidays." He laughed.

Matthew snorted hard. "Oh lord. Emma is Valentine's Day. Guess Sophia's birthday?"

He threw it out there. "Halloween?"

"Got it in one. My little sparkly non-spooky girl."

"You got something backward there. Does that rule out costume birthday parties?"

"What we usually do is let her have her birthday party on the weekend after Halloween. That way she gets both a Halloween and a birthday. Her Girl Scout troop does a party. Her dance troop. Her basketball team." Matthew sighed dramatically. "I'm so abused."

Tyler grinned and popped a French fry in his mouth. "The things you do for your kids, right? That's what my mom would say, usually while rolling her eyes at me. The things I do for you."

"I try. My folks help out a ton—especially now that Emma is older. Otherwise I'd lose my damn mind."

"Sounds like Emma is going to give you a run for your money." He glanced at his watch. He didn't want to leave Peter on his own too long.

"Is it time to get back to work already? That was quick. Do you mind if I hang out, or is that weird as all get out?"

"I have another minute or two. And I don't mind at all. I like your company, and you'd just go back to a hotel room alone. What fun is that? There's nothing weird about hanging out in a bar." Tyler would be on his own for a bit while Peter was on break, and then he'd have to restock and clean up, but Matthew had his book.

"Excellent. Good deal. The hotel is fine, but I'd rather be here with you."

"With me is kind of a stretch when I'm busy, but I know what you mean." He chomped down his last French fry. "You're kind of my new addiction too."

"I'll take that." Matthew squeezed his hand again and stood. "Thank you for sharing your break with me."

"Thanks for not eating all my fries." He winked, picking up after himself. "Looks like your seat is still available." He headed back to the bar.

What would Will have said? *Go for it? You're an idiot? Is this bar it for you?* New York was all he knew. It was home, it was easy, it was safe and familiar. It was easy to get lost in when he really didn't want to be noticed.

He couldn't remember the last time he'd made a decision without Will to help him sort things out.

"I got you, Peter. Go get dinner."

"He's staying, huh?" Peter winked at him. "He's so into you. Like deep. That's cool."

"I think you're right. It's terrifying, he keeps asking me to visit Texas. I'm not ready to send him away either."

"Texas. Wow. That's...that's forever away. Still, it's cool as hell." Peter stared at him for a second, like he couldn't quite put words together.

He sighed. Yeah, that was what he thought. "It's too far. I know."

"I don't know. If Nathan asked me... I'd go. I'd just say yes."

He shook his head. "Okay, one, you're in love with Nate. Two, he's your Dom, and three...you've known him how long? It's not the same thing. I've known Matthew one whole day. One day."

He wasn't going to look too hard at why he was so defensive about Peter's statement right now.

"Okay. Okay, sorry." Peter stepped back, held up his hands. "You're right. It's not my business. I was just being... I'm going to the kitchen. I'll be back in fifteen."

Tyler sighed as he watched Peter disappear into the back. Dammit. He'd apologize after Peter got a break. In the meantime, he'd...totally ignore whatever made him step in Peter's attempt to help him in the first place.

And that meant work. He made a round of the people at the bar, refilled the ice, and restocked the fridge. He ran the mop over the floor because his sneakers were squeaking. He only gave Matthew a couple of quick glances, making sure to smile.

Nobody was mad at Matthew.

Someone came over to Matthew, some younger twink in tight everything, hand on his arm, maybe asking to buy him a drink, maybe asking him to dance.

His eyes narrowed and he grabbed a Dr Pepper from the fridge. "I brought you a Dr Pepper, Matthew." He rested a hand on Matthew's and looked at the guy. "Can I get you anything?"

"I—"

Matthew turned his hand over and held on. "I was just telling this young man that I was waiting here for the best bartender I've ever met."

He refused to blush, but he let it straighten his spine a little. "I try. They're keeping me busy tonight. You have an ID? I'll make you something special."

"I—I gotta—" The kid almost ran off, and Matthew blinked.

"Thank you, honey. He was awful forward given I'm old enough to be his daddy."

Being his daddy was probably what the kid wanted.

"You're not used to every available man in town hitting on you? I'm surprised. You're sitting alone at a bar looking h—handsome and available." Hot. That's what he wanted to say, hot. Was he crazy? Matthew was available and into him.

"Hit on? Me? I haven't been hit on... Christ, honey, since high school." Matthew squeezed his fingers, then drew him to his lips and brushed a soft, soft kiss over his knuckles. "Handsome, though? That I'll take and be grateful."

Oh. Okay. That was a first. A very strange and lovely first that made him tingle and blush so dark he could feel the heat travel up from his chest.

"You're going to make it very hard for me to finish out my shift."

"Should I be sorry?" Matthew watched him like he was beautiful, fascinating. "I'll be waiting right here, honey. No worries."

"Don't be sorry. Just be...patient." He slid his hand from

Matthew's, not taking back, just needing to get to work. "And give me a wave if you need anything."

He couldn't stop smiling, but he turned away anyway and took a drink order from a couple in so much leather he had a hard time believing Matthew hadn't put the pieces together yet. Maybe Matthew didn't have the pieces to put together. He'd asked for gay-friendly. Maybe that was enough to satisfy any questions.

"Hey, Peter." Tyler caught Peter at the freezer. "I'm sorry. Things are weird, and I don't know what I'm supposed to do. I appreciate you listening."

"Sure, man. I'm just a romantic. I know that." Peter smiled at him, the look tentative. "Is there anything we need up front?"

"I know you are. I like that about you." He gave Peter a wink and a pat on the arm. "I've been stocking…it's just the liquor I think at this point." He watched a group walk in through the doors and shook his head. "Looks like we're going to rock until closing tonight."

"Good for business, bad for flirting "

"Shut up." He laughed and got to work.

When he had a second to breathe again it was late. Late enough that Peter was flashing lights and turning the music down. "Goodnight, everybody!" Peter shouted, killing the dance floor lights and turning on the white floods.

He squinted. So painful.

Matthew blinked, dipping his head against the glare, the last Dr Pepper almost dry. "Y'all need some help cleaning up?"

"Thanks, but Les gets squirrely about that, something about insurance. It won't take long. You must be exhausted though. Isn't this past your bedtime?"

"I guess it is, although I'm an hour earlier. It was worth

it. I enjoyed our visits." Matthew looked unsure of himself, then he held his arms open. "Would it be too forward to ask for a hug?"

"A hug. Sure. Not forward at all." A hug. He already knew this was going to be a slippery slope. If not in deed, at least in his own mind. He stepped around the bar, probably looking every bit as unsure as Matthew felt before he stepped into the cowboy's patiently waiting arms.

Matthew gathered him in and held him, the touch warm and solid. He could feel the way Matthew breathed, the softness of Matthew's beard on his temple.

He took a deep breath and held on to the first bit of genuine comfort he'd had in months, shocked to find himself fighting off tears. Matthew was painfully perfect, and he had a much harder time with a second breath than he had with the first.

"Someone I barely know shouldn't feel this good."

"I hear that. You smell good to me. I don't want to go. Do you want—you could come to my room. Just to talk, have coffee?"

"Okay." The answer came out without a thought, it didn't need one.

"Oh." Matthew took a deep breath, and Tyler could feel how nervous the big man had been by the shiver. "Thank you. Where do you want me to wait for you?"

God, he smelled like alcohol and fried food. He was going to have to ask to take a shower. Maybe... "Listen, I smell like a bar and I don't have anything clean to put on. How about I meet you at your hotel in a little bit? Unless you want some coffee at my place."

"I'm easy. I'll be happy to go to yours. I just want to spend more time with you." Matthew kissed his temple.

The kiss made him warm, made him want to lean in for

another one. "Okay. Okay cool. So, hang out at that table by the door, and we'll go in a bit. Soon."

"Sounds like a plan." Matthew reluctantly let him go, moving back toward the table to sit.

Now he was a man on a mission. He used to close up quickly when Will was waiting to head home with him so he'd have company on the subway; he was good at getting the job done fast when he needed to. And Peter was always anxious to get home to his man. The place was clean, the bar was stocked, and they were locking up in less than half an hour. And Peter had only teased him once.

"Cab or subway?"

"I'll call a car for us." Matthew handed over his phone. "Put in your address?"

He took the phone and tapped in the address for his little place in Chelsea. "It's not much. It's a quirky little place."

"I like quirky." Matthew made sure their fingers brushed together when he took the phone back. "I just want to be with you."

"You keep saying that, so I guess I'll believe you. I'm very… I'm just going with my gut." He wasn't sure where his head was at, his heart. Matthew just seemed to have his own gravity, and Tyler had decided not to fight it.

He started running over what his place looked like in his head. Was the kitchen clean? The living room? Did he have milk for the coffee? Shit.

"Me too." Matthew let him have his space, let him breathe. "They're here. Are you—do you still want me to come with? I'll respect it if you say no."

He took Matthew's hand firmly, then glanced up at the cowboy. "Where's the car?"

"Come on. Her name is Alana, apparently. Pretty little

lady with pink hair." Matthew beamed at him and led him outside.

"Have you ever been out running around New York at two thirty in the morning before?"

"I have not. Not once." Matthew didn't look the least bit scared.

"It's busier than you would think in some places and weirdly deserted in others. My neighborhood is quiet, but to get there we'll go through midtown, and that's still busy. A lot of those bars are open until four." It wouldn't be a long ride though.

"Yeah? I don't think they can be open that late at home. I haven't been to a lot of bars in the last decade or so. Just a few." Matthew held his hand, thumb stroking his skin. "What's your favorite drink to make? Have I asked you that?"

"I don't know..." He watched Matthew's big fingers practically swallow his, and he wasn't tiny. "I like the layered drinks like the black Russian. I like simple, pretty drinks like...a J&T. A Johnnie and tonic? That one has guava juice and lime...yummy."

"I make virgin pina coladas once in a while and de-virgin mine. I do like a tequila sunrise sometimes. Mostly I make milkshakes." Matthew winked at him. "I rock at those."

"Tequila sunrise is one of my favorites to drink. And who doesn't like a milkshake? Add a little Kahlua if you want a kick."

"Yes, Kahlua and I are friends. I like a Kahlua and cream sometimes when I can't sleep. What's your favorite milkshake flavor? Coffee? Chocolate? Cookies and Cream?"

"Yes." He laughed and nodded. "All of those. You?"

"It depends. I love a blackberry cobbler milkshake in the

summer. A pumpkin one in the fall. Peppermint and chocolate at the holidays..."

"Oh my God, you really know your stuff. I've never even heard of a blackberry cobbler milkshake. That sounds amazing. You're a milkshake expert."

They rode across town, right past the bright lights of Times Square where it might as well be high noon.

"I live within driving distance of the Blue Bell factory..." Matthew leaned toward him. "There's a miniature horse ranch next door."

He snorted, grinning. "Tempting. Are you going to start offering me lollipops next?"

"I'm sure I have some suckers, but..." Matthew looked at him, eyes wide. "So. Yeah, I said that. Lord have mercy."

He blushed, dropping his face into one hand. "Oh God. I asked the damn question first."

They stared at each other for a while, then they both cracked up, laughing hysterically.

"I swear," he said through his giggles. "I didn't mean it that way. I swear to God."

"Me either. Although, I sure managed to get there, didn't I?" Matthew rolled his eyes, and the chuckles started again.

"It's late. The twelve-year-old boys were bound to come out." The car pulled to a stop. Wow. He'd lost a few blocks laughing. "Oh. This is us."

"Good deal. I can't wait to see."

Two locked doors later, they were inside his building and climbing stairs. His apartment was on the third floor, and three more locks got them in. He was a fairly neat person, but he had a lifetime worth of things in this two-bedroom apartment. He'd lived here and had the same bedroom since he was nine years old.

He turned on the light in his tiny kitchen as they entered

and then went for the one in the living room too. "Sorry if it's kind of a mess. I wasn't expecting guests."

"It's fine, honey. I'm not worried." Matthew took his hat off, turned it brim up and put it on the table. "Is this okay?"

God, Matthew was pretty. Rugged, tan, with those intense gray eyes.

"Oh, yeah. Make yourself comfortable. I'll start some coffee and then hop in the shower." Matthew looked enormous in this small space. He just took up all the air, all the room. But Tyler didn't mind one bit.

"If you'll show me where your coffee is, I'll do that. I'm good at coffee, and you've worked hard."

"Oh. Oh sure, it's um..." *You're so sweet.* "Everything is in the cabinet right above the coffee maker."

"Excellent. Go on and get cleaned up, and I'll make some coffee for us." Matthew unbuttoned his shirt sleeves and started rolling them up.

"Won't be a minute." Tyler backed out of the kitchen, fascinated by the way Matthew very capably settled into his kitchen like he belonged there.

He took a fast shower, scrubbing himself naked-sex clean, even though he had absolutely no intention of having naked sex. He'd had no intention of bringing a cowboy home either and yet, there was a cowboy in his kitchen making coffee.

What the hell was he doing? Why didn't it feel...wrong? Or at least weird?

He found clean jeans and a T-shirt that didn't have a stupid graphic on it, brushed his teeth and combed his hair, decided against shoes, and went back out into the living room.

Matthew had something soft and twangy playing on his phone, and he was singing along, two mugs waiting for him.

"What are you singing?" Matthew looked absolutely comfortable, like he'd been here a hundred times.

"Oh, it's a guy—Cody Johnson? I like him a lot. Been to a couple of his shows when he was a rodeo guy. I always go to the Houston rodeo during spring break with the girls."

"I like his voice. And yours. Did you find the milk for your coffee?" He was ready for a cup, and to sit with Matthew and...sit. Talk. Stare at the cowboy for a while.

"I didn't snoop, but I will now. How do you take yours, and I'll fix us up."

"Milk and sugar, please. I like it pretty light." He leaned on the counter. "Thanks for making it. I feel human now. I didn't want to sit in your hotel room smelling like a bum."

"No problem. I get that. After a hard day's work, a shower makes things right." Matthew made Tyler's coffee first, then his own. "Should we sit?"

"Yeah. Come on." In the living room he sat on the couch and patted the cushions next to him. "Next to me?"

"I'd love to, thank you." Matthew sat and inhaled deep. "Oh, you do smell good."

"Soap." He smiled and sipped his coffee. "It's all the rage."

"So-o-oap? What is this sorcery you speak of?" Matthew's eyes twinkled in the lamplight. "It makes a man smell good?"

"Seems to work." He took another sip of his coffee. "How is it you make better coffee in my coffee maker than I do? That's just wrong."

"I am a lover of the coffee. I seduce it, whisper to it. Tell it how bad I need it."

Lucky fucking coffee.

He decided to live dangerously and caught Matthew's eyes. "I'm a little jealous."

"Well, I have a devious plan. I seduce the coffee, then I start on your cup. It gets right to your lips." Matthew held his gaze. "Once that's solid, I'm going to beg a kiss and see if the chemistry between us is as wonderful as I think it is."

"What if it is? Then what?" That's the part he hadn't figured out for himself. What if?

"Then we see what happens next." Matthew held his hand.

"I'm not going to lose a chance at something wonderful because I don't know what to do."

He didn't believe for one second that Matthew didn't know what to do. Matthew had been steady since the first invitation to Texas. He took a breath, held up his cup, then set it down on the table. "Okay. Then how about we cut out the middleman?"

Matthew put his mug next to his and nodded. "I find you always get the best deal that way. I've wanted to kiss you since lunchtime."

He licked his lips, anticipation making his spine tingle and his heart beat heavily. "It was probably good you waited. I might have said no at lunchtime. You're doing a good job of wearing me down, though. The coffee pot is easy."

"Lunchtime wasn't the right time." Matthew stroked his bottom lip, the touch electric and smooth and sweet and wild, all at once. "Now, though? Now is good."

Then Matthew leaned in, the brush of their mouths an insane amount of input—Matthew's mustache tickled, his lips were soft, the hand on Tyler's cheek was callused and huge and hot.

He closed his eyes, trying to focus on what was important here—not his doubts or his living room—just this feeling, this man, this moment. He made himself breathe, as shaky as it was, and let his lips part, welcoming the kiss.

Matthew moaned softly—Tyler more felt it than heard it—and then Matthew's hot tongue traced his bottom lip, introducing the touch before it came in.

He answered with a sound of his own, something a little tighter than a moan, and reached for Matthew, curling his fingers into soft silver hair as their tongues explored and tasted.

Matthew held him, and with every kiss, every shaky breath, he moved closer, until he was in Matthew's lap. Matthew's hands trailed over his back, moving with slow, steady petting motions, matching their drugging kisses.

It wasn't just a kiss; whatever Matthew had was seeping into his little cracks and crevices and soothing him.

"Matthew." He stroked the cowboy's beard and pressed their foreheads together just to get a breath.

"Damn, honey. You're fine to me." Matthew's eyes were so dark, a deep, rich gray that he could sink into.

"You're...you make me feel...so good." He didn't know. Good sounded so lame, and not big enough. He gave up on words and kissed Matthew again, letting that speak for him. "There."

"Uh-huh." Matthew nodded, and Tyler loved the dazed expression on Matthew's face.

"You have the most incredible eyes."

He needed to let things sink in a minute. He settled against Matthew and drew a hand over that broad chest, the fabric of Matthew's shirt gliding under his fingers.

Matthew seemed to hear him, humming softly as the big man held him, cradling him close.

"Okay. It's wonderful. Now we know." Knowing didn't answer any questions for him though, it just made room for more. He decided not to ask any of them right now. “I kind of want to bottle this feeling.”

Matthew nodded, chin gentle on his temple. “That would be cool—just pull it out and have it whenever things felt rough.”

“Mmhmm.” He sighed happily and sat up, looking for another kiss. “Things do not feel rough right now.”

“No. Things feel stupidly right.” Matthew grinned at him, then gave him what he needed, the kiss slow but deep, like a wave crashing over them.

A cell phone rang—not his—and he decided to ignore it. Nobody he wanted to talk to called at three in the morning.

It stopped, then immediately rang again once, stopped again, then another ring, and Matthew frowned. “That’s the family’s 911 pattern. I got to answer.”

Matthew pulled the phone out. “Sister? Sister, what’s—oh fuck. Okay. Is he—Shit.” Suddenly all the softness was gone from those gray eyes, replaced with a sharpness, an amazing focus. “You need to calm down. Where did they take him, Austin or Houston? I know, I know. Is Jonas on his way? Good. Give me two minutes to figure things out. Take the girls to Aunt Kathy. Have you called Momma and them yet?”

Tyler slid off Matthew’s lap, watching and listening. Rachel’s husband or her kids…something bad was happening.

Matthew took his hand, not letting him get too far. “I love you, Sister. I’ll be home to help with Elias, not that he needs much. Don’t fret. Yeah. Yeah, call me when the surgeon gets there. Love you too. Bye.” Matthew hung up the phone and sighed. “Well, fuck.”

“Who is it? What happened?” He held Matthew’s hand tight.

"Noah was in a bad accident. His girlfriend got a new truck, and they flipped it. Both him and the little girl he's seeing are in the hospital. Noah's waiting for surgery; they think he might lose his leg, and Hannah hasn't woke up. Shit!" Matthew closed his eyes for a second. "Fuck me, this sucks. You sure you don't want to come to Texas, honey? See the sights?"

"I... I can't I have work tomorrow and—" He couldn't just ditch. And even if he could he had to be back for work on Tuesday...that made no sense. "You have to go though, I know. It's family. I get it."

"I do. I need to help. You know—tell me I can text? Call? You're not just some guy. I want to be—I don't want to be a memory to you." There was something so vulnerable, so worried and honest and real about Matthew.

God. This was terrible. He wanted desperately to rewind to five minutes ago and bottle it like he'd said. Freeze time. "Please call. Any time." He got to his feet and made room for Matthew to stand. "I want to stay in touch." They'd kissed, and it was wonderful, but... "This wasn't the what if I was hoping for."

"No. No, me either, but if you change your mind. If you need a change of scenery, you're welcome—no strings, no bullshit. I will buy your ticket. You just say the word." Matthew cupped his cheek. "I have so much to show you."

He nodded and leaned into Matthew's big frame. Maybe he could visit eventually. "Your family needs you, and they come first. Let's talk once you know what's happening."

"They do. Not a memory, right? I want to be real to you." Matthew kissed his temple, the touch painfully soft.

Tyler lifted his head and got a long look into Matthew's gray eyes. "You are real. I won't forget you. I can't." *Kiss me again before you go?*

"I'm holding you to that, honey." Matthew leaned down and kissed him, the touch as intense as before.

He hummed into the kiss and combed his fingers through Matthew's hair, not ready to let the cowboy go.

He knew he was going to have to, but he wasn't ready. He was worried he'd never be ready.

5

Christ on a sparkly purple crutch, Matthew was tired as all get out.

He sighed and shook his head as he made the drive from Sister's to the ranch. He'd offered to pick Noah up from therapy, grab supper for them, his little family, and Momma and Daddy on the way. He'd dropped off Noah, who wasn't walking yet, but it was coming—he'd be on his feet by the time school started. He'd dropped off the food. Now he was heading for Momma's to get his girls.

He checked the time, then told his truck. "Call Tyler."

"Hey! Hi! Hang on!" Tyler shouted into the phone, loud music in the background. It was close to nine in New York, and Tyler was obviously working at the bar. There was a lot of commotion, but then all the noise just stopped, and Tyler was back on the line. "Hey. How are you?"

"Missing you like a lost limb. Fixin' to go pick up the girls. How's work?"

"Busy. I wish you were here, sitting at the bar." Tyler sounded tired. "How's Noah?"

"Doing good with therapy. He will be walking good by the end of summer. I got everyone fried chicken for supper. I wish you were here. The pool is almost done."

"The girls must be excited. Do they dance all summer, or is that done now until fall?" Tyler had taken in interest in the girls and asked about them a lot.

"It's done until fall. Which is good and bad. Bad because I haven't found anyone I trust to help, good because I like hanging with them." Matthew sighed softly and stretched. "I miss you. Bad."

"I miss you too. It's gotten busy here. Pride month is always nuts. Every night might as well be Friday. Good for tips, but it's exhausting." Tyler sighed. "You must get tired of calling me every day and hearing the same thing."

"No." A little, but Tyler was being reasonable. "I'm a patient man. I will just keep asking until you're ready. If you come for the Fourth, we can shoot off fireworks and swim, have a big cookout."

Tyler sighed. "That's a huge tourist weekend here."

Yeah. He was sure it was. *Oh, Deb, I'm a fool. Some things won't ever change.* "Good money for you, then. I'll be hosting this year; next year it's Jonas' turn again."

"Yep. Weekends like that go a long way toward rent. That's cool that you trade it around. This year you'll have to pool for everyone, so that'll be cool. Oh, hey. I need to get back out there. Thanks for calling. I'll text you late like always."

"Okay, honey. Take care of you. I'll be thinking about you." *I think I love you.* "Bye."

"Later. Bye." Tyler hung up. Again. Lately he was hanging up first a lot.

"So, that went well." Go team him. "Lord, Deb. I shoulda

just turned my phone off and had one night with him, you know? Just one night."

He swore he could hear her laughing at him.

On the subway, omw home. You're sleeping, I know, so good morning! I'll be asleep when you read this.

Tyler didn't hit send. Not yet. It wouldn't go through until he got off the train anyway. God, he missed Matthew, and he hated this. He could finally talk because he wasn't at work, and Matthew was sleeping.

Timing sucks, huh?

Their schedules were all off, and there was that hour time difference too. It was frustrating, but they were making it work, right? Sort of. They were making something work.

He closed his eyes for one second and woke up at his stop. His eyes flew open wide. "Shit!" He dove for the doors and just slipped through as they were closing. Woo. Go him. He shook his head as the train pulled away and climbed the stairs to the street.

Hit sent the texts once he made it home and stared at his phone wondering what else he should say.

I miss you. Sorry work was so busy. And he was so fucking tired.

He put his phone down on the bathroom sink and turned on the shower.

His phone rang in answer, Matthew's name popping up. Oh. Oh, not asleep. He shut the shower off again and answered.

"Matthew? What are you doing up? Are you okay?" Matthew got up early. Really early. Should be he worried?

"Fine, honey. Just a touch of insomnia. I'm sitting out here having a Coke and watching the stars. You get home safe?"

"Yeah, but I fell asleep on the subway and almost missed my stop. I hate it when I do that." The shower could wait. He went to the kitchen for a snack and a beer. "It's good to hear your voice. I was just—oh, well you know. I texted you. You're on my mind."

"I get it. I think about you a lot. Was work good?" He could hear Matthew settling in to talk with him.

"It was insane. Great people and everything, but Pride month in a gay bar is a little bit wild. We had three bartenders on, and that was barely enough. A guy came in wearing a thong. That was fun. We had to send him home for pants." His laugh was genuine but weak. He was beat. He popped some bread in the toaster and opened a beer.

"Wow. I've never been to Pride—they have it in Austin and Houston both, but I'm not the type. I'm not a big partier." Matthew chuckled for him. "I'm sure you're shocked."

Not at all. He laughed again. "Not your scene? I bet it's a blast in Austin if the rumors about that place are true. You might like the parade."

"One day we can go together. I'd like that…a lot."

Tyler had to ask. "What do your kids think about you maybe seeing a man?"

"Their Uncle Jonas is gay, honey. He's not very good at monogamous, but he tries." Matthew sighed softly. "I have to tell you, the Flying W has a bit of a reputation of a safe place to come if you're not a straight white guy that wants to cowboy up. I'm trying the whole they'll ask questions when they need to thing."

Whoa. Did he hear that right? Maybe he should have gone for coffee instead of a beer.

"Wait. You run a big gay ranch?" He grinned. This had suddenly become the best conversation ever. Even if it was the middle of the night.

"Well, I got ten cowboys—nine drovers and a foreman. Krissy is my foreman—her wife Lisa is a truck driver that does long haul. Out of the nine drovers I got three straight men, four not-straight ones, a pretty little lesbian from Houston, and a Daniel that used to be a Danielle. I got no idea whether he's straight or not. He's real shy." Matthew sighed, the sound soft. "He'd been beat up pretty bad when Allen brought him home. I got rules—you want to kick someone's ass, it better be because they didn't do their goddamn job or they try stealing from me or worse. I don't hold with folks hating on others because of color or loving or creed or shit."

He had no idea what a drover was, but he didn't care. Matthew was perfect. Perfect. And he was fifteen hundred miles away. "You're a good man." Was he stupid? "I'll come for the Fourth."

Matthew was silent for a second, then Tyler heard, "Oh, thank you, Jesus," in the barest whisper. Then Matthew cleared his throat, voice husky. "I'll send you a ticket. You tell me what day you'll come out."

He inhaled, trying to force down the nerves in his gut. He missed Matthew a hundred times more all of a sudden, and he wanted one of Matthew's kisses so badly it hurt. "I will. I need to check with work, and then I'll tell you."

"That's more than fair. Oh, honey. I want you. I want to hold you so bad." Matthew said the things he was feeling.

"I know. I know exactly. I feel all of that...this ache in my chest, it's awful. I need time with you, I need to figure this out. I'm just...torn. Confused. I don't understand what I'm feeling—" *Oh God, shut up.* He took a sip of his beer to stop himself from saying anything else and ignored how his hands were shaking. He was a fucking disaster. Just like that. He was fine, and then he wasn't.

"I hear you. I need that too. Hell, I want to introduce you to my babies, my land. I want to reach out and touch you. I want to make you breakfast and watch a movie together. There's all sorts of things we haven't gotten to do yet."

"Like anything, Matthew. We haven't done *anything.*" And that's why this made no sense. But if he had learned anything from losing Will, it was that emotions and feelings weren't logical. They didn't progress neatly, and they didn't go away like they should.

Knowing that didn't make anything easier, it just made him feel less...stupid. He sipped his beer and paced the room. He was starting to feel anxious and tried to make himself breathe.

"If your boss lets you, and you need to, come now. Come and stay for a couple of weeks. I can help with rent. You can rest your soul for a bit, breathe and relax."

"I can't think about that right now. I just need some sleep. It's the middle of the night is all. I'm fine." He could take something. All of Will's shit was still in the medicine cabinet.

"It is. You rest hard. I'm going to have a long shower, I think, and then decide what to do next. You take care of you, honey. I miss you."

"I'm sorry you can't sleep." He sighed. "I miss you too. I do. So much." He'd take a shower too, and crash, and think tomorrow.

"Get some good sleep. I'll talk to you tomorrow. Later today. You know what I mean."

"I do. Talk to you tomorrow. Goodnight, Matthew." He hung up, because otherwise they could be saying goodnight forever.

A hot shower would help him calm down. And then he'd sleep. If not, his hands just might shake until the Fourth of July.

6

"Emma, did you check for eggs?" Matthew rolled his eyes as she came out of the house wearing a ladybug costume and a rainbow tutu and her tap shoes. Oh, no. Those damn shoes would fill up with chicken shit in a second. "You can't wear those shoes."

"Daddy!"

"No. Turkey. Go change them and tell your sister to feed the dogs and give them water."

Jesus, he was hot as hell, and he needed to make some lists.

Go get groceries.

Pay bills.

Have one of the guys build a ramp down from the porch.

Hire a pool guy.

Meet with Krissy re finding milk goats for Sophie's 4-H project.

First, though, he needed a big glass of tea. He grabbed his glass and got some ice, grinning at Emma who came back through with her galoshes on. That worked.

"Sister says she's doing her hair right now, but when she's done, she'll feed them."

Matthew didn't roll his eyes. "Is she crying yet?"

"Uh-huh. She wants fishtail braids..."

"Daddy!" He'd heard his name called every which way possible, but that long, drawn-out version with the sob at the end was the one he liked the least.

"Ooh. Good luck!" Emma ducked out the kitchen door.

"Coming, baby. Don't tug yourself bald-headed."

"I hate being stupid! Everyone else does it!" She threw her brush down on the bathroom sink. "I'm so mad, Daddy."

"Yeah, well, I don't mind helping you out." He met her eyes in the mirror. "Hand me your brush, and I'll fix you up."

She handed him her brush with a sigh. "I tried. I watched the YouTube video that Sheri sent me, and I combed my stupid curls straight so it wouldn't tangle and everything. I hate my hair."

"I love your hair. It reminds me of your momma's. It's like the sunshine."

"Aunt Rachel says the chemicals in the pool are going to turn it green, and I need a special shampoo. Did she tell you? She told me she would."

"You've done great with Mamaw and Papaw's pool. I'll find out what she has you wash your hair with there." Lord knew what it would do to his. "Have I ever told you I was still in high school when I found my first gray hair?"

"High School?" Soph sounded horrified. "Well, thank God I have Momma's hair. Poor Em."

"Right?" He started the braiding process, being careful not to pull. "Did I tell you my friend from New York is coming for the Fourth?"

Did I tell you I think I might be in love? Did I tell you I'm a little stupid for him? How about how worried I am that he'll get out here in the sticks and hate it? Hate me?

"You have a friend from New York? Like the big city?"

"Yes, remember? Tyler?" He remembered. He ached with missing the fine son of a bitch.

"Oh, him. Little Tim said he thinks Tyler is your imaginary friend."

"Little Tim needs to learn to keep his mouth shut. He's not imaginary, just a long ways away." Just in a sweet little apartment. Just at a bar. Just not here.

Yet.

"Well he'll know better when Tyler gets here right? You never have friends over. Is he nice?" Sophia patted the braid he was making.

"He is. He so is. He's a good guy. He likes to talk to people." Matthew liked talking to Tyler.

"Will he talk to me? Does he like kids? Does he have any? How old is he? How long is he staying? He can have the trundle bed in my room. If you need it." Sophia beamed at him in the mirror.

"He will talk to you. He asks about y'all all the time, but he doesn't have any babies of his own. I think he's going to need to stretch out, so I'll let him decide where to sleep, but your trundle bed is only little." Hopefully Tyler would sleep in his room, but that wasn't a prerequisite to being here.

"Okay." Sophia looked at him again, eyes shining in the mirror at him, "I'm glad you have a friend, Daddy."

"Me too. I'm so excited for y'all to meet him. Now you got braids, so get on and feed the dogs before they eat your sister."

"Oh is that a thing?" Sophia hopped up and kissed him on the cheek. "I'm gooooiinnnggg, Daaaaddddyyyy." She moved off in a slow running motion, then giggled and took off. "Thank you for the braids!"

"You're welcome, baby. Go on." He headed out to check on Emma and the eggs, finding her sitting on the ground with two hens on her lap, talking to them.

Good lord and butter.

His phone chimed softly, the special text tone that he'd set up for Tyler. It was early in New York, Tyler usually slept long past this hour.

Can I come now? Don't call. Just say yes or no.

Yes. What the fuck? Like he'd say no.

I'm packing. I'll get the next flight. Sorry, we'll talk when I get there. Don't worry. I'm fine. I'm good. I miss you.

What airport? Text me when I'm supposed to pick you up. Oh Jesus. Groceries. He needed groceries. Hopefully Momma and Daddy could take the girls.

I'll text you when I get a flight. Soon. Thank you.

See you soon.

Whoa.

Whoa.

Okay.

He picked up the phone and called Momma. "Hey, Momma, y'all busy? I need some help. I got company coming in and I got to get ready."

He had to do...everything. Today.

Because Tyler was on his way.

7

On the ground. We're taxiing.

Tyler texted Matthew and then looked out the airplane window. Just hours ago he'd been standing in his apartment in New York after another sleepless night, and now he was in Texas. His first plane ride ever, and he wasn't nervous; he'd never felt better, breathed better in his whole life.

Something about the air, it even looked hot in Houston. But he didn't care that the sun was shining, and it seemed like a gorgeous day. Not really. He cared about the guy in the cowboy hat that would be waiting for him in baggage claim.

Waiting for you down here at baggage, honey. Just like that. He'd known Matthew would be there, but to know he was right? That was even better.

Soon.

God, he probably looked like hell. He ran his fingers through his hair to straighten it out, blinked his eyes to clear some of the tired out of them.

It took forever to get off the plane. Tyler tucked his backpack higher on his shoulder as he hurried up the breezeway and into the busy airport, then followed the signs and the crowd and eventually found where he was going. For some reason he'd thought Matthew would be easy to spot, but tall and in a cowboy hat described nearly every man as far as he could see.

"Hey, honey. You look like a breath of fresh air." He turned and there was Matthew, two cups of iced coffee in his hands. "I brought you something to drink. How was your flight?"

He looked up into those deep gray eyes and smiled. "Hi." *Oh, God. You're more beautiful than I remember.* "It was good. Long. It was my first flight ever."

"I'm so glad to see you, honey. You ready to come home with me? You hungry?" Matthew held his gaze, watching him, drinking him in.

"I'm ready." He nodded and reached for his coffee, swallowing hard. "I just packed… I have a suitcase."

"Good deal. Let's grab that, get the truck, and we'll get some food on the way home. You must be starving." Matthew winked at him. "Houston's traffic is hell, but once we get outside of town, it'll be a nice drive."

"Food sounds good. A nice drive sounds better." He jumped when the horn blared, and the baggage belt started moving. "Jesus. Is the place on fire?"

"Possibly. This is Houston." Matthew rolled his eyes. "Crazy busy place. The ranch will be a change of pace. I bought steaks for supper tonight. The pool's done, and the outdoor kitchen is back in business."

Matthew led him to the baggage claim, staying close, offering him slow, happy smiles.

"You have an outdoor kitchen?" Is there anything Matthew didn't have on the ranch? "Steak sounds amazing. It all does. When do I get to kiss you?"

"When we get out of this crush of people. I want to be able to spend a minute or two on it."

"Okay. Perfect." Tyler smiled at that. He'd like a minute or ten too. He grabbed his bag off the belt as soon as he saw it, so ready to get out of this crowd. "Thank you for the coffee, I needed it."

"I always am thirsty to death when I get off a plane. I thought it would be a good pick me up." Matthew took his bag like it weighed nothing and led him out into blazing heat. "The truck is right over here. The big gray dually."

"Big man, big truck. Totally what I expected." He started making a list in his head of all the firsts he'd had since he got up this morning. He had a feeling it was going to be a long, long list by the end of the day. "This will be my first ride in a truck."

"No shit?" Matthew looked utterly shocked, gray eyes wide. "That's...this is going to be the best truck ride ever."

"You know it." He laughed as Matthew put his suitcase in the back and then climbed in. He still couldn't believe he was here. "Whoa. This is nice. Fancy truck."

"Thanks, honey. I like driving it." Matthew leaned into the truck and put his hat brim up on the dashboard. "I like seeing you in it. So much."

"Where are we headed? How long is the drive?" He got comfortable and studied all the bells and whistles in the dash. "I'm not usually in the front seat of a car, either. This is so weird."

Matthew settled in his seat and started the engine, turning the a/c up on high. "Can I kiss you, honey? Please?"

"I've been waiting all day." He braced an elbow on the console and leaned across it.

That huge, warm hand cupped his face, and Matthew

brought their lips together, kissing him like he was precious, like he was welcome and necessary.

He whimpered into the kiss and tangled his fingers into Matthew's shirt, holding on like he needed proof that this was real even though that strong hand and the cowboy's rich scent made it difficult to doubt. He'd made the right choice. He knew it when he looked into Matthew's eyes and he knew it even more now. Matthew was what had been missing.

"Oh, honey. God, I've missed you." Matthew's voice was rough as a cob, and it felt amazing, to hear how much Matthew needed him.

"It doesn't make sense, but I've decided I don't care. This is right." He took another quick kiss and smiled at Matthew. "I can't wait to meet your kids. See the ranch. Everything."

"Lunch first, hmm? What sounds good? Mexican? Barbecue? Burgers?" Matthew put his seatbelt and his sunglasses on, then backed out of the parking space and into the sunshine.

He pulled his seatbelt back on as well and dug his sunglasses and a Mets cap out of his backpack. "All of that sounds good. Man, the sun is bright." He leaned on the console again and tapped Matthew's thigh with his fingers.

He could hardly believe this was happening. This morning he was an exhausted wreck and now he felt great. He was even hungry.

"Let's grab some Mexican then. I have a craving for chips and salsa." It didn't take any time for them to be away from the airport. "Lord, it's good to see you. My babies are so excited to meet you they can't hardly bear it."

"You told them about me? I mean...what did you tell them?"

"That you were my very good friend, and that I love to

talk to you. Sophia offered to let you sleep in her trundle bed. I told her I thought you needed more legroom." Matthew glanced over at him. "I had a guest room made up for you. I want you to know, you're welcome in my room, but I wanted you to have the choice."

Beds. God, he hadn't even considered the whole bed situation, but of course Matthew would have had to with the girls and everything. He knew what bed he wanted to be in, he didn't come all this way to sleep in the guest room. "Oh, the trundle bed. Definitely. Sophia and I will do our nails and talk about boys."

"Sophia would love that. Bone deep. Her daddy might need someone to keep him warm, though."

"Don't you have a dog? What's a ranch without a dog?" He grinned and drew a hand over Matthew's arm from shoulder to wrist, teasing.

"I have Lucys. Westley and Buttercup are my breeding pair. I have three other bitches that I stud out—Lily, Rosie, and Marigold."

"That's a lot of dogs. What are you breeding? I bet Westley and Buttercup would keep you plenty warm. Great names, by the way. One of my favorite movies."

"Mine too. You know about Lucys? Some folks call 'em blue lacys? They're the smartest dogs on earth. Born and bred in Texas. I train them up to work the cattle and the goats."

"I have never heard of them, but I like dogs. No dog is taking my place in your bed tonight, though. Sophia and I can have a slumber party some other time."

Matthew grinned and reached out, stroked his leg. "Good. I want you like all get out."

Oh, that was good to hear.

"That's what I needed to hear you say." He took Matthew's hand and tangled their fingers.

Matthew held on until they turned off onto an off-ramp and pulled into a little building with a sign that said La Senorita. "Lunch."

"Yeah? Awesome. Wow. This is kind of the middle of nowhere, huh?" He climbed out of the truck and looked around at all the open space. "This is a lot of...parking lot."

"Yessir. There's a lot more space everywhere here than you're used to. I love holes in the walls. Hole in the walls? Holes in the wall? Little restaurants." Matthew held the door open for him, and it was a little place decorated in wild colors and ancient Dos Equis posters, but it smelled like spicy heaven.

"Thank you, sir." He smiled at Matthew and went in. "Oh wow. What a neat place. Smells so good."

"Right? I need to decide whether I want those enchiladas or a combination plate." Matthew beamed at the young man that came over. "Table for two please."

They were the only people in the place, and in seconds they had a huge basket of hot chips and a tub of salsa, plus iced waters.

"What do you want to drink, honey?"

"Oh, just a Coke please." He dove right into the chips. "These are warm!" He took a bite. "Oh. Yummy."

"One Coke and an iced tea, please, sir. And can we get some queso and some guacamole? I'm starving."

He watched the server hurry off and dipped another chip into the salsa. "This is so good. I want whatever you're having. I have so much to learn here, I don't even recognize most of what's on this menu."

"Combination plate it is then—enchilada, taco and a tamale. You can taste it all."

"Perfect. I'm so happy to be here with you. I'm up for anything. Whatever you want me to know, see, do, learn. I want to feel like I can do this, you know? I mean, you're not going to move to New York, so..." He was terrified. He felt like he was on another planet and he'd only been here an hour. But it was okay, because this was Matthew's world.

"I'll show you everything." Matthew held his gaze, those eyes smiling for him. "I want to give you a space to breathe, to heal. I want to—shit, honey. I want to love on you and make you happy."

He nodded as the server brought their drinks. "I'm sorry. I'm just slower at this than you are. It's never been because I didn't want to. I want you to know that. It's never been you that I was questioning."

"No apologies. We've spent a day and a half together. I'm the one that jumps in. Always have been. My brother is fixin' to swallow his own tongue." Matthew looked up at the server. "Two number ones, please, sir. Thank you."

"So everybody knows? I hope he likes me." The most important thing was to make sure the girls did, but it would be nice if he could make a good impression on the rest of Matthew's family, they were all so close.

"Yeah. I mean, I haven't been graphic, especially with my folks, but yes. I wouldn't ask you to be here if I was ashamed. That's not good for anyone." Matthew sighed softly, expression serious. "I think about this stuff a lot. One of the things about being a father, everything has a bit of worry about how your babies read things from you. Is it important for them to know I'm bisexual? Is that strange? Do I lie to them? Do I not? What would their momma think? I want to do what's best for them first, and I tell them to tell the truth, first. I need to tell the truth."

"I've worried about this too. I'll do whatever you want.

Tell them or don't, wait and let them ask, whatever you think is best. Do they know about the other people on the farm? Your cowboys?"

"They know that Krissy has a wife. They know that Ben and Little Tim kiss and are in love. They've known them their whole lives, though. Hell, Krissy's Lisa? Was my Deb's best friend in high school."

He wasn't going to stop smiling for weeks. "Well, then maybe it won't be a thing. Maybe they'll just learn you can love everybody, right? Men or women? As far as examples for your kids go, that's a pretty good one."

"I'm trying. I want to make a place that I want to live in. The world outside the ranch might be harder, but my space? I want it to be a good one." Matthew chuckled softly, the sound wry. "It's easy to say that when you inherit a ranch from your grandparents."

"It's not easy to do though. Aren't there people that don't approve? It's not New York. I think it's brave."

The guacamole and cheese dip came, and the smell of spice and tomato was delicious.

Matthew beamed at him. "Thank you. I—I pray I'm doing things right."

"None of us knows for sure, right?" The promise of warm, melty cheese was too much to ignore. He picked up another chip. "Oh...cheese. Good call."

"Spicy melted cheese. At some point, we'll go get queso flameado." Matthew winked. "Flaming cheese is a magical animal, honey."

"What? Flaming? Like on fire?" Surely Matthew was joking. "Flaming cheese."

"Like on fire. It is amazing." Matthew scooped up a big bite of guacamole. "We'll go."

"We will." They had to. And then he'd send a picture

back to Peter, who shared his cheese obsession. "I'm going to weigh a thousand pounds, and I don't care." Actually, he barely weighed a hundred and sixty now, so that seemed pretty unlikely.

"There's the pool, plenty of things to do and see. We'll go on the boat, ride four-wheelers. You'll work up an appetite."

"I hope so. I want to make the most of this vacation." He sipped his Coke thinking about that word and wondering if this was a vacation or a trial run, or what. "I haven't really slept in a few days. I woke up this morning and just said 'fuck it' and texted you. I called the bar from the airport and —" *Quit*. He'd said, "I quit." But Les had said no and told him it was a vacation. "I took some time off. I know I look awful. I don't know what's wrong with me, but I felt much better after I did all of that."

"You've been running hard in your heart for a bit. Maybe you just need to breathe and lay your load down." Matthew's phone began to ring, and he answered. "'Lo? Yep, I have him. I'm feeding him, and I'll pick y'all up on my way home. Yes, we'll be home way before it's time to do feeding. Yes, it's still your turn to feed and water the dogs."

"Rats, they still have to do their chores," Tyler whispered, smiling, and had another scoop of glorious hot cheese.

Matthew's eyes went wide, playful, and he mouthed, "Poor abused babies." Then louder, he kept on, "Emma, what do you really want? No, ma'am. I am not telling your granny anything. She says no stealing the chocolate chips, you'd better not."

"You're so mean. Your friend Tyler would let them have chocolate." He winked.

Matthew snorted, shoulders shaking with laughter. "What? Nothing. I'll see y'all soon. Be good. I love you too.

Bye." Matthew hung up and hooted. "Oh, you are wicked! We'll have to grab some and whatever it is you like for drinks and snacks on the way home."

He laughed. "I may never need to eat again after this. We haven't even had our—oh...here they come."

The server set down plates in front of each of them with tortillas and cheese and beans and sauce and...whoa. "This looks so good."

"We can take home whatever we don't eat and warm it up for later." Matthew poured part of the queso over the enchilada, unwrapped the tamale, and dug in.

He did exactly the same thing, watching Matthew carefully. He was sold from the first bite. "Oh. Mmm." These leftovers would be fantastic at midnight.

"Bueno, huh?"

They ate until he couldn't take another bite. He was full, happy, and Matthew was right there.

Tyler leaned back in his chair and groaned. "That was so good. Thank you. We should go get those girls before they get themselves in trouble."

"We should. We'll hit an HEB on the way." Matthew handed over a card and asked for to-go boxes.

"HEB? Is that groceries?"

"Yessir. The Walmart's another option—if you need swim trunks or stuff."

"I will. I'm not that great in the pool though. I mean, I can swim, I just don't know all the fancy strokes and stuff. I just kind of...fake it." There wasn't a lot of swimming in the city. His mother had made him take lessons at the YMCA when he was young, but otherwise he'd just been to the beach a few times with friends.

"Then we'll stop there. You'll need them. And honey, I can drag myself across the pool, but I ain't no Michael

Phelps. I'm way more of a floaty with a beer can holder or a bubble in the hot tub type."

"Oh, we'll get along well in the pool then. You have those noodle things? I love those."

"We have noodles, floaties of all shapes and sizes, water games—the girls are spoiled rotten." Matthew grabbed the to-go boxes and stood. "You ready, honey?"

"Yep." He pushed his chair back and stood up, following Matthew out to the truck. "So full. God, it's warm here. That's going to take some getting used to."

"It's not terrible warm there in the summer with all that concrete?"

"In July and August yes, but June is cooler. The summer can be brutal. I just wasn't there yet." He grinned. He didn't mind it at all.

"Ah, I hear you." Matthew winked at him. "I bet we'll be able to get in the pool ten months a year, easy." The truck beeped and started up before they got to it. "I'll get the air started."

"Fancy, fancy." He would never see that much money in this lifetime or the next. But he didn't mind enjoying Matthew's luck. He climbed into the truck, feeling the cool air and settled into the comfy seat. This was quite a life, and he wasn't sure he deserved it. But somehow he'd make sure he was worthy of Matthew.

8

They did the Walmart—getting ginger ale and grapes, swim trunks and flip-flops, SPF 10,000 sunscreen, and three new pool noodles. They got chocolate, cheap sunglasses, and some glo-sticks for the girls to play with in the pool at night.

Matthew pulled up to Daddy's, with poor, exhausted Tyler sacked out in the cab. Someone needed some care and rest, a little fun and some loving. "Honey, I'm gonna run in and get the kids. I'll be right back."

"I'm good. We're here?" Tyler jerked awake and sat up, blinking. "I'm good."

"You want to meet the folks? They'll love you." He killed the engine and opened the door, Rosebud and Twitchy—Daddy's bloodhounds—bounding around the side of the house, baying like they hadn't just seen him a few hours ago.

"Yeah. Yeah, of course." Tyler rubbed his eyes and shook his head. "Okay. I'm awake." Hopefully awake enough for a big dog named "Twitchy"." He jumped out of the truck and had hardly hit the ground before the dogs were barking.

"Rosebud! Twitchy! Sit." Two butts hit the ground, tails

going ninety to nothing. "Meet the sniffing hooligans. They're good babies, just loud as fuck."

"Daddy! You said a cuss!" Emma ran out wearing a bright orange sequined evening dress that was at least twenty sizes too big, leaping at him, and he caught her. "Mamaw let us play dress up from her fancy clothes!"

Ah yes. The Goodwill closet. Momma bought up all the formals to cut up for crazy quilts, but the girls loved to 'dress up' in the ones that were still hanging up. "I can see that. Say hello to my good friend, Mister Tyler. Tyler, this is Emma."

"I'm pleased to meet you, Mr. Tyler." She held out one hand. "Welcome to Texas."

Tyler smiled broadly, and Matthew beamed. His babies were so pretty and so polite. Tyler took her hand and shook it. "Hello, Emma. I am very happy to meet you. Your dad has told me so much about you and your sister. Thank you for the welcome. It's my first time in Texas."

"We will show you everything." Emma looked at Tyler, her little face so serious. "We have goats."

Matthew fought his laugh with all he was. "Yes, ma'am. We sure do."

"I have never met a goat, so I can't wait for you to show me." Tyler looked right at Emma, looking just as serious.

"Emma, Mamaw says to come put your stuff away!" Sophia stepped out on the porch and offered Tyler a shy wave. "Hi. Glad you made it, sir."

"Thank you, Sophia. Good to be here." Tyler reached out to pet the dogs and looked at him. "They're better in person than in pictures. Nice work, Dad."

Matthew beamed and tipped his hat, then led Tyler up onto the big covered porch. It looked a lot like his porch—wrapping around the house, with chairs and tables, rockers, huge fans to cool things off. The big difference was that his had a Coke machine and an ice machine that he'd found at this crazy auction. "Come on in." He held the door open. "Momma? Daddy? Come meet Tyler real quick. I got chocolate melting in the truck. Girls, don't dawdle!"

Momma came bustling out of the kitchen drying her hands on a towel. "Tyler! My goodness, it's good to finally meet you. I'm Peg. Matty talks about you all the time, I feel like I know you already." Tyler put out a hand and smiled, but Momma waved him off and gave him a hug like he was family.

Tyler winked at him over her shoulder. "All the time, huh? It's good to meet you too."

"All the time. I thought we'd have a big old to do Saturday—Daddy says he'll do brisket and a turkey breast, maybe sausage. We can swim and play horseshoes and cards and just have a ball."

Oh lord. "What do you want us to bring, Momma?"

"Chips and dips and stuff for poppers. Sister is bringing desserts, and your brother is bringing the beer and Cokes. Aunt Kathy is hiring a bouncy castle for the girls and her grandbabies."

"I tried to tell her that you might like a quiet weekend, since you just got here, but you know Momma." Daddy gave him a pat on the shoulder and reached a hand out to Tyler. "Good to meet you, son. I'm Luke Whitehead."

"Thank you. It's—"

"Quiet weekend." Momma snorted. "We're all so happy to have you here."

"Y'all want to come in and have a beer?" Daddy asked, and Matthew shook his head.

"I got chocolate in the truck. We'll see y'all Saturday. Tyler needs a couple days of rest, I think."

Emma and Sophia came down the stairs together on their best behavior, instead of racing each other as usual, and hugged their grandparents. "Everything is put away, Mamaw."

"Thank you. Go on before your daddy's chocolate melts." Momma looked at him and winked. "Clever."

"I'm a brilliant guy. Love you, Momma. Holler if you need me." He kissed her forehead and winked at Daddy. "Love you. See you Saturday."

"You'll see me Friday. I'm running to the auctions in Luckenbach."

Ah, the goat auction. "Good deal. I got room for another few Nubians and some Boehr."

"I'll keep my eyes peeled."

"Shotgun!" Emma shouted and ran out the door.

"Emma! Tyler gets the front seat. Y'all get in the back seat." He rolled his eyes. "I just need ten or twelve more kids."

Daddy nodded. "See you Friday then."

Tyler looked like he was trying to hold off a laugh as they left the house. "That took me a minute. I forgot what baby goats are called. I almost said something snarky and put my foot in it."

Matthew chuckled and shook his head, just vaguely horrified. "Can you imagine? Two is enough, and they're not teenagers yet."

"I don't know, maybe you need some boys." Tyler grinned and hopped in the truck.

Emma leaned over the console from the back seat. "Where's the chocolate, Daddy?"

"Can't you wait until we get home, piggy?"

"You hush, Sister."

"It's in the cooler compartment in the back. You can have it when we get home. Seat belts."

"Yes, sir."

Tyler buckled in and looked over his shoulder at the girls. "You guys are going to laugh, but I've never been on a ranch. You'll have to teach me everything, okay?"

Emma nodded. "We can. We're cowboys. Sister is learning to do barrels and everything. We got chickens and geese and turkeys. Goats. Cattle. Horses."

"Dogs. We got dogs and donkeys too," Sophia added. "And we're fixin' to get rabbits and maybe llamas."

"No piggies, though, 'cause they stink." Emma bounced and wiggled in the rearview. "And we got a pond with fish! And we planted a garden. We're growing watermelons and corns and cukes and 'maters and..."

Matthew whispered softly as the girls chattered. "We'll be home soon. Five minutes. Our properties butt up on the one side."

"No rush, I'm enjoying this." Tyler smiled and seemed perfectly happy to jump back in with both feet. "Llamas? For real? And I love cucumbers. They're one of my favorites."

"Yeah. Aunt Kathy is too tired to take her of them, 'cause she says you got to give them blowjobs."

Tyler looked square at him, eyes wide. "Is that so?"

He counted to five. Ten would have taken too long. "Baby, you have to blow the sticks out of their fur." He was going to kill Kathy. With a bazooka. "You know, with a leaf blower?"

"Right. So cool. Are you going to blow the llamas with us, Tyler?"

"I—uh." Tyler snorted a laugh out his nose, trying to keep it together. "I can't wait to meet... Aunt Kathy."

And then the giggles won out, Tyler just rolling in his seat. “Oh... God.”

“Aunt Kathy is evil incarnate. She’s an artist. She has two kids, six grandbabies and twelve great-grandbabies. She and Momma are thick as thieves.” And she had a foul mouth. Evil wonderful old broad.

Tyler shook his head and leaned his blond head back in his seat. “Sorry, girls. Yes, I will help with the llamas, and anything else that needs to be done. Not to worry.”

“Daddy, Mr. Tyler likes llamas!”

Matthew chuckled. “He does!” *But does he like blow jobs?*

Tyler glanced at him. “It might be a waste of my considerable skills to blow a llama, however.”

He fought like a beast not to crack a smile. “Good to know. I’ll have to find you something else to...blow.”

“You devise a test and let me know how I do.” Tyler grinned. “Oh, hey! Is this the Flying W?”

“It is! Welcome home.” He hit the button for the huge iron gate, idling as it swung open. You couldn’t see the house from here—the grove of pecan trees hid it, but you could see the line of bunkhouses, the foreman’s house, and the first few barns.

“That’s not the house you showed me a picture of...”

“That’s not our house,” Sophia explained. “That’s Krissy’s house. She’s the foreman. You don’t have to be a man to be a foreman.”

“Oh.” Tyler laughed. “Good to know.”

“And that’s where the cowboys live.” Emma pointed out the window.

Matthew watched as Tyler craned his neck to see everything. “Whoa. I didn’t realize everyone actually lived right here. Wow.”

“Oh, Daddy! Lisa’s semi is in the drive!”

"Y'all ask Miz Krissy before you bother her. She might be sleeping." And lord knew, if Krissy didn't stop them, Lisa would have them in the house making cakes.

"Your driveway is big enough to park a tractor in?"

"Well, we built a space just for it, but we have a tractor barn—the four-wheelers are in there, and the boats and Ski-Doos, and there's a spot for the fifth wheel."

"Boats, plural? What's a fifth wheel?" Tyler was just shaking his head in disbelief. "Crazy. This place is huge."

"We got a couple little bass boats and a nicer speed boat to go on the lake with. A fifth wheel is—"

"The little trailer we take to camping! It has a shower and a potty and a kitchen and beds! It's so fun!" Emma was ramping up.

"It is, Em. Let's take turns talking, though, okay?" They were working on that. Hard.

"Oh. Right, Daddy. Sorry!"

"It's okay, Em," Sophia said. "That's so hard to remember when you're excited."

"Honestly, I'm excited too. I get it." Tyler looked over his shoulder and smiled at Emma. "But we have lots of time. I'll be here long enough to see everything. There's no rush, right?"

"None at all." He made the turn and stopped, nodding to his house. Two-stories, Texas stone, a wrap-around porch, with rose bushes all around. The big old cottonwood in the front held a tire swing, and there were hummingbird feeders and bird feeders dotted all over. "Grab a couple of Walmart sacks before y'all head in, please." He grinned at Tyler. "We're here. Come on in."

Tyler shouldered his backpack and followed, all wide-eyed, looking around and taking everything in. "Gorgeous house. It's so pretty here."

"Do you want to see my room?" Emma slipped her hand into Tyler's and led him up to the porch.

"Y'all. Let Tyler get his stuff in, go pee maybe. He's not going to disappear into smoke." He stood there with all the bags and Tyler's suitcase. "Sophia, put the code in?"

"Yessir!" She typed in a code, and the house unlocked. "Come on in."

The main door opened into a great big foyer with his master suite to the left, the great room to the right, and the staircase to the second floor straight ahead. "You and I are here to the left, honey. Can you open the door and we'll put your things down?"

The door opened into his den—a nice-sized man cave with a TV and his movies, the old leather couch, a pool table and a dart game set up, along with all the neon beer signs he'd collected. "You just walk through to the bedroom."

"This is amazing, Matthew. This is...wow." Tyler crossed the room and opened the bedroom door. "I feel like I'm in some fancy hotel."

Tyler peeked around him. "The girls didn't follow us in. I guess they found the chocolate."

"Undoubtedly." The master was mostly huge king and two dressers. "I cleaned this one out for you, and there's room in the closet. The bathroom's through the door there, and the private porch is through the French doors."

"You cleaned a dresser out for me?" Tyler dropped his backpack on the bed and took the suitcase from his hand, setting it down. "You're so thoughtful. Come down here so I can thank you."

"Yes, please." He sat down on the bed, arms open. He had to fight the tremble in his hands, the excitement that he knew he was going to have to hold in. "I'm so glad you're here, honey. So damn glad."

Tyler sat right on his knees and stroked his beard with both hands. "It doesn't feel real yet, you know? I feel like my feet aren't quite on the ground. Your girls are so sweet, and your home is lovely...but I have everything I need right here in my hands." Tyler kissed him softly, almost as if he were fragile.

He sighed into the kiss, hands draped around Tyler's waist as he held on, feeling like a sparrow in a hurricane.

"I'm here, Matt. It's real." Tyler hugged him, pressing close. "Thank you for letting me just show up."

"Thank you for trusting. You—God, I'm so—You're here." He held on, panting softly, his entire body awake and alive.

He felt Tyler's deep breath, the lean chest expanding against his arms. Tyler leaned back, clear blue eyes locking with his. "Kiss me like you want to. It's okay. I'm not going anywhere."

He didn't hesitate. No sir. He hooked one hand behind Tyler's neck and tugged him in, kissing the fine son of a bitch like he needed to, diving into the sweet lips and letting Tyler know how bad he wanted, how much he'd missed.

Tyler moaned and answered his need, shifting in his lap, hungry fingers digging into his biceps. He plundered Tyler's mouth, wanting to push the sweet body over, strip them down and make love.

For once Tyler was ahead of him. He felt his shirt buttons opening one by one until Tyler got his hands inside, hot palms spreading out across his chest.

"Honey..." He groaned, his body arching like he didn't have an ounce of control over it. His nipples were like little rocks, and his dick ached in his jeans.

"I know." Tyler nodded against his cheek, whispering. "We need this. I should have known that kiss would never be enough."

"We do. I want to... I need to love up on you, honey." He wanted to touch and lick and see every goddamn inch.

"I fed the dogs, Daddy." There was a quiet knock at the door. "And Emma wants to show Tyler the goats."

"And what's for dinner?" Emma's voice followed her sister's. That was Emma, always looking forward to the next meal.

Tyler leaned back, pale skin flushed and eyes shining. "Right. Girls."

"Yeah." He took a deep breath. "I'm going to grill hot dogs for y'all. We ate on the way back, so we'll eat a snack late. I'll be right there, babies."

Fuck him raw.

Tyler slipped between his knees, fingers going after his fly. "What's their bedtime?"

"Uh. N-nine. They go upstairs at nine." He blinked, the sight of Tyler kneeling there making him stupid as all get out.

"Okay." Tyler tugged his cock right through his fly. "You can pay me back then. God, that's a pretty cock, cowboy." But he only saw it for a second before it disappeared between Tyler's lips.

He made a strangled sound, and then every single fiber of his body jerked and went taut, his toes curling in his boot. "Oh, sweet fuck."

He reached out, curling one hand around Tyler's shoulder, his ass clenching as he fought not to thrust up.

Matthew was fixin' to die, and it would be worth it.

Tyler's hands wrapped tight around his ass and tugged, inviting him deeper if that was possible, and wasn't subtle at all. They both knew this was a means to an end. A fucking hot one.

He didn't fight it, his eyes rolling back in his head as his balls emptied in a rush. He'd come a lot in the last bunch of years, but at his own hand. Not...not like this.

"Mmm." Everything about Tyler that had been heated and urgent became slow and sensual, easing him, gentling him back down to earth.

"I—" He blinked down. "Damn, honey. That was...better than llamas."

Tyler snorted and climbed back into his lap. "Told you so."

"You did. Damn. Thank you. I want—"

"Daddy! Daddy, come out! We made y'all iced tea!"

"Sorry," he whispered, but he couldn't ignore them any longer. It wasn't right. "Y'all rock! I'll be right there!"

"Don't be. I wanted you to feel good, that's all. We'll have time later." Tyler kissed him quickly. "I'm just going to freshen up, I'll be right out."

"Take your time. I'm going to go start hot dogs and let them get in the pool, which is what they really want." He stripped off his nice shirt and threw on a T-shirt before heading out to his girls, closing the door behind him.

"Is Tyler coming? When will the hot dogs be ready?" Emma fell in right behind him, following him to the kitchen.

Sophia was already there, stirring iced tea. "Oh. Is Tyler tired? Is he napping in your room? Sorry if we woke him up."

"He's washing his face and just letting himself be quiet a second. Did y'all put the leftovers from the truck in the fridge?" He felt—well, shit, he felt like a trillion bucks, loose-limbed and goofy.

"Yes, sir. They smell good." Sophia sat a glass of tea in front of him. "Is he staying all the way to the Fourth of July party?"

"He is. He can stay as long as he wants." Matthew wanted some time to get to know each other, to work their shit out.

"See? I told you he would!" Emma sounded smug. "We have plenty of time to do stuff."

"We have time, but we have to remember to give him some space, if he wants it. He isn't with our crazy selves all the time normally."

"But Daddy, isn't New York full of a ton of people all the time?"

"Yes, baby, but he lives all alone." And the girls didn't understand, but he felt way more alone in that huge city than on the ranch. He thought, in some ways, Tyler did too.

"Hey. Am I too late for tea?" Tyler joined them, looking relaxed in a clean T-shirt and a happy smile. "I took a fast shower, hope that was okay."

"Perfect." He handed over a glass. "Do y'all want one each?"

"Are there buns?" Emma asked, beaming when he nodded. "Then I want one with cheese and mustard."

"I want just mustard on mine and cooked extra dark."

He nodded and grabbed them out of the fridge. "I'm on it. Dogs are fed? Chickens are in the hen house? Goats have water?"

The girls nodded in concert.

"Then go get your suits on. You can get in while I'm cooking." He had all the paper plates and shit out there in the new kitchen deal. The sooner they ate and swam, the sooner they could go to bed. "You want to come sit and chat while I burn these for the girls?"

"Yes, I'd like that. I've got our tea." Tyler grabbed their glasses and followed him out to the grill. "It feels so strange to be out of the city. I haven't been anywhere in a very long time."

"Yeah? It's going to be a nice night. The sun's going to go down soon." The grill was right near the pool, so he could watch. He had a perfect view of the front acreage too—goats, chickens, the...ah yes. There they were. "Can you see the horses? They're coming up for water."

Tyler set his glass down and followed his gaze, eyes lighting up. "Oh wow! Those are yours? All of them?"

"Those are the ones that aren't being doctored. There are a couple in the other pasture." He lifted his head and whistled. "Sugar! Sugar, what you doing, pretty girl?"

She lifted her head and whinnied, greeting him.

"That's so cool. I want to meet them up close. Can you... I mean, are those the kind you ride? Can you teach me?"

"Yes, and absolutely. We can go out tomorrow, if it isn't rainy. If it's raining, we'll sit in the hot tub and relax and watch the girls play in the mud."

He got the wieners going, chuckling as the girls came streaking out of the house in their swimsuits.

"No running, chicas! Be careful!"

"Yes, Daddy!"

He rolled his eyes as they jumped in the pool.

"Hot tub. Oh, that sounds just as good." Tyler stood close, closer than friends, and tucked a hand into his back pocket. "I'm looking forward to seeing that W tonight."

"You'll see it, honey, and everything else you want." He leaned into the touch. "What did you think of my fancy-assed bathroom?"

He'd traded a few calves for the tile work, and the plumber had wanted two puppies for his sons.

"Oh man, it's gorgeous. And huge. Your shower is like a whole room by itself. It literally is the fanciest place I have ever been."

"I have imagined amazing things we could get up to, in that shower." He had lube and condoms in the bathroom, the bedroom. All over.

Tyler blushed and shrugged. "I got up to a little solo fun, just to, you know, relax a little. Did you imagine that?"

"I was hoping. It means tonight we can take our time together." He turned the hotdogs, his belly going tight at the memory of Tyler's mouth on him. "That before—that was... damn."

"That was an act of desperation." Tyler laughed. "Wait until I have some time to play with."

"The top of my head might come off. Boom." He chuckled softly, the sound cutting off when Emma screamed.

"Daddy! A bug!"

"Scoop it out, honey."

"It's alive!"

"Ooh. I got this." Tyler winked at him. "An alive bug? How dare it! Where is this trespasser?"

"Can you get it?" Sophia was trying to be brave, but Emma was already in tears. "Please?"

Jesus, those babies could fish crawdaddies, but a water bug got in the pool...

"Yep. I got it. Hang on." He watched as Tyler lay down on his stomach and stretched an arm out to catch the bug, scooping it up onto the concrete. "Do we squash these guys or let them run?"

"If you squash him, do it on the grass. They're juicy."

"Ew. Like New York City cockroaches." Tyler kicked the

bug into the grass and made a show of stepping on it. "You ladies okay? Emma? You good?"

"Uh—uh-huh. Thank you." She sniffled softly, then went back to play with her sister.

"You're very welcome." Tyler trotted back over, grinning, and stepped close. "I'm the tough New York bug hunter. Go me."

"You are a prince among men." Matthew chuckled and applauded.

"I love that you can just grill whenever you want. I mean everybody barbecues, I know, just not in the city. Will would have loved this. All this space. He talked about it all the time, wanting to get out of New York. But that's where the work is, you know?" Tyler shook his head.

"I tend to grill a lot. That's why I built the frame out and put the awning up, so I can grill in the rain." He put the hot dogs on the buns and fixed them, putting them on the table. "Do you girls want chips?"

"No, thank you. Can we stay up late?"

Oh, there was no way. Not tonight. "You can get back in the pool until 8:30. Then showers and bed. Fair?"

"I guess." Sophia sighed dramatically and sat at the table, a towel wrapped around her waist.

Emma sat too, digging right in. "Mmm. You got it just right, Daddy!" Emma was never going to give him a hard time about bedtime. She was going to be the one that smiled and nodded sweetly and then climbed out her damn bedroom window. He knew it.

Sophia was going to be his drama queen, but basically good, basically easy.

"What did y'all eat that you're not hungry for a hotdog?" Emma looked at Tyler.

"Melted cheese. Tons of yummy, hot, melty cheese. And things wrapped in tortillas and fried. And more cheese."

"That's just queso, silly. The cheese stuff."

"Oh, it's not just anything. It was heavenly delicious." Tyler rolled his eyes and both girls giggled at him.

"Daddy makes it all the time. He puts Jimmy Dean in it, and it's so good. It's one of my favorites." Sophia beamed at him.

"Well you and I have a lot in common then, Sophia. Cheese is my favorite thing ever."

"Cheese?" Emma wrinkled her nose. "Chocolate is the best thing ever."

"Oh." Tyler looked at her seriously. "Chocolate is a really close second, you're right. I could live on cheese and chocolate."

"Ice cream. Y'all. Ice. Cream." Matthew grinned at them all, loving how Tyler just talked to the babies. "One day we'll all go to New York and have pizza there. It's so good, girls. It's...whoa."

"It's true. It's the best pizza anywhere." Tyler nodded. "And I took your dad for ice cream. He got a strawberry cone."

"Mamaw has a ton of ice cream in her big freezer for Daddy and Aunt Rachel and Uncle Jonas." Sophia leaned closer to Tyler. "A *ton*."

"Do you think she'd share?" Tyler asked, and Emma nodded.

"Mamaw is super nice, unless you're nasty to her or her grandbabies. Then she will cut you."

"Emma!" Matthew blinked. "Where did you hear that?"

"Mamaw said it to Miss SueEllen."

"The hairdresser?"

Sophia nodded. "We went to get a trim while you were gone."

"So it's not just Aunt Kathy..." Tyler grinned at him.

"Momma is a firecracker, no question there." Matthew tilted his head. He was hot, sweaty, and he wanted a dip. "You interested in getting in the pool with the girls, honey? I could use a dunk."

"Why not? I have this snazzy new suit. And then we—uh *I* have an excuse to use that amazing shower again."

No blushing. None. Zero. Zip. "Totally. Gotta wash the chlorine off, right?"

"You got it. Should we go change?" Tyler started backing toward the house.

"Y'all stay out of the pool until I get back, okay?" He met each girl's gaze. They were both good swimmers, but there was no reason to take a stupid risk.

"Okay, Daddy. We'll just play out here."

"Good girls."

Tyler led the way to the bedroom, obviously looking forward to the swim. "I love them. They're so sweet, Matt." Tyler dug through the shopping bag and pulled out his bathing suit.

He beamed, so proud he could hardly bear it. He knew they were good girls, happy and dear and smart—but it felt great to hear it. "Thank you. I love them more than I can say."

"It shows." Tyler had to have known exactly what he was doing when he turned his back to pull on his new swim trunks. Matthew got a quick view of a pert, pale, perfect little ass.

"Mmm...look at that." He hummed and reached out, fingertips trailing over the soft skin. "Pretty pretty."

Tyler leaned into the touch for a second, then slipped away and pulled up his trunks, looking flushed when he turned around. “It’s not nine o’clock yet.”

“Not yet. We’ll play in the pool a while.” Matthew grabbed his trunks and sat on the bed, stripping down. “Then we’ll play in the bedroom.”

Tyler leaned against his dresser and watched him. “It’s weird, but part of me feels like I’ve been here forever already.”

“Yeah? You like it? I have done a lot of updating, since I inherited it. I think it’s a happy space.” Matthew loved it here, his soul was sunk into the space, into the land, into the dirt itself.

“It feels loved. I’m a little intimidated by how fancy it all is, you know? It feels...like you, though. Safe. Warm.”

“It’s just a home. It’s not a showpiece.” He pulled up his trunks and stood, snorting at the idea of this place being fancy. It was a place for mud and suppers and laughing and dust.

“I like it.” Tyler slipped a hand into his as they crossed through the kitchen and gave it a squeeze. “I’m totally going to cannonball into the pool.”

“You totally can.” They went outside to find Sophia and Emma playing with the dogs, Buttercup racing to him when she saw him. “Baby girl!”

She jumped into his arms and he caught her. “Buttercup, Tyler. Tyler, Buttercup. Westley is her man.”

“Hey, Buttercup. You’re a pretty puppy.” Tyler patted Buttercup’s head like someone that hadn’t ever had dogs.

He put Buttercup down, and she sat, wagging happily. “Shake for Tyler.”

She lifted her paw, so dainty, so pretty.

"Oh my goodness." Tyler took her paw and gave it a gentle shake. "Good girl."

Westley watched everything with a suspicious eye, sidling over to herd the girls away from Tyler. "Come here, boy. It's okay." He grinned at Tyler. "Those are his two-legged puppies. He loves them fiercely. Come meet Tyler, Wes."

Westley walked over and sat.

"Hold your hand out with your fingers curled under, Mister Tyler." Sophia demonstrated. "And then when he has your scent and the body language is nice, pet him under the chin. That's respectful."

"Fingers curled...like this? Okay. Hey, Westley." Tyler held his fist out for the dog to sniff.

Westley sniffed him, then licked his knuckles.

"Good boy!" Sophia beamed. "Now, love on him."

Matthew nodded. Excellent. Sophia had a knack with dogs that would serve her well.

"Okay. Hey, Westley." Tyler crouched a little and scritched the dog's ears.

"Do they have dogs in New York?" Emma asked, completely serious.

"Oh, yes. I've seen all kinds of dogs. I just don't have one. Actually, no one I know does. But I've seen everything from big shepherds to tiny little dogs people carry in their purses."

"Aunt Kathy had a purse dog! He got eat up by a gator!" Emma grinned, eyes twinkling. "Can you imagine, a gator stealing a dog out of a purse?"

"Baby, it wasn't in the purse at the time. Aunt Kathy had gone camping and let the little beast out."

"Chomp!" Tyler squinted at Emma and leaned closer to

her. "That's wild. Some of the rats in New York are bigger than those dogs."

Emma's eyes went wide. "Daddy? For reals? I don't like rats. They have the doodleonic germs. Noah said so."

"The—oh for—seriously? That boy!" Doodleonic germs his branded ass.

"I don't like rats either." Tyler straightened up and looked toward the pool. "Are there doodleonic germs in the pool? No? Let's swim!"

"Swimming!" Sophia ran for the pool, taking her sister's hand. "Cannonball!"

Matthew chuckled and walked to the steps. Dorks. Gorgeous dorks.

"Cannonball!" Tyler followed them in, launching himself into the deep end and creating an impressive splash that set the dogs barking.

He eased himself in, the cold water sending shivers all up along his skin. It was always wild—the mixture of discomfort and oh-my-God-that-feels-good.

Tyler popped up, wet-headed and smiling, and swam over. "Oh, this is nice. Come in, slow-poke."

"It's amazing. I'm slow to get in, but man, it feels so good." In fact, it felt like heaven. He hadn't realized how hot he really was.

"This was a good investment. Does it have lights so you can swim at night?"

"Colored lights that I can program." He grinned. "If you're going to do this, you might as well do it."

"Disco swimming. I like it." Tyler dove under and circled him, pinching his butt on the way by before taking off toward the deep end again.

"Daddy! Throw me?" Emma leapt for him, and he lifted

her out of the water and tossed her, laughing as Sophia climbed up his back.

"Gonna jump off your shoulders, Daddy."

"Be careful, baby." He moved to the middle of the pool, not wanting any accidents.

Tyler took Emma's hand and tugged her clear. Anyone would think the man had been around kids his whole life. "Jump, jump, jump!"

Sophia jumped, legs and arms flailing before she hit the water. *Splash*.

"All right, Daddy Diving Board. You ready for this one?" Tyler zoomed Emma toward him, tucked under one arm.

She squealed with laughter, scrambling up his body and leaping off. He let them jump for a while, then he reminded them of the glow sticks. "Y'all can dive for them."

They loved this game, and so did he because it wore them out nicely. He tossed the sticks for the girls, noticing after a bit that Tyler had moved to a quieter spot in the pool where he was watching and floating. The sight of the lean man right there, with his ripped belly and blond hair gone dark with the water, made him want to laugh and pounce and...hell, he didn't know. Lasso something? He casually moved over, settling close.

"You having a good time, honey?"

"I love everything about this day." Tyler's smile looked happy and tired. "I was just taking it all in."

"I'm so glad you're here." He let his feet float up, let himself relax. "Tomorrow I'll introduce you around. Let you meet Krissy and all."

"Sounds good. I might sleep in a little if you don't mind." Tyler flicked a little water his way. "I have a feeling I'm going to need it."

"You can sleep as long as you want. If I'm not in the

house, text. I'll be running around. I've got to take the girls to Momma's, run to the feed store, and pick up a load of shingles for one of the bunkhouses in the morning." He had busy, busy mornings, as a rule. It was the way of ranching.

"Sure, okay. Thanks." Tyler tangled their feet, dragging his under.

"Are you drowning my toes?" He reached out and touched Tyler's hip.

Tyler smiled. "Just until I can drown myself in you."

"Listen to you." Oh, he did like that. So damn sweet and hot, goddamn.

"We got a beach ball, Tyler. Want to throw it?"

"Thanks, Emma. I was just about to get out. How about tomorrow?" Tyler set his feet down and headed for the steps.

"Aw. Please?"

"Baby girl, Tyler's been traveling all day. Chill."

"But, Daddy..."

"Emma Leann."

She sighed. "Yes, sir. Sorry, Mister Tyler."

"You know what, Emma? I'm excited too. But I'm here for a while. If we do everything in one day what are we going to do tomorrow?" Tyler climbed the steps out of the pool. "Whoa. It's a lot cooler now. Are there towels?"

"In that tall cabinet. Feel free to hop in the hot tub and bubble, if you want to." He kept it hot, because all the cowboys came up and used it to soak their bones.

"Yeah?" Tyler grabbed a towel and sat it close by, then slipped into the hot tub with a long sigh. "Oh. Oh that's very nice. Don't let me doze off."

"The bubbler is that dial there on the right." He focused on the girls, letting them have all his attention, racing them and splashing and laughing, letting them have their daddy time.

Tyler relaxed in the hot tub but was obviously enjoying watching them. Every now and then Matthew would turn to check on Tyler and those bright blue eyes were wide open, and right on him. Tyler was still hanging out in the tub as the sun fell low in the sky and shadows took over the pool.

9

Jesus Christ, this place was beautiful. And Matthew's house was like a palace. It was a palace...and Tyler felt like Cinderella.

Without the evil step-people.

In fact, instead of evil step-family, he'd been greeted by real family. Family that acted like they liked him even though they didn't know him from Adam.

He watched Matthew hauling his girls out of the pool. He'd heard something about bedtime and showers. He should probably move too, but the hot tub was heaven. Even if he felt small in it.

Not as small as he'd felt buying boxers in that gigantic zoo of a Walmart—that place was insane—but small.

It wasn't what Matthew intended; he knew that. Matthew had been welcoming and wonderful, but he didn't get it. Tyler had never seen enough money to buy the hot tub he was sitting in. Matthew was loaded. Like, seriously loaded.

Out of his league loaded.

Sooner or later someone in that family was going to

figure out he was just a nobody bartender from New York and tell Matthew he could do better.

So, if he wanted to stay, if he wanted to prove himself to these people, Tyler had one job. To make absolutely sure Matthew understood there was no one better. Because that fact was, there was nothing left for him in New York.

Tyler sighed. He was tired, that was all. He'd get some sleep, and tomorrow he would feel less...lost. He wanted to get some Matthew first, though. The cowboy was even hotter here, in the middle of all of this crazy land and sky and kids... Matthew's smile was brighter than the sun.

Warm hands landed on his shoulders, thumbs digging in. "You look exhausted, honey. You want to skip the steaks?"

"Mmm." Oh, that felt so good. He leaned his head back to look up at Matthew. "Would it hurt your feelings? I'm still full from lunch."

"Not at all. They'll keep." Matthew kissed his forehead, the caress sweet and gentle. "You had a killer long day."

He nodded. "Long but good. And it's not over yet. Did the girls go in? Give me a hand up."

Matthew helped him out and wrapped him in a towel. "They're showering and getting the chlorine off. They're exhausted—they were so excited to meet you."

"Let's hope I live up to the hype." He leaned against Matthew a minute.

"You're exactly who you need to be, honey. And you're here." Matthew held him for a second longer, then began to shut down the lights and cover the hot tub.

"Emma's adorable, and she looks just like you, you're right. And Sophia has that classic beauty thing going on." He tucked the towel around his waist and watched Matthew, not having the first idea what he could do to help.

"She's the spitting image of her momma." Matthew

brushed off the grill quickly and closed it off, turning the gas off at the tank, then turned to him with a smile. "Come on in, honey. Let's dry you off."

"Sounds good." He caught the towel as it slipped off his hips and hooked it around his neck. God, even Matthew's towels were luxurious. "The pool turned out to be a good investment, huh?"

"Yeah, I did some amazing trades for it, so I got a great deal." Matthew opened the door, and the air conditioning was cold as fuck.

"Oh, shit." He tugged the towel off his shoulders and wrapped it around him again, laughing. "Was it this cold in here when we went out?" He danced through the kitchen toward the bedroom looking to get out of his damp suit as soon as possible.

Matthew's laugh followed him, and it wasn't but a few seconds before they had gone through the fancy-assed game room to the huge master. Matthew dropped his shorts, and there was that scar, a thick white W right on his ass cheek.

He reached out and gave it a pat. "Jesus, Matt. That is definitely a W. Wow." It was hard to believe that story was true, but there it was. Funny now maybe, but that had to hurt like hell when it happened.

"Yup. Marked for life." Matthew turned a sweet pink and turned to pull up a pair of sweats. Oh, someone was a little shy about that.

He tugged his suit off, got his suitcase open and dug out a pair of sweats too. "What does the W stand for anyway?"

"My great-great-great-granddaddy registered this brand. He was William Whitehead, and he married a Wilhelmina Winchester. No shit." Matthew grabbed the wet suits and towels. "There's been a Whitehead on this land since before Texas joined the union."

Damn. "That's nuts. I mean, first of all, nobody should be named Wilhelmina." Tyler laughed and grabbed his comb, wincing as he pulled it through his wet hair. It was thick and wavy on a regular day, but the chlorine made it curl up.

"The story is they called her Mina." Matthew came to him and kissed his temple, teasing one curl up out of the way. "You want anything to drink, honey? I'm going to grab me a big glass of tea."

"Sure, sounds great. Do you need to tuck the girls in?" He slid his hand into Matthew's and followed along back to the kitchen trying not to ogle the game room and drool.

"I do. They'll come down, talk about tomorrow, and have a glass of milk." Matthew grinned at him. "Something to know—my eldest is up at five a.m., totally ready to go. Emma? Oh, Jesus Christ. She could sleep until noon."

He leaned on the kitchen counter. "She and I will get along fine. I frequently sleep until noon. Or later." If he slept, which he hadn't much recently. Of course he usually didn't get to bed before four. He kept bartender hours. "Are you an early riser? You are I bet."

"Coffeemaker starts at five o'clock. Every morning, and I'm usually out by six. I'll take the girls to Momma's and drop them off. Emma never wakes up, and Sophia will ask to come with me."

"Five o'clock." He'd be happy if he didn't see five o'clock in the morning ever in his whole life. "That's how it goes, huh? Every morning? Do you ever say yes to Sophia?"

"Depends on my plans. Lots of times, yes. It's nice to take her for daddy time alone. She needs a little more one-on-one than her sister right now."

There was a stampede of feet on the stairs, and Emma and Sophia appeared in the kitchen in their pajamas. "All clean," Emma declared, going straight to Matthew who was setting out two glasses of milk. "You are showing your boobies to your friend, Daddy."

"Am I?"

"Uh-huh. I get in trouble for showing my boobies to people."

Matthew sighed softly, the sound long-suffering. "It's different for boys."

"Why?"

Sophia frowned. "That's not fair. Her chest isn't any bigger than yours."

"I know." Matthew held up one hand. "I didn't make the rules, girls. I'm sorry. I don't have a good answer. That's how life is."

That was funny. At ten, Sophia's wasn't any bigger either. But he could tell she wanted it to be.

"My mom always said 'life isn't fair'. I don't think it's fair that girls grow up to have bigger boobies than boys, but that's how it is. Bummer." He kept a very straight face and picked up his glass of tea.

"There are some boys that wear fake ones, and some boys that get fake ones, but then they're girls, but they—" Emma blinked. "Daddy, can girls that used to be boys show their boobies?"

Matthew tilted his head. "I think that, if y'all are all women, you can't, no matter what. And that's still not fair."

"When you grow up and your generation is in charge you can change the rules. How's your milk? All done, Emma?" Knowing when to change the subject was one of Tyler's bartender skills.

"Are we going to be in charge? Really?" Sophia finished her milk. "When?"

"In eighty years," Matthew shot back. "Y'all are going to Mamaw's early early, so time for bed."

"Can I hang out with you, Daddy? Please? I'll be ready first thing."

"Oof. So early." Tyler rolled his eyes.

"I want to stay with Tyler!" Emma hopped over next to him. "I'll be good. I promise."

"Yeah?" He looked at her and then at Matthew and shrugged. "I mean, I'll be here."

"I... Are you sure?" Matthew blinked at him, like a big owl. "I mean, you're welcome to help, but I want you to know I didn't want you here for that. I wanted you to come for you."

Sophia leaned close and whispered, "Daddy, that didn't make sense."

Tyler chuckled. "I came for you." *For us.* "Emma and I will be fine."

Emma bounced. "It's okay, Daddy? You'll let me stay home with him?"

"I don't see why not. Still. Bed. Now." Matthew winked at Tyler. "I need daddy time."

Me too. Oh, man. Me too. Lots of daddy time.

"Okay!" The girls turned and dashed up the stairs. He watched them go, then raised his glass. "To daddy time."

The look he got was pure, unadulterated heat, no question. "Yes, sir. All the way."

He set the glass down and moved closer. "Can I touch your boobies?"

The flush that climbed up Matthew's body was immediate and dark, and he swore he heard those strong muscles creak. "You can touch anything. Anything at all."

"Good." He spread his hands over Matthew's chest,

sliding them from sternum to shoulders, feeling the muscles shiver. "Should we go rinse off the chlorine?"

"Y-yes." Matthew's nipples went tight and hard, responding immediately, beautifully. "Go start the water, I'll kiss cheeks, and I'll be right down."

He nuzzled Matthew's fuzzy chin and kissed it, feeling himself flush too, his skin breaking out in goosebumps. He wasn't that small, and he wasn't weak, but he'd never been with anyone so strong. It was hard to believe he had this big, beautiful man wanting him like this. "See you there."

Matthew nodded, teeth sinking into that full bottom lip before he turned to go. That was amazing, how much need there was, right there.

Okay. Back to the bedroom. He didn't know about ranches and daughters and trucks, but he knew this. It didn't matter if a bed was in New York or Texas, he was plenty confident. And Matthew had a way of blocking out the whole world for him. He shucked his sweats and tossed them back in his suitcase, took a second to turn the bed down just to give Matthew something to think about, then turned on the water and got into the shower to wait. Maybe he'd wash his hair—soapy bubbles was a good effect.

The bathroom was a goddamn wet dream—all tiled with an open shower with a seat and two huge rain heads, a towel warmer, a tub that he could imagine Matthew in…the whole thing screamed luxury and home at the same time.

Way out of his league. Like, lightyears out of his comfort zone. He liked it though, and Tyler felt okay with that because Matthew wanted him to like it. He scrubbed the shampoo into his hair trying not to worry about how he could possibly fit into a place like this. He had no idea, and he wasn't going to solve that now, so he focused on Matthew.

He'd have to figure it out that was all. He'd have to learn if he wanted to be able to stay.

"Mmm...you are the finest thing I've seen." Matthew's voice wrapped around him like a heated blanket. "I could watch you for days."

He grinned, balls going tight for a second at the thought that Matthew had been watching him, and he hadn't known it. Sweet. "Yeah? How long have you been there?" He turned to rinse his hair, giving Matthew a different view.

"Long enough to be hard as a rock. You want some company?" Matthew dimmed the lights in the bathroom, leaving a warm spotlight on in the shower.

"I definitely want your company." He looked around as the lights dimmed. "Damn, Matt. Are we making a movie?"

"No, sir. You want them back up?" Matthew grinned at him, coming right into his space, hands sliding around his body. "I love the steam and the lights in the shower."

"No, I like it. It's just... I feel like I'm dreaming." He loved the way Matthew's big hands held him. Not a bit of hesitation. He leaned right into them, letting Matthew have his weight. "This is amazing." And a lot. It was a lot.

"I feel the same way, and I'm at home. Does it feel—I don't know, too strange? The first time I went to the Expo, I didn't know how to process the city. It was loud, all the time." All the while Matthew talked, those hands stroked him, finding tense parts and insisting the tension released.

It was strange, all right. He chuckled and shook his head, then caught Matthew's gray eyes. "Honestly? It feels like another planet. I don't understand any of this. It's beautiful, and I like it, it's just..." Bigger, prettier, more expensive, wild. "So different."

"And you're so tired, worn." Matthew tilted his face up

and took a long, slow, almost lazy kiss. "Tomorrow everything will seem easier, I promise."

Not too tired for this. He'd wanted this all day. "It's easier already. Kiss me again." He didn't wait, pulling their mouths together with a soft moan. Matthew grabbed him, dragging them together, holding him up as the man began to devour him.

Matthew's kiss was what he'd been holding on to, what he craved most after Noah's accident forced Matthew to go home early. And Matthew had made sure he couldn't forget, calling every day, texting goodnight, sending pictures. He was here because the cowboy didn't let go of him. And he needed someone that wasn't going to let go.

Matthew groaned, the sound tearing from the barrel chest. "Want you."

There was something primal about those words, about the deep rumble they were spoken in.

"Take me to bed." He reached out and shut the water off. "Take me to bed, baby. Now."

"Now." Oh, yum. Cave cowboy. Matthew muscled him out of the shower and wrapped him in a towel, all the while walking to the bed.

They toweled off a little more once they got there, but he wouldn't swear they were totally dry before Matthew lifted him off his feet and set him in the sheets. He was burning up and they were cool against his skin. He reached out and took Matthew's hand, giving it a tug. "I want this. I want all of you."

"I got you." Matthew covered him, one leg pressing between his to nudge his sac and spread him. "Gonna help you fly."

Tyler believed it, unable to stop his moan or the way he spread wide open for Matthew, offering him everything. He was so hard every nudge, every accidental touch made him gasp and stoked a fire deep in his gut. He drew trembling fingers up Matthew's arms and down his back, everywhere he could reach. "Please."

"Anything." Matthew rocked them together, beard so fucking soft on his throat. "Tell me what you want, honey."

"I want you to touch me. I want you inside me. I want everything to go away except this. Except us." It was an easy answer to a complicated question. He wanted his whole world to be Matthew.

Matthew pressed an indentation in the headboard, exposing a little secret drawer, and he pulled out a condom and a little bottle of lube. He set them down, and then went back to touching Tyler with a focus that made him dizzy. His nipples were stroked, made hard and stiff while Matthew rubbed against him.

This was unreal. He arched into Matthew's hand and moaned and hooked his heels over Matthew's ass. Secret fucking drawer. He reached between them and pushed his fingers through the fuzz over that broad chest, finding the spots that made Matthew shiver.

Matthew cupped his ass, humped him for a second, like he'd lost control of his hips, then he eased back, kneeling up tall and letting him see all that strength, the lean hips, the broad shoulders, the thick, needy cock.

He dragged his gaze from Matthew's cock all the way up to those pretty gray eyes. Breath catching, making him gasp. "You're so beautiful."

Matthew grinned, the look surprisingly sweet. "Listen to you."

Matthew grabbed the lube, slicking his fingers. "I haven't done this in a long time, honey. I want to make it good for you."

He wasn't worried. He was surprised, but he understood what Matthew was telling him. He smiled. "Take your time, baby. I'm pretty sure you've got this."

"I think I remember how it goes." Those thick fingers traced along his cock, held his sac for a second, and then slowly circled his hole.

"Yeah." His hips rolled up off the bed. "That's...that's how it goes."

"Jesus, you're burning up." Matthew pressed, but didn't penetrate him. Not that pass. Or the next.

Tyler might have to kill him.

But when Matthew pressed in, one hand wrapping around his dick, he thought he might not.

"Good." Tyler nodded, sucking in a rough breath. It was good, but it wasn't enough. He arched into Matthew's fingers and covered the hand on his cock with his own, squeezing slightly. "More."

Matthew grunted, and one finger became two, and he began to stroke, pulling hard on Tyler's prick.

Yes! The word stuck in his throat and disappeared, replaced with a low groan. He let go, both hands reaching for Matthew. When they didn't make contact, he dropped them to the bed, balling the sheets into his fists. He bucked, not sure whether to ride Matthew's fingers or thrust up into his grip.

"So tight." Matthew leaned down, losing the grip on his cock to suck the tip in and taste him.

"Fuck." He was going to short-circuit. Maybe he was tight, maybe Matthew's fingers were just huge. Either way, everything the cowboy was doing felt amazing. "Matt... Matthew."

"Mmhmm..."

Fuck, he felt that all the way down his shaft. He reached

for Matthew again and combed his fingers into that thick, dark hair. “Baby” He tipped his head back, shoulders twisting in the pillows, and tried not to roll his hips up too hard, but he just couldn’t stay still. His goosebumps gave way to little beads of sweat, cooling his hot skin. He tugged hard on Matt’s hair. “I… I need…”

“Me too.” Matthew pulled away and grabbed the condom, getting it on with shaky fingers. He watched impatiently, gaze alternating between the look on Matt’s face and those busy fingers. Once the rubber was on, he reached for Matt, pulling him down for a kiss.

“It’s good, Matt. Just breathe, baby. It’s so good.”

“Hell, yeah. You’re going to feel like heaven around me.” Matthew slicked himself up, hand moving in short, almost brutal strokes. Then Matt leaned down to press against him, that heavy cock nudging his hole.

He spread again, knees going wide, eyes locked on Matthew’s. He knew what he was in for, he’d had that thick, beautiful cock in his mouth already. He gave a little nod and rocked up to meet Matthew halfway.

The mushroom head popped in, and they both gasped and stilled, their eyes meeting.

“Oh fuck.” Okay, knowing was different than experiencing. Matthew was fucking huge. He took a deep breath and relaxed as he exhaled letting Matthew slide in farther. They both moaned and he hauled his knees up higher.

“Fuck, honey. Heaven.” Matthew’s hips moved in the tiniest little thrusts, easing himself in deeper and deeper.

He was so…full. Matthew was everywhere—inside, all around him. He hooked his fingers at Matthew’s nape as they rocked together. “Heaven. Yes.”

"Kiss me." Matthew began to move, thrusting nice and slow, driving into him and dragging over his gland.

"Oh! Oh, God." He shivered and hauled on Matt's neck, pulling their mouths together, tangling their tongues as Matt stole his breath. They found a rhythm and went with it, and Matthew gave him every inch, gray eyes staring into his.

He tried to hold that gaze but sometimes it was too much, too big...he'd get too close, and he'd have to close his eyes for a second. But every time he looked up again, Matthew's eyes were on him. Focused, steady.

He didn't really want control though, he wanted to lose it, for Matthew to have it. It didn't take long, Matthew hit just the right spot just the right way, and Tyler rocked up hard, body begging for more.

"Yes." Matthew nodded and began to slam into him, just hitting that perfect spot, over and over.

That was it; he was gone. He couldn't breathe. His ears filled with their sounds, his vision narrowed to Matthew's face, and he came so hard he saw stars, balls emptying in an aching rush, his climax tearing through him like Matthew had shot him with lightning.

"Oh honey." Matthew watched him, then those gorgeous eyes closed, and Matthew took him, driving into him with short, hard thrusts, filling him up.

He held on, blinking his eyes clear even as his body was still trembling and his lungs fought for air, so he could watch too. "Yes," he managed to say, willing Matthew to take everything he needed. "Beautiful."

"Need you." Matthew's body went tight, lips drawn back in a grimace as he shot.

Matthew didn't have to say it for him to know it was true, he could see it in that look, feel it in the way Matthew had held him. "Baby. So beautiful." Tyler stroked Matthew's face, combed fingers through his beard and his hair, panting along with him and talking him back to the room.

"Damn." That was so sweet, how that single word grew syllables when Matt was melted.

"Mmm." He pulled Matt down into the sheets and did the honors, touching gently as he removed the condom. He slipped out of bed to toss it and clean up a little, then crawled right back into Matthew's arms. That was about the end of his energy too, he was suddenly exhausted.

"Mmm..." Matthew wrapped around him, holding on and keeping him close. "Sleep good, honey. I got you."

"You're amazing. That was...everything." He felt heavy and already half asleep. He hoped Matt understood, he was just so tired.

10

Matthew's phone rang with Sister's picture at seven in the morning. He'd already taken Sophia to breakfast, picked up feed and shingles, and was heading to the grocery. "It's your Aunt Rachel. Go ahead and answer it."

"Auntie Rache! I got to come with Daddy! We had breakfast at the diner, and I had pancakes!" She did love to get up and go.

"Well aren't you a lucky girl." Rachel's voice came over the speaker. "Are you being helpful?"

"The feed was too heavy, but I stayed by the car like Daddy said." Sophia bounced. "Daddy got us a playhouse for the backyard! Like a big one!"

"Did he?"

"I did." It was on sale—it was really a big shed, so he could use it after. "How's it going, lady?"

"I'm fine. Noah's doing well. Momma called to tell me she met your...friend." Oh. Look at Rachel being discreet. "She said she was disappointed you didn't stay."

"Tyler was exhausted. He needed a quiet night."

Momma was a turd, but he wasn't surprised she was telling stories on his happy ass.

"Ha. I'm sure it was very quiet." She snorted. "So she says you're bringing poppers on Saturday? I'm doing desserts. What does Tyler like? Chocolate? Berries?"

"He likes chocolate. I like berries..." he teased. "I'm over to the grocery. You need anything? I can drop it off on my way home."

"I think I'm all right, thank you. Are you going by the house to pick up Emma? Alan went over to help Daddy with the Wi-Fi."

"Emma stayed in bed. Tyler said he'd keep an eye on her, and Lisa's home for a week. Krissy said she'd be there in the pool all day."

"Nice of you to let Tyler sleep in. City boys probably aren't used to rancher's hours. How long is he staying?"

Three sentences, so much subtext. Rachel could be so much like Momma.

"He's used to working the night shift. Six a.m. isn't his thing." He shook his head and rolled his eyes at Sophia, making her giggle. "He's welcome here for as long as he wants to stay."

"Well, I look forward to meeting him on Saturday. Momma says she bought sunscreen..." Rachel laughed. "She really said that."

"Yeah. There must not be much sunshine up there. He's lilywhite. I'm going to buy more at the store." He chuckled. Sunscreen, hamburgers, chips. Lord, he needed to get home and fire up the grill. "I'm cooking burgers for lunch. I'll let them know at the house."

"Might as well tell my boys then. Momma will call them. I swear she thinks I starve them both."

"Noah!" Sophie liked her cousins. They were older and interesting.

Rachel laughed. "I better get to it. Call me when you have a minute to yourself."

He had to grin. He knew she'd called him in his truck at seven in the morning because she thought he'd be alone. At least he knew she was calling to ask real questions too, not just the ones she'd asked for Momma.

Sophia looked at him as Rachel hung up. "She wants to know if y'all are boyfriends."

"Does she?"

"Uh-huh. If you want to date him, you can. He seems nice, even if he sounds like a TV show."

Oh, that was a good one. He had kind of been worried Tyler wouldn't understand either of the girls at all. "A TV show?"

"Uh-huh." She nodded. "Like the ones with lots of policemen and stuff. It's cool."

Well okay then. "Do you think he'll like it here?"

"Well, duh. It's like the best home ever! And we can go everywhere." There was no doubt in her voice whatsoever. None. And didn't that make him feel ten thousand feet tall? "Don't miss your turn, Daddy."

"No, ma'am. No missing." He made the turn into the little store and parked. "Come on, chica. Let's grab some stuff. We'll get some kolaches while we're here."

"Emma likes those."

"She does." He grabbed his hat and laughed as she followed him out the driver's side. "Monkey."

"Ook ook ook. Come on, silly Daddy. We got to make a million burgers for all the hungry cowboys."

"Yes, ma'am. We do." All the hungry cowboys and one beautiful Yankee.

11

Okay. Tyler didn't know ranches, but he knew how to be a house guest. He showered, cleaned up the bathroom, made the bed, got dressed and then tucked everything neatly back into his suitcase. He stashed it in a corner with his backpack where it wouldn't be ugly and in the way.

Now he needed some coffee.

He padded barefoot out to the kitchen, thinking he should probably check on Emma. It wasn't late, his eyes had popped open about eight, and he'd made himself get up. He'd promised Matt they'd be okay. He could nap by the pool later or something.

He hadn't seen eight o'clock in the morning in eons. Well, not sober anyway. Jesus, the sun was bright.

He hadn't been this perfectly sore in ages either. Every step he took reminded him of Matthew.

There was a coffee cup in the sink, a carafe and a clean cup on the counter along with two notes.

The one for 'Emma' said—Good morning, baby. Be

good. You cannot get in the pool unless Tyler or Lisa are out there. I will bring you breakfast. Love you. Daddy.

His note was folded, written in a blocky, masculine cursive. Hey, honey. Hope you slept well. Don't forget I cleaned out that one dresser for you and there's room in the closet. Make yourself at home. Coffee is in the carafe. I'll bring doughnuts and kolaches. Making burgers for the crew for lunch. Text if you need anything from the store. Last night was amazing. Love, M.

"I had totally forgotten," he said out loud as he reread the note, grinning stupidly. Last night had been better than amazing. All it was missing was a good morning kiss, and he knew without a doubt that was coming. The third time through the note he ran his thumb over the "Love, M" part, folded it back up and stuck the note in his pocket. His fast-moving cowboy.

No sign of Emma yet, so he poured himself some coffee and googled "kolaches" on his phone. Yum. No bad there.

He wandered over to the window and peered out at the pool and that neat outdoor grilling space. He hadn't even heard Matt get up. He must have been dead to the world. That was the best night's sleep he'd had in forever.

Matthew had held him, all night.

Two women came up onto the patio—one in jeans and boots opened the cabinet under the grill, shaking the propane bottle, the other in a one-piece swimsuit that started checking pool chemicals.

Damn, Matt had a busy house. He'd met more people in the last day than he knew in New York. Well, he hadn't met these two, but he had a feeling he knew who they were. Must be nice to just have people taking care of things for you. Not that Matthew didn't do things, he was up and out of the house by some disgustingly early hour after all.

Okay, so go out and introduce himself or run up and peek in on Emma? Maybe it was weird for a grown man to go peek into a little girl's room? He didn't know. He didn't know about kids.

He bet they knew though, so that settled it. Matt said to make himself at home, right? He'd just take his coffee out to the pool.

"Good morning!" The woman in the bathing suit called out when she saw him.

He picked up the pace, stopping on the other side of the pool. "Good morning."

"Are you Tyler?"

Okay, that was still weird. Everyone knew about him already. "Yes, hi."

The lady in the baseball cap nodded to him. "I'm Krissy, the foreman. This is my girl, Lisa. She's home for the next week. Bossman said I could borrow a cup of coffee, I'm out. You mind?"

Did he mind? It wasn't his house. Or his coffee. "Please, help yourself." She took a couple of steps toward the house and he got an idea. "Hey, um. Krissy? Can you peek in on Emma for me? I didn't know if... I'm supposed to be watching her this morning, but I didn't know if that would be weird, you know?"

"Not weird, but sure. She's probably in the family room sleeping on the sofa. She gets scared when it's too quiet." She glanced at Lisa. "You want a cup of coffee?"

"No, babe. Grab me a Coke?"

"Sure, what kind?"

"Diet Dr Pepper."

He chuckled. Something he didn't have to learn. He made a mental note...not weird and check the sofa if

Emma's not in bed. Also, what did too quiet mean? This was the quietest place he'd ever been.

He pulled a chair up and sat, watching Lisa. "You drive a truck, Matt said?"

"Yes, sir. I drive two weeks on, one week off. Love it. Been doing it for almost ten years now. Paid off my rig and everything." Lisa grinned and winked at him. "And this was a great idea on Matthew's part. He's the best boss ever. Just ask Krissy."

He didn't doubt it. "I believe that. He's a good man. I know he was excited about the pool, for the kids. And hanging out here is pretty sweet, huh? Could do worse for vacation. This whole place is beautiful."

"It's amazing. Krissy says he talked about you constantly. It's nice to know you're wanted." Lisa's face lit up when Krissy came out the door. "How's my Emma?"

"Sound asleep with the TV on, her elephant in one hand, Sophia's ostrich in the other." She put the can of soda on the pool coping, then stood. "Bossman says he's heading back with shingles, feed, and a goddamn shed that Sophia talked him into. I'm going to wrangle men and get them moving, I guess. Lord have mercy, that man spoils those girls something awful."

He felt pretty spoiled too. "Thanks for looking in on her. I just wasn't sure. I know exactly two kids and they both live here." He grinned, feeling a little sheepish. "I have a lot to learn. About a lot of things. Like, everything."

"Well sure. This is like a hospital or an airport. It's a whole weird little town. Hell, Miss Rachel lives one way, the folks live the other. We got ten cowboys here. There's a ton to learn. Enjoy it."

"Yeah, Jonas is the one that got away. All the way to

Austin. Crazy bastard." Lisa winked at him, then ducked under the water.

"I'm trying to." He sipped his coffee. "It's been a whole day. So far so good." Really good. He shifted to the edge of the pool when Lisa came up for a sip of her soda. "He called me every day after he came home for Noah. Every day."

"He's never once brought anyone home to meet the kids. Losing Deb damn near took him to his knees, but he stood back up. I can't wait for you to meet Rory and Bullet."

He knew how much Matthew loved Deb. It was in his eyes every time her name came up. "Rory and Bullet..." Tyler didn't know those names. They could be people, or they could be dogs. God, he was an idiot.

"Matthew's first boyfriend and his husband. Bullet's a commercial artist in Houston. They have a beautiful baby boy. Uh... Justice? I think his name is Justice..."

The ex was married. Excellent. "Oh yeah? Are they local?"

"Outside Houston. Not too far. Y'all should run to Galveston and everybody do the beach." Suddenly her face lit up again. "Mija! Good morning!"

Emma looked surprisingly young, worried. "Where's Daddy? Can I call him?"

"Of course. Are you okay? Come sit, we can call him on my phone." He held a hand out to her. "Did you see he left a note on the counter for you?"

"Uh-huh. He's bringing breakfast." She pulled a little chair over and sat right next to him, eyelids going heavy again. "Oh, I do like the sunshine."

"You are your daddy's girl." Lisa laughed softly, shaking her head.

"Have you done, like, all the morning stuff? Brushed

your teeth and...things?" And things. He rolled his eyes and pulled out his phone.

"I just read my note and came out. I'll go pee and brush my teeth when I put on my swimming suit."

"Okay. That sounds good." He dialed Matthew and put it on speaker. He didn't know what was up, but it didn't matter. She looked worried and she wanted Matt. "I'm calling Daddy now, okay?"

"'Kay."

"Hey, honey. I'm almost home. Gonna stop at Ground Up for fancy coffees. You want?"

"Daddy! Get me a strawberry coffee? I miss you! Come home."

He grinned and winked at Lisa. "I miss you too, Daddy! Can I have a caramel macchiato, please?"

Matthew laughed, the sound booming and wonderful. "You can. Tell Lisa that I'm bringing Krissy an iced hazelnut mocha, and that I picked up a case of Diet Dr Pepper for her?"

"I'm right here in the pool, honey. Thank you! Krissy will kiss your toes. She's off rounding up the guys."

Tyler chuckled. "I think you've covered everyone within earshot now." This whole exchange was worth getting out of bed early for.

"I'll be right there. Love y'all. See you in a few."

"Love you too, Daddy! I'm going to go to the bathroom!"

"Okay, Em!" Matthew chuckled. "Bye, honey. See you in a sec."

Tyler tucked his phone back in his pocket, grinning. "Well that was fun. Emma, don't forget your teeth. Oh! And make your bed too, okay?" That was what his mom always said. Make your bed.

"Yes, sir. I'll put our stuff upstairs." She stretched and then bounced away, happy again.

"And the world gets to spin again. Yay." He rolled his jeans up and stuck his feet in the water. "He's the best Dad ever. Matthew told me he's a little worried about telling them. You know, about me. He just doesn't know how they'd take it."

"Em doesn't remember her at all. None of it. Sophia remembers enough to worry, but he doesn't lie to them. He tells them the truth and just lets it be."

He nodded. "I think that's great. I just...it's really important that I figure them out." This was their home, he really wanted to get along.

"Totally. Matthew loves them to distraction, but they're easy to love. I just hope you like us—this life. It's wild and different. There's never a second something's not happening."

There was never a dull moment in the city either. It just wasn't the same kind of busy. "I'm a New York City bartender, I know wild. Just not this kind of wild."

"That's right! Krissy said you were a bartender. Can you make a paloma?"

He nodded. "Yep." He liked them too.

"Can you make a margarita?"

"With my eyes closed." In every incarnation that existed.

"Can you tap a keg?"

He laughed. "I sure as hell hope so."

"Well, damn. You'll fit right in here!" Lisa grinned at him. "Life of the party. Shit, give Matthew a minute and he'll have a bar put in out here. The girls beg for virgin pina coladas."

Oh, he would enjoy that. He could make drinks for the barbecue. It would give him something to do, something familiar.

"Bring it on. I can make a virgin anything." He looked at her and raised an eyebrow. "Why does that sound wrong?"

One pierced eyebrow lifted. "Better than making anything a virgin..."

He chuckled and stood. "I better go check on Emma. It was great to meet you. I'll be out for a dip later I'm sure." A dip and a nap in the sun. Well, in the sun under an umbrella.

"I'll be in here watching lesser men work for a living."

"It's vacation! You let me know when you're ready for something stronger than Dr Pepper." He gave her a wave and headed inside. "Emma?" He called making his way through the kitchen to the stairs. "You okay?"

She came be-bopping down the stairs, wearing her swimsuit and a rainbow tutu. "I'm dressed!"

"You look beautiful. Rainbow is my favorite color." He took his mug to the carafe and poured himself a warm-up.

"Can you do my hair, please, sir?" She held out a brush and a fuzzy blue hair tie.

He put his coffee down and took them from her. "I'm going to tell you a secret. I know nothing about hair. But I am a super-fast learner, and I promise to be very careful. You just have to tell me what you want. Okay?"

"Can you not pull hard, and put it up so it's not in my face?" God, those eyes were just like Matt's. Just.

"I will do my best, and you tell me if it's too hard, okay? You can teach me." Why did this make him nervous? It was a ponytail, right? How hard could this be? Just don't hurt the girl. He looked at her hair, which was thick like Matt's too and shook his head. He was going to make a mess of this.

"Ready?" He started brushing, carefully, gathering her hair into his other hand. "You have very pretty hair, Emma."

"It's like Daddy's, not my momma's. Did you know about her?"

He started at the bottom, finding it fairly easy to brush.

"I know your Dad loved her, and I know she was pretty because he showed me a picture. Hm. He told me other things. She waited tables in high school..." He kept brushing, letting Emma lead this conversation because he was a little out of his depth.

"She died. She had cancer and went to live with Jesus. Daddy was real sad, but he says that it's not right, to be sad forever. You have to honor God by having laughs and puppies and love."

That was beautiful. It sounded just like Matt, but better, because it came from Emma. "Your dad is a really smart guy. And he's right. Love is the most important thing." He knew his mom was in Heaven because that was where she wanted to be. He didn't know about Will. He just knew Will wasn't in pain anymore. "I lost my mom too. But I know she'd say the same thing."

"Oh." Emma stopped and turned around, pushing right into his arms and hugging him tight. "I'm sorry! Me and Daddy and Sister will love you, and you can play with the puppies all the time."

Whoa.

Tyler hugged her, but it took everything he had to hold the tears back. Something was definitely wrong with him. He could handle anything right now except people being nice to him. "Thanks." He cleared his throat and tried that again because he sounded like he'd swallowed a frog. "Thank you, Emma."

She squeezed him again, then let him go. "Now, fix my hair. Mamaw would say I looked a mess."

"Yes, ma'am. We can't have that. Your dad will be home

soon." He took a deep, deep breath and then got back to work. "What are your plans for today?" He changed the subject because he wasn't planning on losing his marbles in front of an eight-year-old.

"Today is my day to get the eggs. I'm going to swim lots and help Daddy feed cowboys. Daddy loves that, to feed folks."

"Right, I heard we're having a cookout. I guess I'll get to meet everybody. That will be fun." Using the definition of fun broadly to include worrying about being put on the spot. "I think I'm going to help too."

"Everyone is nice, but you have to be super-duper nice to Daniel 'cause someone beat him up, and Mr. Allen brought him home. Daddy says to ask before you hug him, 'cause he's got hurt bones."

He didn't randomly hug people the way kids did, but he understood. Matthew had told him about Daniel. "I'll be careful." It sounded like, if he needed a quiet moment, he knew who to go sit with. "Little tug." He wound the hair tie around her hair then twisted and pulled the hair through. It wouldn't win any glamor prizes, but it would keep the hair out of her eyes.

"Thank you!" She took her hairbrush and ran to the front door. "Daddy! Daddy's home!"

He caught himself smiling and followed her to the door, waiting for Matthew to get out of the car. "Hey, you. You need a hand?"

"Can you help with the—"

"Oh my God, Sister! It's a playhouse!" Emma's squeal pierced his eardrums.

He laughed. "Let me get some shoes." He jogged back to the bedroom to tug on his sneakers and hurried back out to the truck. "Nice playhouse. Word is you spoil your girls. I don't see what they mean."

"I have no idea what you're talking about. I bought ice cream." Butter wouldn't melt in Matt's mouth.

"Did you get strawberry coffee?" Matt looked so good. Smiling, happy. He wanted a kiss. "Let's get it inside before it melts."

"I did. Two strawberry coffees, a caramel macchiato, an iced hazelnut, and an iced latte with three extra shots." Matt leaned down and kissed him, just a peck, but the girls were right there. Damn.

"Thank you." He grinned at Matt, making sure Matt knew that kiss was appreciated. "Girls, there's groceries to bring inside."

"Sister, it's a playhouse," Emma whispered, and Sophia nodded, so smug.

"Daddy says it's ours. All ours. We can hang curtains and put bean bags in and have sleepovers." She grabbed a bag of groceries. "We have to put it under the big tree so there's shade."

Emma grabbed two sacks and followed her big sister with huge eyes.

He grabbed the flats of coffee, noting that Krissy was already on her way over. She must have seen Matthew pull in. "Is that everything?"

"I've got the big cooler with the cold stuff." Matthew grabbed a huge Yeti out of the back of the pickup. "Hey, lady."

"You bought them a playhouse." Her grin was barely—barely—held at bay.

"Yep." Matthew didn't hide his smile.

"I suppose my cowboys are going to have to put the damn thing up."

"Yep."

She finally lost it, laughter filling the air. "It looks amazing. We can turn it into storage when the girls outgrow it."

"That was my thinking. Tax write-off, you know."

Tyler held out the coffee. "Which one are you?"

"The latte with the most shots."

He should have known. "Um...probably that one, closest to you on your right?"

"Yep. Looks like." She pulled it out of the tray and took a long sip. "Oh, that'll do it. Thanks, Boss. We'll get over here to deal with the shed—playhouse—in a bit. I know the girls will be anxious to get in it." She tugged on her cap and headed back toward the barns.

"Was Em good for you?" Matthew asked, hauling the cooler like it weighed nothing.

"She taught me how to put her hair up, and we had a good talk. She's very kind. She has a big heart." *She made me cry and I adore her.*

"She's a good girl. I think I'll keep her." They got inside and started unloading ten thousand tons of hamburger supplies and chips and Velveeta and dips.

"Is this lunch or a party?" He laid things out, organizing them on the counter so they could see what was what.

"Velveeta means queso, Tyler!" Emma bounced next to him.

"Mmm. Cheese." He grinned at her. "I think Lisa is still in the pool."

Emma's eyes lit up. "Can I Daddy?"

"Let me make sure she's still out there. Hold up." Matthew stuck his head out of the kitchen door. "Hey, woman! You mind if these hooligans come in with you?"

"Bring it on!" she hollered back.

"Go on." Matthew came back, chuckling. "Just a lunch. Ten cowboys, Krissy and Lisa, four of us—that's sixteen. Plus Momma and Daddy and the boys—that's twenty, assuming Noah's girlfriend and that little boy that's attached to Elias aren't here or there aren't folks that don't stop by. I planned for thirty."

"Yay!" Emma grabbed their strawberry drinks and went running.

Sophia took off upstairs. "Getting my suit!"

Thirty people? What did a party look like? How much did it cost to feed them all? He leaned against Matt's back. "Lisa said you should set up a bar...since you know a bartender."

"Do I now?" Matthew bumped their shoulders together. "If you want to, I'll take you in to buy some supplies later this week. If you don't, I'll buy a couple of tubs of margaritas for the freezer and have beer."

"Could be fun. I'd get to know everybody, right? And it might be nice for people to know I can do *something*. Other than pretty up your pool I mean."

"Sounds like fun. We'll make it happen. Today, we'll feed hungry cowboys and maybe take a ride and go look at the pond and stuff."

"Sounds great." The pond sounded quiet. He might need some quiet after meeting all those people. "I can't wait to meet everyone. Emma was so sweet. She said I needed to be careful and not hug Daniel too hard—and to ask first. I think we're going to be good friends, she and I."

"She wants to take care of the whole world. She's very concerned about people's pains." Matthew chuckled as Sophia ran outside to swim. "And Miss Sophia wants to make things, damn the consequences."

"The best pieces of you." He leaned very close and whispered, "I ache in all the right places today."

Matthew's eyes lit up, and he grabbed Tyler and kissed him hard enough that his toes curled.

He threw an arm around Matt's neck and held on, grinning and breathless. "I'm not kidding. I'm looking forward to a soak in that hot tub later. Damn, cowboy."

"Mmm... I'm ready to enjoy that. No horses for you today, hmm?" Matt's little wink was adorable.

"No." He stretched and winced, playing it up. "Not the ride I had in mind."

"I'll have to rub you down tonight, honey. I'll cure what ails you."

"I'm cured. I'm a true believer. I have subscribed to the Book of Matthew." He gave Matt's ass a squeeze. "Are we making burgers out of these now or sticking the meat in the fridge?"

"Let's let it sit in the cooler. It'll stay a good temp."

He stuck the ice cream in the freezer and picked up his coffee. "I had forgotten you cleaned out space for me. I should go unpack. Hang my coat up and stay awhile, like my mom used to say."

"You want a second of company?" Oh, that was interest there.

"Yes." He reached up and scritched Matthew's beard. "Maybe two seconds."

"Maybe four or five." Matthew danced him down the hall toward the bedroom.

Oh, he loved dancing, and he could follow any lead. "Did you have a good morning with Sophia? She seemed excited."

"Lovely. She's a morning girl, and she always has the

best debates with me." Matt hummed and twirled him, rocking him right back into his body.

He laughed through the little twirl and leaned close when he could. "Emma was a little worried, I think. I'm not sure if she forgot I was hanging out with her or just wasn't quite as ready to be brave and without you as she thought. She did fine, though."

"She wakes up slow, and she dreams. God, the nightmares. They kill me."

He stepped through the bedroom door and headed for his suitcase. "Oh that sucks. I had them too as a kid. I still dream a lot." Not always good dreams, not until very recently.

"I'm not a huge dreamer, but when I do, it's a doozy." Matthew closed the door behind them and locked it.

He hid his grin, wondering how much actual unpacking he was going to get done with the door locked. He decided to pretend like that was still the plan just for fun and gave Matt a little show bending over to open his suitcase on the floor. His tease hadn't accounted for how sore he was, and he couldn't stop his tell-tale groan as everything below his hips stretched and burned. Man, that felt just right.

"Mmm... Does that feel as good as it sounds?" Matt's hands landed on his hips, thumbs digging in his lower back.

"Hurts so good. Mmm." He stretched lower, this time on purpose and let Matt's fingers go to work. "That feels so good."

"That's the point, right?" Matt's hands were sure, strong, rubbing and dragging on his skin.

"Mhm." He straightened up and let Matt steer him toward the bed. "Is there more?"

"More points? More massage?" Matt eased him down and straddled his ass, rubbing his back now.

"I don't care, just keep doing...that. All of that." Tyler sighed, sinking into the comforter, letting his eyes close. "You have good hands."

"I work with them a lot. Jesus, you're fine to me."

Matt's voice was husky, almost a growl, but warmer, infinitely more sensual.

"I'm so glad I just...got on that plane." He wriggled out of his T-shirt and tossed it. He'd panicked. He'd needed air. He'd needed Matthew's air. "You're the most beautiful man I've ever seen." Tan, strong, solid.

"Thank you. Don't think anyone's ever said that to me before."

"I don't believe you." He didn't. Surely Deb had told him how handsome he was. "But if that's true, that's just another reason why I'm glad you showed up at my bar."

He knew he mumbled the end of that, Matt's hands felt like heaven and he was going totally boneless. He told himself not to doze off. If all he did was sleep what would Matt think? What kind of house guest would he be?

Still, Matt's hands were hypnotizing, so warm and the bed was so soft, and he knew better. "Thank you, baby," he muttered, so relaxed there was no fighting it anymore.

12

"Daddy! Watch me!"

"Boss, where do you want this shed?"

"Boss, can I have your keys? I need to move the truck."

"Bubba, I need you to sign the paper I emailed you."

"Bubba, can I stay at yours after Momma's shindig?"

"Boss, you'd best turn that burger."

"Son, can you send someone out to help Noah with his chair?"

Matthew signed and directed, watched and flipped and chopped and answered and sent.

He pondered just going to work in the barn some. No one would notice.

"Daddy! Watch me!" Emma waved her arms and jumped.

"Cheese for the burgers. And buns." Lisa came down from the house with her hands full, in a flowy cover-up and flip-flops. "You keep the plates out here someplace, right?"

Momma kissed his cheek. "I just love this new outdoor space, Matty. Where do you want me to put my salad?"

"Just set it on the counter. There should be spoon deals

in that weird little drawer." He pointed with his chin to the stack of paper plates.

"What else do you need, Matt?" Lisa put her sunglasses on. "You want me to pull ketchup and stuff out of the fridge? Watch the girls? Where's your man?"

"Here! Here. I'm here, sorry." Tyler came out of nowhere in his trunks and a T-shirt that read, "Not Throwing Away My Shot," and went right up to him for a kiss. "Sorry. I crashed so hard."

"No worries. You're on vacation, honey." Matthew was not going to blush at the look Momma gave him. No way. "Lis, can you grab the mustard and ketchup? Does anyone need mayonnaise?"

"I'd love some." Tyler looked sweet and a little sleepy, still. "You want me to get it?"

"Hang on, Tyler, I think..." Lisa had her nose in the minifridge. "Yep. There's some here."

"Thank you."

"Hey, Uncle Dub." Elias walked up with a huge watermelon. "You remember Sam?"

Sam was a tall, bean pole, and very hard to forget. "Hello, sir."

"We're gonna swim. Cool?" Elias put the watermelon on the counter.

"It is. Where's your brother?"

"Uh—Papaw has him. He's wanting to get in the pool too."

Okay, damn. "Have Little Tim run and help?"

Tim was the size of a Mack truck, and the sweetest man on earth. He could carry Noah, if he had to.

"You boys go ahead, I'm on it." Lisa gave Matt a nod and headed for the crew at the playhouse. "Kris!"

"Just lunch, huh?" Tyler leaned on him. "What can I do?"

"Just lunch." He couldn't remember the last time he was in this house without a bunch of folks for one meal or the other. "Can you please open the buns and get the first pack out? They'll all serve themselves."

"Yeah, sure." Tyler got to work laying out buns. He looked completely comfortable when his hands were busy. "Seriously, this is a lot of people for lunch. You do this a lot?"

"Once a week or so. It's a good way to build family. It's bigger in the summer. In the winter things slow way down." But right now they were calving, building, moving cattle, raising up all the babies. He needed his cowboys fit and happy and ready to work.

"Neat. Crazy, but neat."

"The playhouse went up like a dream, Boss. It's good to go." Krissy pulled a bottle of water from the cooler. "It'll be cute with some curtains and all."

"You can decorate it for us." Matthew met Krissy's glare head on, managing to keep his face straight.

"I will beat you to death, Boss." Krissy went over to the triangle on the porch, ringing it good and hard.

Tyler nearly jumped out of his skin. "Okay. So I'll know to expect that next time."

Krissy glanced over at Tyler and laughed. "Welcome to the ranch, Yankee." She gave Tyler a chuck on the shoulder with her work gloves and walked past him, probably headed to talk to Lisa and the girls while the cowboys got food.

"Yes, Tyler. Welcome to the ranch." Leanne, one of the sweetest cowboys he'd ever met, came up to Tyler, shook his hand. "Krissy's a hard ass. Don't worry about her."

Tyler was all smiles. "Thank you. We actually met this

morning before I'd even had my coffee. We're good. I didn't get your name."

"Leanne Gentry. I work with the horses, and I have some veterinarian training, so I'm always in the barns."

"That's cool. Matthew pointed the horses out last night. I've never seen them up close. They're beautiful." Tyler reached for another package of buns to put out. "You're going to take me for a closer look soon, right, Matt?"

"We'll go riding, honey." He would put Matt on one of the old steady riders, one that the girls were safe on.

"I'm game. It was good to meet you, Leeann."

"Matt, can I grab a rare one for Noah? I'm not going to roll him through here." Alan grabbed a plate. "No cheese for him."

"Where's Hannah?" he asked, dishing up a burger. Noah and that little girl were joined at the hip.

"She's at physical therapy. Her mom's bringing her by, and Mamaw Whitehead said she'd run her home after supper tonight."

"It's good to know they're both getting better."

"Thank you. You must be Tyler. I'm Alan." Alan stuck out his hand. "Rachel had a hair thing and...honestly I think she was glad to be rid of us for the day. She says she'll see you Saturday."

"Sure. Good to meet you."

"Yep, you too. Gonna run this over to Noah." Alan nodded and left with the burger.

"You'll help me when I forget everyone's names, right?" Tyler tickled his elbow.

"God yes. No one expects you to remember, honey. Shit, I forget sometimes." Which wasn't true. His job in the world was this—to organize folks, make them happy, encourage them to work.

"I was kidding. I'm not going to forget, I'm a bartender. It's my job to get to know people. This is just a lot of new people all at once. They're nice, though. Everyone's really nice."

"They try." He winked over, going for comforting. "They are cowboys. Things can get wild now and then."

Wild. Things could get downright western.

Hell, he'd just bailed Ed and Jimmy out a few weeks ago for fighting down to the bar.

Tyler laughed. "You forget I work in a gay bar. Might be a slightly different wild, but it's still wild." Tyler bumped shoulders with him. "Your burgers look really good. I think the kids are coming over."

"Have one." He put together one with cheese, one without. "Can you put mustard on the cheese one and ketchup on the other, please, sir?"

"Mustard on the cheese one..." Tyler scooped up the mustard and ketchup. "And ketchup on...all set. For the girls? Oh, and here come your parents."

"Both with cheese. They'll make their own. Emma is the ketchup." Matthew grinned at his babies. "Having a good day?"

"Uh-huh. Can we have popsicles after burgers?" Sophia grinned at him, nose all freckled from the sun.

"Yes, but not in the pool, okay." The red dye was nasty.

"I see my boy's already put you to work." Momma patted Tyler's hand. "I don't think there's anyone on this ranch that knows how to sit down."

"It's all good." Tyler shrugged. "I like to keep busy. I wouldn't want to sit down today anyway."

"Ha!" Krissy and Lisa were waiting behind Momma and Daddy and they started laughing so hard they had to take themselves right out of line.

"Oh. I didn't mean—uh. Wow." Tyler blushed bright red like he'd been out in the sun for a week.

Matthew didn't even begin to know what to say, so he didn't. He just fought his grin. He'd been a kid when him and Deb were married, and he'd never felt like he was grown enough to tease with Momma and Daddy. Now he was old enough, but he didn't quite know how. Christ, he was going to get an earful from Sister tonight. "Get your burgers, y'all!"

"Yes, sir!" Everyone who hadn't eaten yet lined up and the first round of burgers, and most of Momma's salad and half the watermelon was gone.

By the time he got his lunch, the girls were having their popsicles with Momma up by the new playhouse, Hannah had showed up and was sitting with Noah on the steps in the shallow end of the pool, and Daddy was chatting with a bunch of the boys. Tyler had wandered off to eat and was sitting on the steps up to the house, sipping a Coke.

He leaned back against the house and rested, breathing where he—

"Daddy! Bull! Bull!"

Matthew was running for the fence before he even thought, before he looked, whistling up his dogs. He and Krissy hit the gate at the same time, hollering and waving their hands, desperately trying to distract Nutterbutter from whatever had caught his goddamn attention. Someone threw Krissy a rope, and he pulled his Colt from his ankle holster.

The dogs were nipping and biting, and that slowed the big black asshole some.

"Come on, you bastard! I don't want to shoot you." He stood his ground while Krissy threw a loop over one horn and pulled hard.

The bull turned on a dime, and he grabbed the fence and pulled himself over. Little Tim showed up on Cimarron, grabbing him and dragging the bull out of the near pasture.

"Good deal." He holstered his weapon and loved on the pups, praising them. "And you, Miss Em. Good eyes!"

"Just luck, Daddy."

Krissy coiled up the rope and stalked off. "C'mon, Jimmy, let's go see how he got out."

It took a minute, but everyone went back to what they'd been doing. Except maybe Tyler, who was standing instead of sitting, looking like he didn't know what to do next.

"Hey, honey. That was Nutterbutter. He's a shit." He grabbed a hamburger and tossed half to each dog.

"That was...intense." Tyler's brow furrowed. "And you carry a gun."

"Yep." He stretched up, his back popping, and Daddy came over.

"Shit, boy. Look at you, clearing that fence. You're younger than you appear in the rearview."

"No shit on that."

"That was a pretty impressive jump." Tyler stuck his hands in his pockets. "Where did he come from? Is everything okay now?"

"He pushed through some fence. He's my top producer because he's still so active, but he can't be tromping around up here. I imagine he heard all the fun and wanted to join in." Nutterbutter had loved working, loved showing off still, but he was headstrong and smart as fuck. Still, at fifteen a straw, it would have been a shame to kill the evil shit. "The guys will find where the fence went down. No worries."

"Remember that time you shimmied up that tree when Radar got out?"

"Up a tree?" Tyler looked horrified.

"I had to climb up there and get him down like a fireman." Daddy laughed, and he loved that sound.

"How old was he?"

"I don't know. Matty? Maybe four? Five?" Daddy shook his head. "Little."

"Lord yes. I saw that big beast, and I swear fire was shooting out his nose." He remembered how scared he was, how he'd frozen in the live oak like a cat.

"Jesus. That's dangerous." Tyler rested a hand on his arm. "Are you okay?"

"I am." He wouldn't be maybe, after an hour or two he'd have a little adrenaline let down. And him and Krissy were fixin' to have a come to Jesus meeting about the fences. "You? You look a little rattled."

"Yeah. A little. I've never seen anything so big and angry in my life. I thought it was ready to kill somebody." Tyler took his hand. "And you actually hopped that fence to get in there with it? That's insane."

"That's the job. We have a dozen buckers, plus the regular livestock, the horses—they all have minds of their own. It takes a bit to get used to the whole big critter thing." He didn't remember not riding, not knowing the livestock, but Deb had been incredibly worried at the beginning. She'd been a townie, and her eyes the first time she'd seen him with his arm up to the shoulder in a cow...

It had been a bad date.

"It's a fucking scary job." Tyler shook his head. "And where I come from you don't pull out a gun unless you're going to shoot someone with it. Talk about making my heart race."

"Well, I was hoping I didn't have to." Matthew winked at Tyler, hoping to ease the worry. "I love that crazy old bull, but I couldn't risk my girls."

"No, no. I get it, I just…it's just a lot. I'm glad everyone is okay."

"Funny thing." Daddy squinted at Tyler from under his hat. "Most of these boys wouldn't know what to do with themselves up in New York either. You just give us a little while." Daddy tipped his hat and headed for the pool.

"I will," Tyler called after him.

Matthew didn't know what to say, really, so he held his tongue, just smiling at Tyler every so often. "Soon I'll have to show you the rest of the house. You haven't seen the library, the media room. You have rooms to explore. My office is up there over the garage."

"You have time to sit in an office?" Tyler leaned on him. "I don't believe it."

"I am up there a couple days a week, sometimes. If it's slow." That little lean, the pressure and warmth, that did it for him. "I usually just check my emails at the kitchen table."

"I can't wait to see everything. And don't worry, if you're busy the girls can show me around." Tyler grinned. "I can ask them all about you."

"Oh lord." He could just imagine. Actually, he had no idea what they'd say. They were basically healthy, happy, peaceful babies.

"Uncle? Are there more hamburgers?" Lord, Rachel's boys were eating machines.

"Yeah, turn the grill back on. There's more," he hollered back.

"I'll make 'em," Daddy said. "You show Ty all the roses and stuff."

Tyler snorted a laugh. "Yes. Show me the roses, baby. He's funny. I mean, I love flowers. But I guess he thinks that's more my speed?"

"No. No, come on, you'll see." Oh, this was going to be fun.

He led Tyler around to great-granny's roses that led from the side of the house. They were huge now, bushes that grew well over Tyler's head. The roses were in the last stage of their first bloom, the scent strong and familiar. "My great-granny planted these, and we've all cared for them. They lead to a—well, come on, you'll see."

The folly had fascinated him as a little boy. A little set of facades made to look like an Old West ghost town, with doors that opened into a big old circus tent. The big meeting area behind had been remade a dozen times, and it wasn't safe for the kids to play in anymore, but he couldn't tear it down.

"Oh wow." Tyler worked his way around it, eyes wide as he brushed away growth and tested what it was made of. "What is this? This is so cool."

"They used to have dances here, revivals, weddings. Bridge parties. I used to want to sleep out here, but it was already dangerous." He loved it though. There was something wonderful about it, but more than that, it was history. Their history.

"So neat. It's actually really cool just like this. Have you ever thought about fixing it up?" Tyler stepped in just a little to have a look.

"All the time, but when? I mean, maybe when I'm ninety and I'm not taking care of grandbabies and critters. One day, huh?" It was dirty and damp, and he could see where critters had been in there.

"I think it could be neat." Tyler came over and hugged an arm around him. "The roses are amazing, and they smell so good."

"They do." And this was a perfect, romantic spot to steal

a kiss, so he did. He cradled one hand behind Tyler's neck, tilted his head, and brought their mouths together.

Tyler had obviously been craving the contact. He made a soft sound and leaned right into it, fingers reaching to stroke Matt's beard.

"Mmm..." He could lay Tyler down, right here, and love him into oblivion.

"I've been watching you. You're hot as fuck taking charge out there, everyone looking up to you." Tyler's hand was warm as it slid across his back and teased him, tucking into his back pocket.

"Just doing my job, honey." But the words pleased him, heated him. He always told his girls to learn to accept a compliment. "Thank you. I'll take hot as fuck."

Tyler gave him another kiss. "Watching you do your job works for me. Like whoa."

He could stay out here all day, but the kids would start looking and, fuck, it was hot for his Yankee. "Come on, let's get you some more sunscreen."

"You could just stick me out there in the middle of the field for planes to land. Or spaceships. I glow compared to everyone else here." Tyler's hand slipped into his as he led them back around the house.

"You'll be fine. I'll keep you lubed up." Oh, didn't he feel clever?

"Promises, promises. And please don't say that in front of your parents, I've already humiliated myself today." And there was that blush again. Not as dark as before, but Tyler's skin was pale enough he couldn't miss it.

"They'll be heading home soon, I bet. I'm a grownup. They've heard worse. Jonas can be filthy when he's pushed." His brother was sharp as a razor.

"I just want them to like me." Tyler shrugged.

"Tyler!" Emma came running over. "Tyler, Noah wants to know about New York. Come tell him all about it? He's so bored sitting there. Please?"

"Sure, I can do that." He got a smile and a wink. "He probably wants to know what the bars are like."

"Tell him they're awful." Matthew scooped Em up, nuzzling her with his beard and making her giggle. "Are you having a good day, sweet baby?"

"Oh, the best. The best! Mamaw says we can spend the night if we want. She wants to make us sundresses, and she's going to take us to the store to pick out fabric."

"Gosh, Matthew. We'd miss them, wouldn't we?" Tyler teased. "Come on Em, take me over and introduce me to Noah."

"Okay." She grabbed Tyler's hand and tugged him over. Goofy girl. She had a good heart.

Hopefully no one was plotting to dunk Tyler in the pool.

13

In less than twenty-four hours Tyler had gone from having nothing and no one to Matthew's fancy ranch and more people and family around than he'd ever had in his life.

Sure, he worked in a crowded bar, but it wasn't the same. That was work. This was...life. He was used to going home to quiet and solitude. The minute he'd tried to step back a little today, a giant, scary fucking bull had tried to crash the party.

Things were winding down now, though. The girls were off with their grandparents, the cowboys were getting ready to go in for dinner, and the teenagers had been dragged home by their father.

And unlike the bar, everything was spotless and put back together like there hadn't been twenty people here an hour ago.

Matthew was in the kitchen making coffee, humming deep in his chest, wearing nothing but his jeans. It was casual, easy, and quiet.

Oh, that was exactly what he was craving. A little quiet, a lot of Matthew.

He wandered into the kitchen, also barefoot and in jeans, though his were more fitted and lighter in color than Matt's were. He liked the way Matt's sat on his hips, loose but comfortable, showing off a little fuzzy trail of hair in front that disappeared under the waistband.

He whistled softly, trying out his high school Spanish. "Hombre guapo."

Matthew chuckled and beamed, spinning once playfully before he bowed. "You want a cup? There's damn near anything you might want to drink if not."

"I'd love one." He stepped up behind Matt and slipped his hands around to those hard abs. "You made a mean hamburger, cowboy."

Look at those muscles ripple, just for him. "Mmm... thank you. Man burn meat. Thank you for chatting with Noah and his girl. They felt very grown."

"They're great kids, and they've had a hard dose of reality lately. I was happy to talk with them. Noah is crazy about her, huh?"

"Yeah. I hope she's on birth control." Matthew sighed and grinned. "He's supposed to be using condoms too, but if they're both using it, they're super safe."

"He's a smart kid, but if you ask me, she's smarter." Tyler kissed Matt between the shoulder blades and went to get the cream out of the fridge. "I think they're probably fine."

"He's hoping to be back to two-a-days by August. Rachel says it's about a fifty-fifty chance." Matt handed over his coffee. "Want to sit a while?"

"Maybe out on the porch...or one of the porches?" The house had a lot of porches. "Fifty-fifty is good. That means it's possible. I'd put money on him."

"Come to my porch. It's got a great fan." Matt led him through the man cave and the bedroom, to the little screened in porch with a sofa and a ceiling fan.

"Oh, this is great. Right off the bedroom and everything? I love this house." He let Matt sit first and then joined him, tucking himself under one strong arm. "What a great view from here too."

"Isn't it? This is my happy place, or one of them."

The fireflies started showing up, little lights flickering on and off, putting on a little show for them.

"Oh, Matt. They're so pretty. I've seen them in Central Park a couple of times, but not this many. So romantic."

"They're one of my favorite parts of summer. This is the part you remember when you're old."

"How would you know? You're not old yet." He'd gotten that vibe from Matthew in New York too. Like Matt was settled, rooted, ready to grow old. His feet didn't have roots yet. "We're just starting out."

"I don't mean I'm old, but I am... I guess looking forward to the whole thing—seeing things in fifty years. Sixty."

"I hear what you're saying." Tyler tucked a hand around one of Matt's thighs. He felt like he was always slowing Matt down. "You move fast, baby. Don't rush there. Look forward to tonight, like I am. To tomorrow. You'll get there eventually."

"I do. I know." Matthew took a sip of his coffee, eyes fastened on the land. "Pretty night, isn't it?"

He figured he'd hit a nerve and let it go. He knew too well even tomorrow wasn't promised, he couldn't look at fifty years down the line. Tyler wanted it, but that wasn't enough to make it happen. "Beautiful. Perfect."

It did make him curious though, if sitting here—sitting here with *him*—was easy for Matt, or not.

He had a thousand questions, all of them zipping through him, and Matthew sat there, and he wanted to know what was in there.

"So are you quiet because you've already moved on to some other train of thought, or because you're stuck on this one?" Not the best question to start with maybe but it was what came out. "You can tell me, you know."

"I was thinking about how everyone always says that I'm still, unless I'm moving, and if I'm moving, I'm racing."

He smiled, he got that too. "You feel like you can't win? What do you want to be doing?"

"Right now? This is perfect. I don't get a lot of chances to sit and relax."

"I believe that." He sipped his coffee and leaned a little harder into Matt, soaking in the solid comfort. He wondered how much Matt kept busy on purpose. "We'll just hope Nutterbutter stays put."

"Krissy found the fence. It'd been cut. I've got the boys watching tonight. Hopefully it was a prank." Matthew's lips tightened, and there was a quick flash of ferocity there.

"Cut? Like on purpose?"

"Yeah. There's a series of fences between the bulls and the family. The bulls and the cows. The bulls and the goats. You know." Matthew shook his head. "I mean, I even do my loading at another gate. I'm careful."

So, if it wasn't a prank it was the Flying W's reputation. That's what he was hearing. It was a pretty dangerous prank. "Hopefully just some stupid kids or something, right?"

"That's my hope. If not, someone's going to have a bad day."

"For some reason, I thought I left guns and trouble behind when I left New York." The truth was, all he knew about guns was that they killed people. He'd heard them go off several times in his life, but he'd never held one. He'd never fired one. He'd never even seen a real gun up close. Today, he'd learned they also could kill wild, dangerous animals, which was probably a good thing.

"Oh, honey..." Matthew hugged him hard. "I wish, but we live with snakes and bucking bulls, wild boar and coyotes, and to be honest, the periodic asshole that sees a nice house in the middle of nowhere with little girls in it. I'm armed because I don't know when I'll have to use it. I've *had* to fire a weapon a dozen times in my life, but it's been because I was protecting my land, my girls, my life here."

"I get it. I'm not afraid." He felt absolutely safe in Matthew's arms. He wasn't going to pretend it didn't worry him, but like the city, it was probably a bad idea to totally let your guard down here too.

"Good. I'll protect you. You're one of mine, and I'll defend my people to the ends of the earth."

He had no doubt. Anyone could see how Matt felt about those girls every time he looked at them. They were going to grow up safe and confident. "Maybe it's not too late for me to learn a few things too."

"Oh, I bet you learn a metric fuckton, in not a whole lot of time. Ranches are like tiny cities. They have their own rhythm, their own heartbeat."

"A metric fuckton." He arched his head back and grinned at Matt. "Do you kiss your boyfriend with that mouth?"

"In fact, I do. I could do a number of things to my boyfriend with this mouth." Oh, that was a naughty grin.

"Mmm. Promise?" He nuzzled Matt's chin, the fuzzy beard tickling his nose. He'd never imagined himself with—well, with anyone, but especially not with someone so fuzzy.

He loved it on Matt though. It was soft and warm and masculine.

"I do." Oh, he could listen to that deep, rich tone in Matt's voice forever. It seemed like it was his—like it belonged to him and him alone. One of Matt's hands slid over his back, dragging over his skin.

Sitting like this he could understand the appeal of thinking far ahead; of holding on to someone that long. Building something that could carry them into the future. It made more sense. He sat up so he could see those gray eyes clearly. They looked darker in the evening. "This might not sound right, because I've never said it before. I've never felt what I'm feeling right now either. But I think—I'm really pretty sure I'm in love with you."

"Oh. Still? Even with the crazy bulls and family and everything?" Matthew kissed him, the kiss painfully soft.

Still. Because of course Matthew knew before he did. He really shouldn't be surprised. He'd have laughed but he was busy right now, trying to return Matt's kiss, to understand it.

"I know they say there's no such thing as love at first sight, but they're wrong. It's not as often as the books say, but it's real. I saw you, and my heart stopped for a second." The whisper fell between them.

He didn't move, frozen by the truth in Matt's words. "You smiled. That stupid cut in your hand had to hurt but you still smiled at me. You have the most amazing smile."

"It's amazing to want to smile at someone again." Matt stroked his cheek, the lines beside his eyes deepening.

"I'd given up. I didn't want to get close to anyone again." He turned his head and kissed Matt's fingers. "But you didn't give up on me."

"No." Nothing more. Just 'no'. Matthew held his gaze,

and Tyler swore he could feel the love there, the steady belief.

"Okay," he said, as if Matthew had asked him a question. "So, we'll try really hard to be sitting right here fifty years from now, then."

"Fifty years works for me." Matthew took another kiss, this one sharp with hunger. "Then I'll work for another fifty."

Oh, he was so ready for some cowboy. "By then I'll be more useful for sure. For now, I'll stick to what I'm good at." He put his coffee down on the little side table with Matt's and climbed over to straddle Matt's thighs. "Work for you?"

Matt's gaze dragged over him, sure as a touch. "Fuck yes."

He took Matt's face in both hands, thumbs playing over stubbly cheeks, admiring. "Beautiful." He kissed Matt with intent, looking for more of that heat. Matt had done so much for him, but he didn't need help with this.

Tyler wanted to take Matt away, get him out of his head, make him lose control.

They were in an empty house. Hell, he wanted to make Matthew scream.

He slid his fingers down to Matt's shoulders, over strong biceps, across to that warm, bare chest. "No kids, no bulls, no parents, no cowboys...just me and you. And a long, perfect night."

"Oh." That single gasped word was offered with a tightening of Matt's belly, a tell-tale roll of those hips, proving how much Matt wanted him.

"That's right." His fingers traveled down to Matt's belt and worked it open. "I'm all yours. Any way you want me. Anything you want." The top button of Matt's worn jeans popped open easily, and he reached for the fly.

"I want everything." Matt's prick pushed at his zipper, like it was attempting to get to Tyler's hand.

He stroked it through the denim and then set it free, catching the full, hard weight in his fingers and caressing it gently. "Oh, baby. That's an inspiring sight."

"Jesus, you got this touch that I feel in my soul. Deep."

"Deep." The rumble in Matt's voice made him shiver and his breathing shallow and quick. Tyler pushed off Matt's knees and stood to slip out of his jeans and boxers, then tossed them on the back of the couch. "I like the sound of that."

"I do too." Matt licked his lips, then leaned down, rubbing his beard along Tyler's shaft, making his eyes cross.

He tangled his fingers in Matt's hair. "That's...whoa." Prickly. A little painful. Worth it.

"Yeah? You want more?" Matt stroked again, this time nudging his balls with the fuzzy chin.

He braced one foot up on the edge of the sofa to give Matt more room, laughing softly at himself even as Matt made him moan, blushing. He was embarrassed that it felt so good; it seemed silly, but it wasn't. It was a crazy, amazing turn-on that he never would have expected. Matt hadn't touched him with anything other than that wonderful beard, and just that little tease was making him ache.

The soft brushes continued for a few long minutes, and then they began to be interspersed with hot touches of tongue and barely-there kisses.

"Jesus... Matt." He scrabbled at Matt's shoulder for balance, fingers gripping the big muscle there as well as he could.

"Right here, honey. Loving on you." Matt dragged his tongue over the tip of his cock, pushing in hard.

Loving on him. So sweet. "Right here," Tyler whispered,

as if he couldn't believe it. He slid a hand as far as he could reach over Matt's back, curling over him. The motion made it easy it seemed for Matt to suck him in, tongue sliding over his cock, the pressure around him perfect.

"Oh fuck." He lowered his foot back to the floor so he wouldn't fall over. The wet heat, the careful friction felt so damn good. "Yes, babe. God."

Matt gave and gave, sucking him, head bobbing over him and pulling him in. Somewhere was a voice suggesting he slow Matt down, hold off longer. He was supposed to be seducing Matt, wasn't that the plan?

Fuck it. He tuned that voice out and focused on Matt's amazing mouth and the sweet need building in his balls.

He could do it after. This first.

Matt's hands found his ass, pulling him in and then easing him back, over and over.

It snuck up on him. Tyler straightened up, fingers tangling in Matt's hair as his balls drew up, and every muscle went tense. "B...babe. I..." He gasped, sucking in air, trembling on the edge of the cliff for what felt like forever, every nerve on fire. One of those hot, heavy hands cupped his balls and rolled them, pushing like Matt was demanding his orgasm.

He bucked and shot with a cry that stuck in his throat even though his mouth was wide open to let it out. He braced an arm on Matt's shoulder lightheaded from the rush and just trying to breathe.

Matt groaned, forehead resting on his belly. "D-damn, honey."

Tyler huffed, panting between words. "That's supposed to be my line, isn't it?"

"Mmhmm." Matt chuckled softly. "Been a while since I did that."

Tyler pushed Matt back and collapsed in his lap. "Could have fooled me. That was stunning. Thank you." He reached a hand between them to find Matt's prick again.

Matt wore a pleased, shocked, needy expression, and Tyler would have been impressed if he hadn't been so surprised Matt could show that much at once.

"You look a little like you forgot how much you like men." Tyler grinned, fingers curling around Matt's hungry cock and giving it a light squeeze. "Oh, this is very nice."

"I have the faithful gene. I admit it." Matt bared his teeth. "Wh-when I'm with a person, I'm all in."

"Good. I'm taking all your chips, and I'm not giving them back." He stroked Matt's length, watching his cowboy's face.

"Your hands." Matt spread and set his feet, beginning to move into his touch.

"My hands." He shifted to kneel beside Matt on the couch and tasted a hard nipple with his tongue, still pumping Matt's heavy prick evenly. "My mouth, my ass. Anything you want, babe."

"Everything. I want you, lock, stock, and barrel." Matt blinked at him, eyes dazed, unfocused. "My beautiful man."

He shifted off the couch and stood. "Hold that thought, lover. Don't... I'll be right back." He gave Matt a quick kiss and took off into the bedroom. *Rubbers...lube...*he dug what he needed out of the nightstand in a hurry because he didn't want Matt to lose that hot little high.

Matt was sprawled out, looking debauched and needy, hand working his cock in an almost lazy rhythm.

How the hell did he land...that? That gorgeous, sweet, wild, shameless cowboy. "Keeping it warm for me?" He tore the foil packer open and waved the condom in front of Matt's eyes.

"I was. I was rubbing and thinking about you."

"I like that." He gently brushed Matt's hand away and carefully rolled the rubber on without hesitation, making his intentions clear. "I do know how to ride, you know." He liked how flirty that sounded, even if it was cliche.

Matt chuckled softly, hands reaching for him. "Oh, I do thank God for that. I'm ready to admire."

He let Matt's strong hands pull him in, practically lifting him as he moved to straddle Matt's thighs. He put some lube on his fingers and kissed his lover hard as he made Matt's cock good and slippery. Matt opened up to him, tongue sliding along his, and Tyler could taste himself there, just barely.

Jesus, that was hot.

He walked his knees a little farther forward and lined up, wanting Matt to get a little taste, a little tease. "Want me?" he whispered into their kiss.

"Fucking burn for you." There wasn't the slightest hesitation in his cowboy.

"God, the things you say." Tyler leaned back and took Matt in with a heavy groan as the head of the thick cock pushed past his muscle, stretching him just right as he was still a little tender from the night before. He sank down, taking Matt in as deep as he could manage and paused a second to get a breath.

His lover wasn't making it easy. Matt's head was thrown back, cords of his neck standing out. Tyler swore he could hear the heavy muscles in Matt's forearms creak.

He started to move, gasping at the friction and the pressure as Matt filled him up. He focused, listening and watching, trying to respond to what his lover needed. The cowboy was distracting though, he couldn't ignore Matt's intensity and all that tan skin.

It didn't take long for Matt to find his hips, to tug him down and fill him, the pressure damn near overwhelming.

"Matt!" He got the message. He moved faster and took his lover in deeper, bouncing in Matt's lap as Matt pulled on him. It only took a slight rock of his hips for Matt's prick to find that perfect spot inside him and set every nerve on fire again. He rode the sensations, giving himself the jolts while Matt's hips fed the fire, slamming up toward him.

Tyler shifted his grip, one hand bracing around the back of Matt's neck and the other taking hold of his cock. He didn't have to work too hard, it slid through his fingers every time Matt moved, but he wanted to be ready when Matt was. "Fuck. Fuck, babe."

"You're gonna shoot on me, make me smell like you." Matt's words made his eyes go wide, the pressure inside him getting heavier.

"Yeah. Yeah, soon." He gulped air and came down on Matt hard, stars shooting past his vision. "No not soon, babe. N...now!" No joke. He gasped and rocked in Matt's lap, coming for a second time, as if he'd hadn't in days.

He felt Matt thrust a few more times, then a rough cry winged out, filling the air.

He leaned forward, tucking his forehead against Matt's jaw, breathing hard. That was the best sound ever; the sound of Matt, always so capable and in control, just letting go.

"Fuck. Fuck, honey. I needed that." Matt chuckled, chest moving under him.

"Uh-huh." He leaned harder, wanting more contact, wanting to be held. "Love this porch."

Matt's arms wrapped around him. "Lord, yes. It's a good place."

"Mmm. This is perfect." The ranch could go ahead and be crazy town tomorrow. They had this tonight.

Matt nuzzled his temple, humming softly. They had the sounds of the ranch—cattle lowing, the buzz of crickets, a periodic bark from a dog.

"Shower? And then a snuggle. What do you think?"

"It's a good plan, honey. Shower, snuggle, and I might let you have the remote."

"Wow. That's love." He shifted with a groan that sounded like he was ninety. If he woke up tomorrow and couldn't move he'd just float in the pool all day.

But for tonight, he was going to get his man into a nice hot shower, bundle them both into bed, and lose himself to sleep in Matt's strong arms.

14

"Lord have mercy." Matthew wiped his forehead, the back of his neck. Daddy was bringing a dozen new goats in and they were trying to all build another goat shed. The sun was beating down, and his head was with his lover in the pool.

He could use a cold drink, a dip, and a sandwich.

He really, really could.

Kris pulled up in a four by four and hopped out. "Water, y'all!" she shouted, like someone had been listening to him think. "Is now a good time for a break, Boss?"

"Yeah. It's looking good." He met her eyes. "Tell me why I run a ranch again?"

"Got me." She laughed and handed him a bottle of water. "Don't let that pretty Yankee of yours get you questioning your life choices."

"Shee-it. This land needs a Whitehead on it, and that's me, until they bury me here." Then his girls would run it—his money was on Sophia, to be honest—and his grandbabies and great-babies. The thought suited him to the bone. "Speaking of Tyler, though, I'm fixin' to check in on him, maybe get in the pool for a second."

"Must be good to be the boss," she shot back, and Matthew flipped her off.

"That's me. I spend my days eating bonbons and my nights dancing."

She pinned him with an amused look. "That's what you call it now? Dancing? Y'all had me going for my gun. I thought it was coyotes."

Oh, fuck a doodle god damn doo. He was glad he could blame his burning cheeks on the heat. "Watch it, woman. You know how many times I had to convince the girls I didn't need to take my gun and check on you and Lisa?"

Kris didn't look the slightest bit embarrassed. "Don't you just love a warm night?"

"You know it." He'd never done that before—not because Deb had been a prude, because that woman knew how to seduce a poor idiot—but because he hadn't built that porch yet.

"I'm freed up. I can stay here and finish this with the boys. What time are we expecting your daddy?"

"Give him two and a half, three hours. He's toodling." Daddy loved his wanders taking the back roads. "You make sure you drink enough water."

"Yessir. Take the ride, leave the water. There's a couple of flats back there." Kris tugged a pair of beat-up work gloves from her back pocket.

"I'll walk up. It ain't far." He grinned and tipped his hat, then headed up to the house, checking on this fence post, this horse, this momma cow on his way.

He clomped up the stairs to grab him a Coke and get in the shade.

"Marco!"

"Polo!"

Wait. Was that the girls?

"Marco!" That was definitely Ty.

"Polo!" He knew those giggles all too well.

"Are you ladies playing fair? You're not out of the pool, are you?"

Well, shit. Momma must have brought them home early. He had to find him a lady to come watch the girls during the days.

He popped open his can and wandered around to see what was what in the pool.

There was a happy but ear-splitting squeal as Tyler caught Sophia by the arm and tore off his blindfold. "Ahha!"

Sophia sighed dramatically, but she was grinning and trying so hard not to laugh.

"Daddy!" Emma hauled herself out of the pool and ran to him.

"Hey, baby girl! I'm sweaty and stinky. When did y'all get home?" He kissed the top of her head and waved to Tyler and Sophia. "Hey, y'all!"

"Right after shopping. Mamaw had a hair appointment. Tyler said it was okay for us to swim with him."

"That was super nice of him. Did y'all have lunch?" He took another drink. Lord, he was tempted to get his swim shorts on and jump in.

Tyler hung on one of the pool ladders. "I asked if they were hungry, they said not yet. Are you coming in?"

Sophia got out of the pool and walked over to get her kiss. "Tyler is good at pool games, Daddy."

"Is he? Excellent." He rubbed their noses together. "You know, I think I will. I'm hot and gross. Let me change."

It didn't take five minutes to get inside and pull off his work clothes, throw on a pair of trunks.

The girls and Tyler were chatting, holding hands and floating on their backs when he got back to the pool.

"Not even a swimming hole?"

"Nope. There are some public pools in some places, but not close to where I grew up. This is a treat." Tyler kicked his feet gently.

"So how did you learn to swim then?"

"I had a very wise mother who made sure I took lessons. She worked really hard to pay for them too."

"Daddy works hard so we can have stuff like dance lessons too!" Sophia's smile lit everything up. "It's the same thing!"

Sweet girl—he did work hard, but it was because he wanted to, not because he needed to.

"It is. You're very lucky girls. I appreciate you sharing him with me."

"No problem." Emma chuckled, the sound making Matthew smile. "There's a lot of him."

"Uh-huh. A way lot," Sophia added.

"Do not make me beat you both." He walked down into the pool, shuddering at the sudden chill.

"So mean." Tyler let go of the girls' hands and swam in his direction. "Hey, you. Did the goats get here yet?"

"Not for a few hours. Soon. The new pen is almost done though." He sank down to his chin and gasped as his heart skipped a beat. Whoa.

"It's not that cold." Tyler floated up and gave him a kiss. "You're just that hot."

"Kissing!" the girls squealed, and he laughed, spinning Tyler around before diving to get his girls. He grabbed one in each arm, squeezing and smooching before dunking underwater with them.

Emma came up wriggling. "Tyler! Help!"

"Oh no! A damsel in distress!" Tyler took her hands, pretending to pull with all his might. "Can't...break...free!"

"Harder, Tyler! The sea monster has me!"

Emma squealed, Sophia climbed up his back, and Matthew roared, playing along. This was the best game. He loved the sound of laughter.

"It's the hairiest sea monster I've ever seen! Maybe... maybe it's ticklish?" Tyler's hands landed on his hips. "Get him, Em!"

"Tickledaddy!" Emma squealed, her little fingers digging into his ribs. Damn, she could poke.

"I'm gonna get you!" He roared playfully, tackling both Tyler and Em.

"Don't splash, Tyler! It's against the pool rules!" Sophia shouted, so serious.

"Oh. Sorry!" Tyler laughed, hanging on him. "Rules, Daddy."

"Rules, huh?" He took a chance, kissing Tyler and dunking him at the same time.

Tyler tugged him down, returning the underwater kiss and sneaking in a grope the girls couldn't see. His eyes went wide, and he gasped, getting a mouthful of water.

He came up sputtering and laughing like a dork.

"You okay, cowboy? I'm CPR certified, if you need mouth to mouth." Tyler was laughing too. The little shit swam toward the ladder.

"Let's get him, girls," he whispered, swimming up to grab Tyler and spin him around, the girls grabbing Tyler's feet and tickling.

"Hey!" Tyler shouted, grinning and wriggling in his arms like one of the girls. "Hang on! I'm the guest here, is this how you treat your guests? Hey!"

Guest his ass. They'd said things that was way deeper than guest. "You're not a guest, turkey. You belong here."

"Yeah, turkey!" Emma parroted, pouncing on Tyler and gobbling at him.

"Daddy doesn't have guests." Sophia said solemnly. "Like, ever. Right, Daddy? You're new."

"He is new, but he's welcome. Family." A lover. A friend. Someone to spend years with.

"Family means I get to dive off your shoulders. Come on, Tyler!" Emma hauled on Tyler, and Tyler pretended to resist.

"I don't know, this family is kind of crazy. Do I want to be family?"

"Too late!" Emma tugged and Tyler let her win, laughing.

Sophia settled in his arms for a second. "Hey, Mr. Daddy. I love you."

"Hey, Miss Sophia-Bedelia. I love you more." He smooched her, then he took off with her, making her fly across the pool.

Krissy pulled up in her truck and hopped out, stalking over to the pool with smoke shooting out of her ears. "Hey, Boss. Sorry to interrupt, but Jimmy found another whole section of fence down and we've got strays to round up. The shed's going okay but I didn't know if you wanted to supervise that or ride out with me. Little Tim's getting the horses."

"Motherfucker. I'm coming." He met Tyler's eyes, the girls knowing not to even fuss at him about cussing. "Can you please watch them until I get ahold of Momma or somebody?"

Tyler stood and gave his arm a squeeze. "Don't worry

about calling your mom. We're fine. Do what you need to do."

"Thank you. Girls, be good." He kissed Tyler hard, then he hauled himself out of the pool. "What the fuck is going on, Krissy?"

She handed him a towel and followed him in. "This isn't kids, Boss. This is testing to see where they can get the most cattle out."

"Get the boys to move everyone to the near pasture. Leave Daniel to get the goats settled. We'll ride out and check this shit out. Stupid motherfuckers, trying to steal shit from us." He put on his jeans and boots, grabbing a T-shirt from the drawer.

"I'm on it. I'll meet you at the barn." Krissy turned and marched out.

He grabbed his phone, his .45, and an energy drink on his way out. Tyler had the babies. Sophia and Emma both knew how to call Mamaw. Shit, Daddy would be there in a couple of hours. It was all good.

They were already playing and giggling in the pool as he headed out, he wasn't going to worry about them. He could see tons of movement up by the barns as he got closer, the cowboys and horses swarming, Krissy shouting. Even Lisa was out helping where she could.

He got Violet saddled up, the black mare stamping and restless, feeding off their emotions. "It's okay, girl. We'll run."

Krissy climbed up on her Beau, a broad-shouldered bay, and came around beside him. "We're ready, Boss."

"Let's do this." He nodded to Little Tim, and they took off, trailing Tim's dust.

Assholes. Fucking asshole. He felt a dull rage build up in his chest and he swallowed it back.

He'd deal with this, then he'd go home, and they could have a couple beers and meet the new goats.

15

Hanging out with the girls in the pool was one thing, but they were all pruny and waterlogged and probably had had plenty of sun, so Tyler had hauled them inside for lunch.

"Okay." He stuck his nose in the fridge and looked around. There's a ton of leftovers, guys. What are you in the mood for?"

"Grilled cheese?" That was Sophia.

And then Emma asked. "Peanut butter and banana sammiches on crispy toast?"

"Yeah, okay." That was a no on leftovers. He looked around for cheese. He could do this. "Emma, pick a banana, please? Sophia, grab bread for everyone? I'll have grilled cheese too. Where's the peanut butter?" He put the cheese on the counter.

"Is it nasty bananas or yummy ones, Sister?"

"Yummy. Nasty bananas are for smoothies and Mamaw's bread." Sophia grabbed the loaf of bread and a tub of butter. "Daddy keeps the peanut butter up above the fridge because we ate a whole jar one afternoon and puked. We were little. He just holds a grudge."

He laughed. "I bet he does. Have you ever cleaned up peanut butter puke? Ugh. No thank you." He'd cleaned up enough at the bar to know any puke was too much puke. He looked up at the cabinet over the fridge, then went and got a chair. "Even I am too damn short. Shit. Don't tell your father I said 'damn'." *Shit*. "Or shit either."

Both girls started to giggle, the sound merry and a little wicked.

He got the jar down and put the chair back, giggling along with them. He was going to get himself in so much trouble with these two.

"Okay. Sophia, what pan does your dad use for grilled cheese? Can you get it out for me?" He found a butter knife and handed it to Emma. "You can spread the peanut butter how you like it, kiddo."

"The one on the stove. It was great-granny's. It gets hot."

The huge iron skillet sat on the stove like a monster.

"Tyler, you got to put the bananas in it and stir, don't you? And spread when it's hot?"

"I'll help you, Em. I know how." Sophia had the smugness that only an older sibling could.

"Thanks, Soph. I appreciate the help. Any tips on the grilled cheese?" Stir in the bananas? He stared at the skillet—he'd never used cast iron anything. If Sophia wanted to show off a little he'd let her. "Do I put butter in this thing, or just on the bread?"

"Daddy just puts it on the bread. Do you want a different skillet? Daddy only ever uses that one, but Momma used other ones."

"Can you show me where the others are?" He needed to

get the job done, it didn't matter if he did it Daddy's way, right?

Sophia pointed to a cabinet and he found much more familiar frying pans inside. He even dug one out with a lid. Perfect. Okay. He had this. He put together two sandwiches and tried to keep one eye on Sophia so he'd know about this peanut butter concoction the next time.

"Emma, why don't you pour some drinks for you and your sister?"

"Cokes?" Oh, that was a hopeful look.

He wanted to be indulgent because Emma was so sweet, but Matt had left him in charge, and he wanted to get it right. "Does your dad have a rule about sodas?"

Emma started to shake her head, but then she sighed. "Daddy says not for lunch or breakfast. They're not good for us."

He nodded. "He's right, they're not. But you were honest, and I appreciate that, so can you girls agree on one to share?"

"Oh...can we have a cocktail, Sister?"

Sophia nodded. "Get the orange juice."

"Did someone say cocktail? Because I am a bartender, you know." He flipped the grilled cheese in the pan grinning at the brown melty perfection.

Sophia's eyes went wide. "Oh, can you make a fuzzy sunrise? Daddy puts orange juice in Sprite and it's so fancy!"

"I can." He could do even fancier...maybe for dinner. He pulled the grilled cheese out of the pan and stuck them on plates. "Is Emma's sandwich ready? You girls sit and I'll make your cocktails. Straight down the middle or triangles, Soph?"

"Triangles." She peered at the sandwich. "You did so good! It's so pretty!"

Emma teared up. "I want a pretty sandwich too."

Oh man. Tears. *Shit. Be strong, brother.* "I'm sorry. You asked for peanut butter, Em. Maybe tomorrow?" He cut Sophia's sandwich into triangles.

"Hey," Sophia sighed, the sound long-suffering, and then she whispered. "Em, dude, breathe. I'll share—halvsies?"

Emma blinked at her sister. "Yeah? For reals."

"Sure. It'll be like lunch sandwich and dessert sandwich."

He stared at Sophia for a second, thinking how proud Matt would be of her right now. She'd saved his bacon twice by taking care of Emma, and they were just making lunch. "Thank you, Sophia, that's really nice of you." He gave her shoulder a squeeze.

Emma smiled as she took her seat and he split the sandwiches between them. "Lunch sandwich, dessert sandwich...and cocktails coming right up."

"Yay!" Emma dug into her grilled cheese, and Sophia winked at him. She was so much more grown up at ten than Em was at eight, and he had to wonder if it was because she had those extra years with her mother.

He watched them talk and eat as he made their drinks, frothing up the orange juice first with some ice in a covered bottle before pouring it into glasses and adding the Sprite. They both reminded him of Matt in different ways, even if Sophia did look more like her mom. She had Matt's way of looking after people, and Emma had his generous spirit.

He cut a slice of lime and couple of strawberries into spirals for garnish and set the drinks down on the table. "How'd I do?"

Both girls went wide-eyed, like he'd done magic.

"Oh, wow."

"Sister, it's so pretty."

"And a strawberry!"

Score one for the man that didn't know how to make peanut butter and banana.

He pulled up a chair and dug into his own sandwich, which he'd cut in half, not triangles. He was such a dork. "So we've had enough swimming for a while right? What do you girls want to do after lunch?"

"Did Papaw come yet?" Emily bounced in her chair. "Can we go see the new goats?"

He shrugged. "We can go find out."

"I want to make curtains for the playhouse." Sophia looked at him. "And take our beanbag chairs out there."

"That's an idea. Curtains will be pretty and help keep the sun out. Do you have fabric?"

"Mamaw has a whole closet full." Sophia shrugged and grinned. "She makes quilts."

"Well, let's see how the day goes. I can't drive you over there. Do you guys have summer reading or anything for school?" He always had in the city. Three or four books a summer, and challenges too, where he'd read a certain number of books and win a prize.

"We do! You know about the library?" Emma sipped her drink. "Oh, this is nummy. Do you have a library where you live?"

"I do. There's the big New York Public Library. Very famous, big statues of lions in front of it. There are smaller branches too, but this is the cool one." He pulled up a picture on his phone to show them. "See? Where's your library?"

"That's big!" Sophia blinked up at him. "Daddy buys books for our library, and Aunt Rache pays Miz Culpepper."

Emma nodded. “The library is in Uncle Jonas’s house, ’cause he lives in the city.”

“Oh! Right. He told me about all the books he sends home from the convention in the city. That’s how I met him, you know. He came into my bar after the convention one day.” His handsome cowboy had ordered a Cuervo and a Bud Light. He remembered that moment well.

“He did.” Sophia gave him the most serious look. “He went to find books, and he found you. He told Krissy you lit up the room.”

Emma chuckled. “That’s because Tyler is blond like you, Sister.”

“He did, huh?” He smiled, hoping his little bit of sunburn would cover up his blush. “Maybe because I’m so pale compared to everyone here. It was good to be found.” Man, these girls. He was falling in love fast.

“Were you scared to be alone? Like in the dark at home?” Emma asked.

Tyler looked at her, right in those little, curious, eyes. “No. I wasn’t. My mother raised me there. My friend used to live there with me. It was a place full of love. I got a little lonely sometimes maybe.” More than sometimes, but she didn’t need to know all of that.

“Oh. Is that because you’re big? I get scared alone in the dark all the time, and I have to get Daddy or Sister. Daddy’s *never* scared.”

He wasn’t so sure about that, but the faith these girls had in Matthew made him proud. Matt was a great dad.

“I was scared sometimes at night as a kid too. It’s totally normal.” He gave her hand a pat. “I was scared by the bull the other day. I’d never seen anything like that.”

“They can be scary.” Sophia sounded totally sure of

herself. "Daddy says that they're smart enough to be wicked, and that's why they're so expensive."

"I believe him. That bull definitely wanted a hamburger." He winked at Sophia.

He noticed the way Emma was watching him. "Something on your mind, Em?"

She got shy for a second and shook her head. "No."

"No? Are you sure? You want to know something about me? About New York?"

She took a deep breath. "Are you and Daddy married now?"

Whoa. That only took two days. He must have blinked at Emma a second longer than he should have, because she shook her head.

"Sorry."

"No, it's okay." *Hopefully*. He was just going to be honest. These girls were way too smart for him. "We're not married, but I understand your question. I… I do love your dad. And I know he loves me. We're not married, but we're definitely together now."

"Are you going to live here? There's room. You can keep your books in the library here."

"Em, we can't ask that stuff. That's like, grown-up stuff. Noah told me."

"Hey, you can ask. If we don't want to answer the question, we just won't. Okay? It's cool. He's your dad, so you get to know some of these things." He and Matt needed to have a parenting talk; he was flying blind here. "And I'll just be honest. I know I'm invited to stay, and I know I want to stay. So that's where it is right now." He had to get back to New York eventually to clean out his apartment and get his stuff. And how weird was it to even think about that?

"Cool. I like you. You're nice." Emma yawned. "Can we watch *Moana*, please?"

And that was that.

There was something about being eight he'd like to revisit.

"Yep. We'll watch *Moana*. Help me clean up?" He got up and headed for the sink with his plate. The girls followed him, more than happy to help, to participate.

Maybe they'd have a nap.

16

The fence was down, for sure. Someone had cut the wires over damn near fifty feet of fence.

Rage bubbled up inside Matthew, acidy and vicious. "Goddamn it! Did you see tire tracks?"

"Yeah." Jimmy gave him a wave. "They stop by that crop of rocks over there and head out toward the tree line. I'd say they drove in off the county road."

Krissy counted the boys off into teams. "Go see who you can round up, bring 'em up to Little Tim in the near pasture. Keep count and keep in touch. Jimmy, Ed, stay with us." She looked at him. "Want us to check out the tracks, Boss?"

"I do. We need to put up some barriers back here—maybe get the backhoe out here and dig it out so they can't drive out here." It wasn't like they could get the money out of them that he could. No way. So this was personal.

Fuckers.

Krissy took Ed and rode off toward the trees, leaving Jimmy with him. "If they wanted to steal the cattle, why cut the fence here? That's what I'm thinkin'. Why?"

"You think they're intending to pull them into a trailer

and run?" That made the most sense to Matthew. "They can't think they're just trying to steal random livestock. All ours are branded."

"This is a lot of fence just for letting cattle out. And everybody knows your brand. Are they just—whoa, shit."

Krissy and Ed were riding back at a good clip with a pickup on their heels that was honking and kicking up a long line of dust.

"Come on." Oh, he didn't fucking think so. This was his land. His home.

He leaned down and spurred Violet on, eyes fastened on the truck.

When the first shot came and Ed fell, it took him a long minute to figure out what the hell.

"Motherfucker!" The next two shots came from Krissy, who whirled around in her saddle and took out the truck's front tires. As the truck started to swerve, Matt caught Ed moving out of the corner of his eye and Jimmy scooped him right up, riding back toward the fence with him.

"Go! Go!" Matthew started shooting, refusing to let these sons of bitches steal anything—men, cattle, anything.

There were four of them. Given that they were with him and Krissy, it was damn near even.

Damn near.

A shot hit right at Krissy's mount's feet, and he reared, sending her flying to the ground where she all but disappeared in the tall grass. Fuck.

Matthew laid down a line of fire as he headed toward Krissy. He heard the windshield blow out, heard the cracks of return fire.

"Boss! Boss, it's Vernon."

"Who?" Fuck, did he send Violet back riderless? She was

a big fucking target, and his people would be coming for him. He sent off another shot, hearing a cry. Bingo.

"Vernon, asshole. The bastard I caught stealing straws the second day after we hired him. You had me call the sheriff?"

"Oh. Shit." Yeah, he vaguely remembered that. He'd been in the hospital with Sophia. She'd caught pneumonia and had been so goddamn sick. "You hurt?"

"Some."

Fuck. Okay. He slid down, grabbing his extra ammo from his saddlebags, and slapped Violet's flank. "Go home. Get the others."

He bent to check Krissy. "How bad is it?"

"Well. I landed—" Krissy grimaced and shook her head. "Think my shoulder's out. Not my shooting hand, that's a blessing. You want to give it a pull?"

It was definitely out; he could see it. It would be nice and purple eventually, to match the shiner she obviously didn't know she had yet.

"You got it. Hold up." Matthew held his breath, listening for footsteps and hearing only his heart beating in his ear. "Brace yourself," he whispered, then he got a knee against her ribcage and wrapped his hands around her upper arm. "Ready?"

Krissy looked away and took a breath. "Not a bit. Go."

He pulled, and she paled, but didn't say a word, didn't squeak.

"I'm going to kill you, tear those little girls apart, set your house on fire, and shoot those bulls." The voice dripped with venom, and Matthew could no more not respond to the threat against his daughters than he could decide to breathe water.

"You'll fucking try." He whipped around and shot. He

didn't monologue, he didn't play games, and he didn't have time to be anything but sure.

Even when two more shots rang out and fire spun him around, making him dizzy.

"Boss!"

"Don't let them near my girls."

17

The nap was good; all of them dozed off not ten minutes into Moana. But Tyler woke up to shouting.

He stuffed his feet into flip-flops, left the girls sleeping, and hurried out of the house to find cowboys in the drive and horses and chaos out by the barns. "What the hell?"

Were those police cars? *Shit*. Ambulances.

Fuck, fuck. "Matt?"

He scanned the mess for Matt and didn't see him, or Krissy either, but he saw Lisa and jogged that way. "Lisa! What the hell is going on?"

"There was a shoot-out, I guess? Y'all have to go the other way! Pick them up off the access road." Lisa ran past him to the cops.

What? Shoot-out? What the fuck? Pick who up?

And where the fuck was Matt?

He looked around, feeling out of place. He didn't know anybody, and nobody had time for someone so completely useless.

A truck and trailer pulled into sight, Luke in the

windshield frowning deeply. He wasn't going to have any answers but at least Matt's dad was a familiar face. He stepped up near the driver's side door and waited, feeling about as foolish as he looked.

"What the fuck is going on, son?" Suddenly Luke looked so much like Matt, that it was scary. "Are the girls okay?"

He looked back at the house which still—thankfully—looked quiet. "They were napping when I left them, so they're fine. But I just got out here, I have no idea... I don't know where Matt is. Lisa said there was shooting...? I need to know where Matt is."

Whatever was going on out here, he couldn't help. No one would let him anyway. Matt would tell him what he could do. "I'm sure he's fine. He's fine, right?"

He could feel the panic growing in his chest, rising in his throat. *Matt's fine. He's fine.*

"He'd better be, or I'll kick his branded ass. Joshua! Joshua Peters, what the fuck is going on?"

Wow. That was loud.

Someone with a badge came up. "Luke. There's been a report of a shoot-out. I need to know how to get the EMTs out there."

"Matthew?"

"That's the rumor. Please, sir. Can you get us back there?"

"Back where? Someone tell me where the hell they were!"

A cowboy ran up, a bloody streak over his cheek. "The fence was down back near the access road. That's where they are. There were four in a pickup, the boys are holding them, two are hurt. Krissy says the boss cain't be moved. Come on, Sheriff."

The sheriff and the cowboy left at a run, and Luke grabbed his phone. "Mother. Our boy's been shot. Get your ass up here." Then he hung up and stared at Tyler. "Okay, what the hell happened?"

He'd stopped hearing much after he heard Matt couldn't be moved. He'd just about stopped breathing too. He looked at Luke and blinked. "I...what?" *I was watching Moana with the girls.*

"Tyler!" Luke raised his voice, but he wasn't angry. He was just very serious, gray eyes like Matt's but older staring into him. "Why was my son out there?"

"He was—" He blinked again, his brow furrowed as he thought about it. "We were swimming with the girls, and Krissy came over and told him a big section of fence was down and the cows were out. He rushed out there with her and a bunch of the guys on horses. I told him I'd watch the girls and I—we didn't know about any of this."

"Okay. Shit's fixin' to get real for a bit. Like stepping on a fire ant hill real. Can you handle the girls?" Luke's phone started ringing and buzzing in his hand.

"Yes." Yeah, that he could do. "I can. I will. I have them." He looked at Luke's phone, not that he'd have any idea who was calling.

"Good. Thank you. Make coffee." He answered the phone. "Rache. Your brother's been shot. Don't know. Call Jonas? Tyler's staying with the girls. Yes. Gotta go. Momma, are you headed over? I need to deal with these goats."

"We can get the goats, Papaw." Sophia was standing there, white as a sheet with her sister. "Just unhook the trailer for us. The three of us can unload them."

"Oh. Girls." Tyler held his arms open for them. He wanted to get in someone's truck and go to Matt, see him and be with him. But these girls were Matt's whole world, and Matt would want them safe and cared for. He'd go. Later, he would go when things had calmed down and he knew what was going on. "We can do it, Luke. The girls will show me, and we'll get it done."

Emma came to him, but Sophia was focused on her grandfather. "You have to go get Daddy and Krissy. You *have* to."

"I'm going, girl. You get them goats in a pen and watered, okay?"

That was Matt's fierce love for his family in her.

"Yessir." She nodded. "We can do it."

Tyler caught Luke briefly. "Call when you know something? I'm in Matt's phone. Please."

"Of course. Yes. As soon as we find him, okay?" Luke started unhitching the trailer. "Aunt Rachel and Uncle Allen will probably come over to help with the feedings, but I'm not sure."

"Today is my day for the dogs, Em is doing chickens, and we'll feed and water the goats. Do I need to milk Bean and Vera?"

"Do you remember how?" Luke asked, and she nodded.

"It's hard, but I can."

"That's my girl. Y'all cowboy up now. I'll call."

Then Luke was gone, leaving him with two little girls and a trailer with a bunch of tiny goats.

"We need to get ropes and get the dogs out. They'll help." Sophia sighed softly. "Em, dogs. I'll grab some rope."

"Okay!" Emma ran off toward the house.

"I'll help." He followed Sophia, grateful for the tenacity and confidence of a ten-year-old. "You just tell me what to do. I'll learn." At the very least he could carry more rope than she could.

"You see the new pen? We're gonna have to get the little

goats over there from the trailer." She started to look a little worried. "The dogs will get them if they run and herd them back."

"Okay." *So not okay.* "We got this. You and I will, uh... kind of pen them in with the rope? Yeah? And we'll have Emma hang out by the gate and close it after they're in."

Well, this was one way to keep his mind off things.

"You think we could? They can jump some, but they're just little." Sophia led him to a garage and opened a door on the outside of the building. It was filled with rope and bits of leather and mousetraps.

"I think maybe, yeah." He had a look at the ropes and found a couple with loops already tied on the ends. "Just shoo them all in and count on the dogs to help. Teamwork, right?" Then again, they could end up with baby goats all over the place and he'd be chasing them around until sundown.

"What if we tie them all together in the trailer first? Then we'll just make them be like kindergarteners in the hall."

"Oh." He looked at Sophia and smiled. "I like it. Let's try that."

Sophia seemed pleased, and they gathered up rope. Emma was waiting with the dogs when they got back, and Sophia climbed right into the trailer and got to work. It turned out his job was mostly just making sure she didn't run out of rope.

"Emma, can you get the gate open?" He called as Sophia was finishing up.

"Uh-huh. Is Daddy okay?" That was a question he didn't want to hear.

He jogged over to her and crouched lower. "What did

you tell me earlier? Your daddy isn't afraid of anything. I haven't heard yet, so we're going to hope he is, and we're going to take care of his place like he'd want us to until he gets home. Okay?"

"Okay." Emma grabbed his hand and squeezed it tight. "I'll get the gate. We can do this. We *can*. Sister says so."

He squeezed back and winked at her, starting to believe it himself. "She's pretty smart, huh? We've got this." He kissed her forehead and jogged back to the trailer.

"Okay, Soph. Emma's got the gate. You lead, I'll help them get out. Ready when you are."

Sophia had a fierce look on her face, and she took hold of the rope, a midsized silvery looking goat at the end. "Look, goat. Your name is now Jolene. You are the leader. You and me, we're going to your pen. Now. Jolene. Come."

Jolene stared at her.

Tyler snorted, grinning. "You know, my mother used to say I was stubborn as a goat. I had no idea what that really meant until right now. Go on, Jolene! Give her a tug maybe?" Somebody got them all in, there had to be a way to get them all out.

Sophia tugged Jolene out, and then goats started spitting out the back of the trailer, bleating and shaking and being goats.

"Okay, Buttercup. Do your thing and keep them in line." Sophia sounded tickled.

"Which one is Buttercup?" Tyler brought up the rear and hustled them along. "Do they always smell this bad?"

"Buttercup is the dog, and they sometimes smell worse." Sophia tugged again, the dog nipped at heels, and they were moving. "Boy goats stink."

"Right. Sorry. Duh." The dog. Jesus, he'd seen more in

two days than in two years in New York, and he was already forgetting shit. "Get ready to close that gate, Emma."

"Ready Ty-Ty-McTyleroso!" She beamed at him, so cute.

In fact, the dogs did a lot of the work for them once they got moving, and suddenly they were all through the gate and into the new pen. "Hey!" He gave Sophia a high-five and a nonchalant little side hug. "That was a brilliant idea!" He waited for Emma to climb over the gate and gave her a quick hug too. "Okay. We'll untie them and then water, yes? And then what else did Papaw say?"

He tugged his phone out of his pocket. Still no word. No news was good news, right? He swallowed hard, forcing down the panic and worry that was roiling in his gut. Even if it wasn't good news, he had girls to look after and...dinner. And chickens. Whatever. Anything to keep them all busy.

"Dogs and chickens, then we have to make coffee and food for family and cowboys." Sophia nodded to him. "We're the ones in the big house, so we're the ones that provide."

Someone had heard that over and over, Tyler would bet.

But food for...he could make enough cocktails to go around no problem, but food? For all those people? He was going to need some help. "Your dad feeds everybody every day, huh?"

"Daddy feeds somebody every day, but when stuff is bad, that's when everyone comes, you know? It's like...it's our job —taking care of things, because we can. And if we can, we *should*."

His phone began to ring, Matthew's name coming up.

Oh, God. Please be good news.

"You ladies get water for these guys, okay?" He walked away to take the call. "Hello?"

"He's been shot twice. He's in the ambulance with Peggy

and they're heading to St. Marks. He's awake, talking, pissed as hell. Krissy is heading too. Two of the assholes are heading to the hospital, two are heading to jail."

Tyler froze a second, letting all of that sink in and trying to get a breath. Pissed off meant Matt was okay. He'd be okay.

"You got all that?"

"Yes. Sorry." Right. All business. Okay. "Thank you. The girls are fine, the goats are in, I'm about to start thinking about food, but I have no idea how to feed so many people. Who should I call?"

"Hold up. Sister, where's that chili at?" There was a muffled answer. "Get in the big freezer in the garage. There's a bunch of chili frozen. Put it in the slow cookers. There are three."

"Oh wow. Great. Thank you." He took a big breath. Maybe he wasn't going to have a nervous breakdown today after all. "Please tell Matt his girls are just fine and I—I'm... thinking about him." *And I love him.*

"I will. Thank you, son. We needed the help."

"You're welcome. Let me know if there's more news. I'm going to get dinner going." They probably could have handled this without him. One of the teenagers or someone would have been here. But it was good to hear he was useful, and even if he wasn't where he really wanted to be right now, he was in the next best place. He was here with Matt's girls. He hung up and headed for Emma. "All done here?"

Emma was covered in water, head to toe. "Yep! Doggies are fed and watered. Sophia's doing the goats."

There were worse things in the world than water.

"Tyler! Help!"

Uh-oh.

He ran to Sophia, who was on her butt in the mud next to the biggest goat he'd ever seen, a bucket and a stool upended beside her.

Worse things…like mud.

He kicked off his flip-flops rather than lose them in the muck. "What happened? Are you okay?" He offered her a hand up.

"I was trying to milk her, and she kicked me, and Daddy got *shot*!"

Oh man. "Hey. Papaw called me just now. Your dad is okay and going to get looked at in the hospital." He pulled her up and caught her eyes. "He is pissed off. And the guys are all going to jail."

"Yeah? He—he's okay? You promise to God?" Poor baby, she was trying so hard to be brave.

"The doctors have to look at him and it sounds like he's hurt, but yes. I think he's going to be okay." He tucked a stray length of platinum hair behind her ear and smiled at her. "Can I tell you something? I'm scared too. But you have been smart and kind and helpful today. Everything your dad would want you to be. It's hard, but you're doing great. You've helped me a lot."

"Yeah? I want to cowboy up. I'm just…milking goats is *hard*."

"You need some help? I'm a little bigger, it might be easier for me. We can finish together and then get you both inside to wash up. Emma's all wet too." Milking goats. Him. Peter would never believe it.

"Please. You rub with your thumbs on the sac, and then pull. If you can start her, I can help, but she's so nervous."

Together they managed it. Mostly. Sort of. There was a lot of giggling and missing the bucket, and then they had to get in. They had to make chili and coffee and clean up. He hustled the girls inside and sent them upstairs to shower, and only felt a little guilty for collapsing in a kitchen chair for a minute.

Coffee. Slow cookers. Frozen chili.

Wait for another call, or a yard full of cowboys.

Then maybe half a bottle of tequila.

18

"I want to go home, goddamn it!" Matthew had been poked, prodded, and he was done. His man and his girls were at the ranch, and he was leaving!

"Son, they have to surge on that shoulder, you know that. It'll happen in the morning, and you'll be heading home by noon." Momma was too calm for color TV.

"Give me my phone."

"They're fine. The girls are fine."

Sure, but what if Tyler freaked out? Matthew had lost his shit the first night in New York; everything had been too new, too big. Too much.

"Daddy said Tyler was fine too." But she didn't argue again, she handed his phone over with a sigh. "Don't get yourself all worked up, son. You need to get some rest."

"Are you going home?" he asked, knowing what the answer was.

"No. Your sister will be here soon to keep me company."

He rolled his eyes and dialed Tyler.

It barely rang.

"Hello? Matt?" Tyler shouted into the phone. "Hang on…just…hang on a second it's loud as hell over here."

There was a shuffling sound, and the voices faded to a dull roar in the background. "Hey. Matt?"

"How are my babies? You have them? He said he was going to hurt them." Matthew knew that it hadn't happened, but he needed Tyler to tell him it hadn't happened.

"I have them, and they're safe. They're stuffed full of chili and pie and are zoning on the couch watching TV." Tyler sighed. "Nobody's going to hurt them. First of all, there are four cop cars in the driveway, and second, I'd put myself between them and anyone who tried. Are you okay?"

"I got shot." That wasn't important. "How are you? Are you okay?" *Do you still love me?*

"It's good to hear your voice, babe. Really good. I'm fine." Tyler sounded a little revved up. "Jonas is here. There are people everywhere, trucks and cowboys, and there's more food in the kitchen than I've ever seen in one place in my entire life."

"Jonas? Lord…he's not as scary as he seems." He was just…fierce. Fierce and a little grumpy. "They're going to do surgery first thing. I'll be home by noon. Are you sure you're okay?" He wasn't okay. He didn't want to be here, have surgery, get put under. He didn't want it at all.

"I miss you, but I'm fine. I was… I was freaking out for a minute but honestly, the girls and the goats didn't give me time to think much. I wish I could see you, but I've got Emma settled, and Sophia's in a good place, and I want to keep them from worrying."

"I appreciate it. What did you tell them? Do they know I'm hurt? Did you tell them they were safe with you?" His mouth wouldn't stop running.

"They know. They have ears, and Sophia is smart. I told

them you were going to be okay and... Matt. You would have been so proud of them, Sophia especially. You were hurt and they were worried, but they knew there was work to do, and...we just got it done. We got a little muddy, but we got it done." Tyler sounded pretty proud of them himself.

"Oh, y'all..."

Momma waved to him on her way out the door. Thank God.

"Oh, honey. I'm so sorry about this. Are you really okay?"

"I'm... I'm keeping it together. I want you home. Nothing bad will happen during your surgery tomorrow, right? You'll come home to me? Promise you'll come home?"

"I swear to God. I want to come home now, but they got to take the bullet out and all. Nothing's going to happen. I'll be home." He felt sick, but he didn't know what else to do.

"Okay." He heard Tyler's deep breath and heavy exhale. "Okay. We'll be fine. Does it hurt a lot? Is anyone there with you?"

"Momma is here, Rachel. It aches, but they have it all immobilized." Whoa. Go him. That was a twenty-five-cent word.

"Sounds awful. Are you bored out of your mind? Wait. Look at this." A second later a picture popped up on his phone of his outdoor kitchen and the yard and driveway with all kinds of people milling around. "It's the most polite crowd ever."

"Show me the girls? Please? Don't wake them. I just need to see them."

"Oh. Yeah, sure. Let me go inside." The next picture was of his girls crashed out on the couch. Emma had her head in Sophia's lap, and Sophia was leaning against a pile of pillows.

He closed his eyes for a second, taking a shuddering breath. "Thank you. I want to come home."

"Krissy is home. She stopped over to check on the girls too, and then Lisa took her back to their house. She said Jimmy's going to be in the hospital for a few days but he's going to be okay." He got another pic, this one was a selfie of Tyler leaning against the kitchen counter and Tyler had put a little stamp in the bottom corner that said "I love you".

"You look good. You look like you belong there." He tried to get a selfie, and he only dropped the phone three times before he got one to send.

Tyler laughed softly. "Man, I milked goats today. Goats. Me. At this rate I'm going to be a cowboy in no time. Oh, look at you. I should let you rest. You look tired, babe."

"Not yet. Not yet. I won't sleep. I got a TV though, and there's a weird little bed here for Momma." He felt like his heart was racing, like his blood pressure was soaring.

"Okay. I wasn't really ready to let you go yet anyway. I might never be. I love you. This is crazy. Is it always this crazy?"

"This is pretty crazy, but it's a ranch. It's a ranch with a lot of moving people." It was the only life he knew. "Have I said thank you?"

"Not yet, but that's okay." There was that soft laugh again. Like Tyler was trying not to wake the girls. "Sophia saved my butt today, so you can thank her too. You can say it in person tomorrow. If they don't let you come home, I'll try to come see you."

"I'll be home. I need to come home." He hated hospitals. He hated feeling weak, and he hated not being with his family.

"That's what I want to hear. But listen. Don't worry, okay? I'm fine, the girls miss you but they're fine. They trust me, I think. Jonas is going to stay the night. We've got this. And no one is going hungry for sure."

"I'm glad you're there. You and the girls are the most important." He'd never gotten shot before. Never. He voted to avoid it in the future. It was pretty much a pain in the butt.

"And you. You're the most important too. Don't forget that, okay? Well, you and Jolene, the lead baby goat."

"Jolene the...there's a lead baby goat?" That had to be the girls' doing. Had to be. Maybe.

"Oh yeah. We had quite an afternoon unloading baby goats from the trailer. We didn't lose any. The dogs were helpful." Tyler sounded amused.

"Wow. Did someone milk? Did you say you milked the goats?" He tried to imagine this, Ty on the little stool, milking away.

"I got the milk out of the goat. I'm not sure you'd officially call it milking because Sophia and I were muddy and wet before it was over, but we did it. She says we have to do it again in the morning, so let's hope practice makes perfect."

"Lord, and no one took video? Seriously. Life is so unfair." He started chuckling, the sound bubbling out of him.

"If there'd been anyone to take video I'd have made them do the miking." Tyler laughed too. "And I don't know what Emma did. I think maybe she took a bath in the water she was trying to give the animals. She was soaked head to toe. We got good and dirty today. But everyone cleaned up fine."

"Emma is dangerous with a hose, God knows." He shifted, swallowing his groan. Fuck, that was sore.

"Are you still on the phone, son?" Momma came back

with a cup of coffee in her hand and Rachel in tow. "Sister, tell your brother to get off the phone. He's tired and he needs to rest."

Rachel looked at him, crossed her eyes and stuck out her tongue, then reached over and put Tyler on speaker.

"Tyler, quit trying to have phone sex with the injured one," she said. "He's hurt his smart hand anyway. You'll need to help him get off."

"Rachel!" Momma's voice blended with his, and then he cracked up.

"Dude, even this clueless Yankee is ambidextrous," Tyler said, louder than he needed to. "What's wrong with you?"

"There you go. Welcome to the family Tyler!"

"Honestly." Momma sat hard in her chair. "You're worse than Kathy."

Tyler laughed. "Kathy? Like, give the llamas blow jobs, Kathy?"

"That Kathy." Rachel came close and kissed Matthew's forehead. "You're flushed, Bubba. You need to lean back and relax."

"Lie down, babe. Get some rest. I need to get the girls into bed and clean this place up."

"I'll be home tomorrow to help. Sleep well. Call me if you need me."

"You do the same. Ask someone to call me after your surgery? I love you."

"Love you."

Rachel and Momma both stared at him, wide-eyed.

Fuck a doodle doo.

19

With kids and animals and Matt's ranch schedule, Tyler hadn't seen two a.m. since he'd left New York. He didn't want to be seeing it now, but he couldn't fucking sleep. He'd been alternately pacing and staring at the ceiling since he'd tucked the girls in.

That had been a long, emotional process, but he'd managed to get them both down, and once their eyes had closed, they'd crashed. It had been a long day. Even Emma, who'd been pretty anxious, was out cold when he last checked on them.

Fifteen minutes ago.

For the fourth time.

He'd tried warm milk—nasty stuff. He'd tried listening to music. He'd tried counting sheep, and that had almost worked but as he dozed off, they'd turned into baby goats and run amok, and as they all went charging off a cliff, he bolted upright, wide awake.

That was when his heart had started pounding and it hadn't stopped.

Texas was scary as fuck. Scarier than New York could

ever be. At least there he knew things. He knew his place. He understood everything. Here, he was constantly surprised, constantly off balance, constantly busy...

Charging bulls, flying bullets, people everywhere; he wasn't cut out for this shit. He picked up his phone and opened his travel app again, staring at the flight that was going out in the morning. He tapped it. It was pricey, flying last minute, but if he went while Matt wasn't home and Jonas was here to watch the girls that would be easiest.

All he had to do was tap "Book Now".

He could apologize later. Matt might even pretend to understand.

He'd been here twice before today, but this time he could do it. He could do it right now. Click the button, pack his shit, call an Uber.

Tyler sighed, shaking his head at himself. He could do it, but he would be a giant chicken-shit asshole.

He closed the app again. After everything Matt had done for him, everything that had happened, if he was going to go, he needed to stand up to Matt and explain it.

He sat heavily on the bed and looked at the empty half where Matt should be, chest so tight it was hard to get a breath. This place was crazy with Matt here, but it made no sense without Matt in it. What if Matt didn't make it through surgery? What if he was more hurt than he let on? What if those assholes came back? What if—

What was it going to take to stop his hands shaking?

He looked at his phone once more and scrolled to Matt's number. He needed to talk to Matt so bad it hurt. His thumb hovered over the number, but he knew this time that he wouldn't make the call. It was one night. Matt needed his sleep and Tyler needed to...what did Sophia say? He needed to *cowboy up*.

They'd said goodbye earlier. He'd said, "I love you". If anything happened, Matt knew. Unlike Will. Tyler would never know for sure what Will thought.

He stood up and wandered out of the bedroom again, leaving his phone behind. There was nothing that thing could help him with tonight.

He wandered out into the kitchen and peered into the stuffed fridge, shaking his head at all the comfort food. These people knew how to take care of each other, didn't they? God, what a fucking lousy day. Poor Sophia and Emma...what would he have done without those girls?

He wandered up to check on them again, laughing softly despite himself thinking about the determined little look on Emma gave him as she'd said, "We can do this". Matt's eyes in a baby face. And Sophia, trying so hard to be brave, to be the big sister, to prove something to him like his opinion mattered. He was proud of them. Genuinely proud, and he realized, with a little awe and a little wonder, that he'd miss them terribly if he went back to New York. He'd miss them because he cared about them. They'd found some little spot in his heart that he never knew wanted children and he loved them.

He stuck his head in Emma's room to watch her sleep, suddenly horrified to find she wasn't there. Heart pounding again for a different reason, he hurried down the hall and checked the bathroom, but it was empty.

He opened his mouth to call Emma's name when Sophia came shuffling out of her room with Emma in tow. "Oh..." Oh, thank God. "Girls?"

"Uncle Tyler." Sophia moved right into his arms, and Emma followed.

Uncle Tyler... Oh wow. "I'm right here. Are you okay? Did something happen?"

"We can't sleep," they said as one sisterly unit, and he couldn't tell one voice from the other.

"Me neither," he admitted. Not one wink.

"I'm worried."

"Can we call Daddy?"

"Oh, I wish we could. I almost did, but he needs his rest before surgery, and we have to be brave for him."

"I don't feel brave right now," Sophia admitted softly.

"You know what? I don't either. But we can help each other, right? I'll tell you what. Let's have a sleepover."

Emma peered up at him, eyes hopeful. "Yeah?"

"Yes. Get your favorite friends and your pillows and come on downstairs."

Emma hopped up and down and took off down the hall. "Thank you, Uncle Tyler!"

Sophia let him go and wiped tears from her eyes like she was good and done with that, thank you very much. It was as sweet as it was beautiful. "Thank you."

"You're welcome. Go get your stuff and bring Emma down okay?"

"Yes, sir." Sophia took a few steps away and stopped to smile at him over her shoulder. "Love you."

Tyler did his best not to gasp, thinking maybe his heart might explode. He managed a slow nod. "I love you too, Soph."

Nope. No airplanes. He wasn't going anywhere. Everything he loved in the world was in this crazy house, living this busy life, and taking care of each other just because that's what family did.

20

"Good eggs."

Tyler leaned against the kitchen counter, sipping his coffee and watching Jonas eat. It was oh-my-fucking-God early, and Jonas was dressed and about go do… something. Outside. Fix fences. Ranch stuff.

He hadn't slept except for a couple of desperate hours around four a.m. when his body shut his mind down for him. Otherwise he'd been awake. Like, *awake*. He'd just given everyone bowls of ice cream and they'd climbed into Matt's bed and watched *Animal Planet*. He'd stayed awake until they finally dozed off and then he'd let his eyes close too.

The girls were still sound asleep. He was only up because Jonas had knocked on the door at five thirty and asked for eggs.

"The sausage is almost done." Just the thought of real food at six in the morning turned his stomach. He was a bartender. He went to bed at four and got up at noon. But Jonas was here to work today and was doing Matt and Krissy a big favor, so eggs and sausage were happening.

Was he a bartender, though? He was pretty sure he was signing on for shoot-outs, bulls crashing picnics, a crazy huge family and milking evil goats.

And Jonas.

Talk about the polar opposite of Matthew—whipcord lean and short where Matt was tall and broad, with piercing dark eyes, fierce and angry where Matt was easy-going and joyous.

Krissy tapped on the door and let herself in. "Lord, man. What are you doing up? You don't have to wait on this asshole."

"I'm adjusting to ranch life." He tried, but he sounded about as enthusiastic as a bartender at six a.m. could be. "There's coffee. How are you feeling? Shouldn't you be resting up?" He found her a mug. At least he made good coffee.

"I'm fixin' to feed. You know you're not—Matthew didn't bring you here to cook for folks." Krissy poked Jonas in the chest. "And you. You need to stop being all imperious. You aren't the lord of this manor, dickhead."

"Pardon me?"

"You want to be all macho and shit, you go back to your fancy-assed club and be. You want to cowboy up, cook your own fucking eggs."

Oh, Jesus Christ. What now? A brawl in the fucking kitchen? "It's cool, Krissy. I got this." He said that, but he still backed up about five feet. Maybe six.

Jonas stood up, eyes icy, jaw tight. "Bitch."

"Fudgepacker."

"Carpetmuncher." Jonas stepped into Krissy's space, then he grabbed her up. "Jesus, girl. Y'all scared me."

"Sorry. Careful...watch the shoulder." Krissy's voice

sounded a little tight to Tyler, but she returned the hug like she meant it.

Thank God.

"Jesus Christ." He exhaled hard and bent over, bracing his hands on his knee and feeling a little dizzy. He'd had about enough of adrenaline for a little while. "I thought you were going to have a brawl in Matthew's kitchen. I was ready to throw this pot of hot coffee on the two of you. Fuck."

Suddenly he was moving, Krissy and Jonas putting him on the sofa and stretching him out. "Easy, boy. In and out. We were messing with each other."

"He's had a bad time of it," Krissy murmured. "The boss will kill me if I break him."

"Yeah, he's in love, and you know Matthew."

"I'm *not* broken, I'm just..." Tired. Worried. Frazzled. Maybe a little terrified. Just a little bit. He waved his hand. "Matt's in surgery. The sausages are burning." He was fine, he just needed some coffee. He'd texted Matt after he got the eggs going, but he didn't get a response. That probably meant Matt was being prepped for surgery already.

"I'll get the sausages." Krissy disappeared, leaving him with short, skinny, and intimidating.

"Matthew's going to be fine. The big doofus is too fucking lucky to die." Jonas didn't look terribly worried. "What do you think of ranch life so far? You bored yet?"

"Ha." Bored? Was he serious? Tyler stared at Jonas. "Well, let's see. In the last three days I got on my first ever airplane, rode in my first truck, had my first queso, met dozens of people—and those are just the ones you guys are related to—and another twenty or so cowboys. A bull tried to break up the cookout, my lover was shot, I got soaked in goat milk, and Matt and I had sex for the first time." He sighed. "I tried to keep two sweet little girls from fretting over their father. Oh...and then...and then some skinny version of Rambo woke me up at five thirty a.m. Do I *sound* bored?"

He sounded hysterical actually, and he knew it. He sighed. "Sorry." He tried a grin. "You're better looking than Rambo."

"Fuck, I hope so." Jonas nodded to him. "You'll be okay. Trial by fire, and that's the truth. This whole deal is just the good lord's way to make sure you got your shit together."

R u up? Matt. It was Matt.

"It's him." *Yes, babe. I'm here.*

His phone rang. "I want to come home. Send someone to get me."

"Isn't your mom there?" He looked up at Jonas, partly relieved and partly worried. "Are you allowed to come home? Are they releasing you?"

Jonas looked up from his own phone. "He's stoned, man. Just agree. He won't remember this."

Okay. That was good. Better. "You know what? Never mind. Yes. Someone will come bring you home. I promise."

"Okay. I'm real tired, and I miss the hell out of you. Do you miss the city? Do we need to get your things, honey? You got to have important things."

"Today, all I need is you. Come home, and we'll rest. We'll talk about the other things later." He did need to get his things soon, but God, that sounded so good. Some rest, with Matt. Just a little quiet.

"Sister says she's going to come to the house to meet you. I told her maybe next week. We need a couple days."

To meet him? What the hell, Matt was stoned. "Sounds great, babe. I think a couple of days to ourselves will be perfect. Don't worry about a thing. Jonas is here, and he's going to handle everything." He winked at Jonas.

"Jonas is a turd. One hell of a big brother. Oh, they say it's time, honey." Matt's voice got sharper. "It'll be about forty-five minutes, then recovery, then home."

"Tell him goodbye, son," he heard Peg say.

"I'll be here. You be good and listen to your doctors. Love you." He was going to tell Matt that every chance he got, whether Matt was going to remember it or not. Life was too fucking short for someone not to know. "Bye, babe."

"Love you. See you soon."

He heard a rustle, then Peg's voice. "It should be quick. He just needs the bullets out and repair done. He's mostly exhausted. Seriously."

"Thank you. It was good to talk to him. If he asks again, we're all fine here." He took a breath and leaned back into the couch cushions.

"Thank you for hanging in there. He had faith you would have the girls."

"I do. They trust me. Take care of him and keep me updated? Thank you." He hung up because too much more of that was going to get him all worked up again.

"Go eat your breakfast, Jonas. We got shit to do." Krissy handed him another cup of coffee. "Folks will start coming by at nine, dropping off food, looking for gossip. Can you handle that?"

Did he have a choice? "Yep. I'm good." He sipped the coffee and let the bitterness ground him. "Thanks."

Gossip. He didn't have any, so they were going to be disappointed. And where the hell was he going to put more food? He had enough to feed a crowd already, which was handy since by lunchtime it sounded like they'd have one.

"Momma will take them all home with her." Jonas nodded like he knew something. "I'm staying with her. If the girls want, they can come with us tonight, but I bet you they want to be close to their father."

"Thanks. I'd bet money Matt will want them home too." Everybody safe under one roof. He had no doubt. "Thanks for being here to help out. I'm still pretty useless around here."

"Shit, we need you here. We're three guys down, and Bubba won't relax if he thinks those girls aren't safe." Jonas met his eyes, so serious. "Those little ones are his soul. He's trusting you with them."

He nodded. "I know." He understood the trust Matt put in him, and he wasn't scared of it. He was starting to understand why Matt moved so fast too. This life didn't give you a lot of time to think about anything. He'd been here a very short time but already felt protective of Emma and Sophia.

"Uncle Tyler, where's Daddy?" Sophia rubbed her eyes, looking like death warmed over, heading for him.

Uncle Tyler. That was just so...he'd never get tired of it. He gave her a smile and fudged the truth just a little. "He'll be home in a couple of hours." He patted the couch next to him. "Say hello to Krissy and Uncle Jonas."

She went to Jonas and Krissy, hugged them both, and then came to him, snuggling right in. He pulled the blanket around her, and she sighed, almost asleep again.

He looked at Krissy and shrugged. "There wasn't a lot of sleeping in the house last night, so they're going to need a quiet day. They usually do things with dogs and chickens and... I don't even know. Can you guys handle that for them today?"

"I can." Krissy's smile was warm. "You worry about the girls and making sure the boss is comfy and settled for a few days while he recovers. We'll handle the ranch."

"Thanks. Really. That's really nice of you." Comfy and settled was about how he was starting to feel. Maybe he could get in a nap right here before people started showing up.

"Come on, lady. Let's get to work." Jonas gave her a grin and a pat on the ass.

"I will bite that hand off, Mister, and feed your skanky ho self to Lisa."

Oh, that was nice. Krissy was quick.

"So I'm a ho because I didn't show up with a truck and a bottle of tequila, move in and never leave?" Jonas winked at him.

"Yeah, that's so why. Come on, tell me stories about the big city while I work." She grabbed Jonas by one arm and dragged him out.

Tyler looked around the quiet room. God, that was so much better. He tucked the blanket higher over Sophia and sipped his coffee. He should probably sleep, but the quiet was just so nice right now.

Did he miss New York? Why did Matt have to ask him that question? He was just trying to keep his head above water here.

But it was good to know the worry was on Matt's mind. They'd talk. Sometime soon, they'd talk. First they needed to just get Matt home.

21

Matthew hurt something fierce, but he didn't so much as peep, because Momma was already panicking about him coming home so soon.

He didn't care.

He needed his house, he needed his family, and dammit, he needed his lover.

"You want anything to eat, son?" Momma asked, and he looked at Rachel, panicked. God no. Barfage.

"How about a limeade after he gets home, Momma? We can go together."

If it didn't hurt to move, Matthew would squeeze Rachel's hand in thanks.

"Oh," Momma frowned. "I don't know if we should leave Matty alone. He's going to need help."

"Momma, Tyler is there. Krissy is there. Lisa? There. Jonas? The girls? A dozen cowboys? Let. It. Go." Oh, go Sister!

Momma let out a long-suffering sigh. "Honestly, Rachel."

The car ride was quiet until they pulled into the driveway. “Do you want us to take the girls tonight?”

“Can I call? I don’t know how they’ll be.” If they needed him, he would be there for them.

“We’re home, Matty. Just ask them. No pressure, right, Momma?” Rachel’s tone made it clear there was only one right answer.

“I’m only trying to help.”

“We know, Momma.” Rachel parked and looked at them both. “You okay walking, Matt? You want me to get Tyler to help?”

“I’m okay. Seriously. I could probably have driven, but —” It had been damn good not to have to.

He eased himself out of the truck, breathing through the pain. He’d get in, have a sandwich and a pain pill, and watch TV.

As it turned out, nobody had to go get Tyler, or his girls, or any of the folks already milling around his house. “You’re home!” Tyler’s kiss was sweet and gentle on his cheek, but his girls were a little less subtle, wrapping themselves around him.

“Are you okay, Daddy?”

“We missed you!”

“Easy, girls.” Tyler sighed. “What did we talk about? Easy.”

“Do you have stitches?”

“Did you keep the bullets?”

“Do you want a drink?”

“Or a sammich?”

“Tyler, honey, please.” *Help me.*

“Girls.” Tyler didn’t shout, but his tone was stern. “Go in and clear off the couch, please. Peg? Would you…?”

"Oh. Yes, of course, Tyler. You heard him, inside, girls." Momma herded Emma and Sophia away.

"Let me clear out your kitchen." Rachel gave his good elbow a little squeeze and followed Momma inside.

"Sorry. They've been worried. Are you okay? You want to lean on me?" Tyler didn't wait for an answer, ducking under his good shoulder.

"I know. I'm home now. Glad to be here too." Tyler smelled so good—like home. He made it up the porch steps, feeling better already. "Lord have mercy, hospitals are nowhere to be."

"No. They're awful. Come in and sit, and I'll shoo everyone off." The way Tyler held him was more than help, it was care. "I've got the door."

"Thanks. I have pills to take here in a bit. I think Momma has them." If she didn't, Sister did, but someone would let him know.

"I'll get them. Couch? Straight to bed?" No one so much as said hello that he noticed as they walked in, someone must have been running serious interference.

"Couch. That way we can all four nap together. I know y'all didn't sleep either." The girls would settle with a show, and he could snuggle with Tyler. "We need a couple days of quiet, please God."

"Jonas and Krissy promised." The girls were sitting quietly on the couch on their best behavior but watched him with worried eyes as Tyler got him settled. "I'm going to get your dad his medication and something to drink. You may sit with him, one at a time, if you promise to be gentle. Emma first. Like you told me you are with Daniel, okay? Super careful."

Emma nodded, and Tyler waved her over.

"I'll be right back, babe."

Tyler went back toward the kitchen, and Emma slowly slid over next to him. She rested a little hand on his leg. “Hi, Daddy. I’m glad you’re...h...home.” He heard her hold back a sob with all her might, but her eyes were watery when she looked at him and one tiny little tear rolled down her cheek.

“Oh baby, come here. Soph, you too. My girls. I missed you last night. I didn’t sleep a wink because we all weren’t together.”

Sophia settled next to Emma, and he drew them both in, his heart slamming around in his chest.

“You’re okay, Daddy. We’ll take care of you with Uncle Tyler. We’re going to watch movies and eat snacks and relax. Together.” Sophia was trying to be so brave, so grown.

“Yeah? Perfect. I’m ready for a couple of days in our big blanket fort.”

Emma nodded and leaned against him, quiet and close. “Was the hospital scary?”

“They were super nice. I had two nurses—Van and Denise. They were the sweetest folks, and they talked to me and brought me ice, but you know what?” He made it as dramatic as he could. “I haven’t eaten since breakfast yesterday.”

“What?” Emma eyes went wide.

Sophia gasped. “Yesterday? Aren’t you hungry?”

“I am. I was thinking about a little half a sandwich. Mamaw is heading to Sonic to get me a limeade and some tater tots.”

“I’ll make you a peanut butter sandwich, Daddy. Emma, you stay here in case he needs help.”

“Okay.” Emma nodded. “I’ll keep you company, Daddy. Uncle Tyler will be back soon too, don’t worry. He’s like you. He keeps his promises.”

Oh, he loved hearing that. "Does he? Did he help you girls last night?"

"Uh-huh." Emma nodded. "Sophia said he needed help too, so we all helped each other. And then I had a bad dream, and Sophia was already awake, and we had ice cream in your bed. Uncle Tyler even put on the big TV in your room!" She perked up a little and made a face. "*Daddy*. He puts chocolate on his strawberry ice cream. Ew! Did you know that ost-er-ich-es-es can run faster than a horse?"

"Really? Because Violet's pretty fast…" God, he loved her so much that it made him a little queasy. "Where did you learn that?"

"Last night on the *Animal Planet* show. They're weird. We were laughing watching them run."

"Hey, you two. I have your meds, babe." Tyler put two pills in his palm, sat on his other side and held out a glass of water. "Your mom put the straw in, she said it would be easier."

"Thanks, honey. I'm a little clumsy with all of this mess." Stupid sling. Stupid surgery. Stupid stitches. "I'll be right as rain in a day or so."

Tyler snorted. "Yeah, okay. Those must be good drugs. You're delusional."

"Am I delusional, girls?" he asked, cracking up when Sophia appeared with half a peanut butter sandwich.

"No, Daddy. You're hungry."

Sophia balanced the plate on his knee and climbed up next to Emma.

"Take it slow, babe. See how it hits your stomach." Tyler's voice was soft, his touch lights and gentle.

"If y'all want anything from Sonic, tell Mamaw." He leaned back, telling himself he wasn't queasy, that it was just relief from being home.

"Ooh!" Emma sat up, jostling him slightly. "Come on, Sister. Let's get slushes!" Emma tugged on Sophia, who rolled her eyes but grinned at him as Emma dragged her off.

"They got burgers and corny dogs and all, honey. You ought to get whatever turns you on."

"There is so much food out there. I don't need to eat for a week." Tyler's hand tucked up under his shirt and rested hot on his belly. "You don't have to pretend like this doesn't hurt, and like you're going to be fine tomorrow. We both know that's not true."

"I'm so tired. I needed to come home to you." And that was the God's honest truth. He needed his family, his heartbeats.

"Rachel's getting everyone to go home. Jonas offered to take the girls to your mom's with him, but I wasn't sure... I thought you might want everyone here tonight."

"I think we all need to be a family tonight. We can just watch movies and eat popcorn and rest." He met Tyler's gaze, seeing the deep tired there. "We need some time, just the four of us, hmm?"

Tyler nodded, looking relieved and getting a deep breath. "Hopefully the girls will sleep now that you're home." The girls. As if Tyler hadn't been up with them. "We'll get you all drugged up and comfy in a bit so you can too."

"How's Krissy? Lisa keeping an eye on her? She's got to be tenderized." He knew that shoulder would pop in and out for the next week or so. Shoulders were weird that way.

"She's badass. She's all taped up, but she came by this morning early to grab Jonas, and she's been out there doing her thing. Jonas went out with a bunch of guys to fix the fence." Tyler shook his head. "They're...fun together."

Shit. Tyler had no idea. "Those two are like fire and gasoline. If they weren't both queer, they'd be married."

He'd seen them both tear each other up, seen them fight back-to-back in a bar fight. Jonas would kill anyone that spoke against her, and in the same breath snarl at her to cowboy up. He didn't pretend to understand them. He didn't have to. That was the good part about being family. You loved them, even when you felt like nothing made sense.

Tyler grinned. "It got a little hairy for a minute. I almost tossed hot coffee on them both. I have a whole arsenal of strategies to break up bar fights."

"Oh, honey. I'll pay damn good money to see that. Seriously. Those two sometimes need the hose turned on them—literally." Oh. Oh, fuck. That was funny as all get out. He could see them both, mad as hell and dripping.

"Jonas is a character for sure. I haven't gotten my head around him yet, but I will."

"The house is empty, and we're taking the girls to Sonic." Rachel poked her head in the room. "We'll feed them and bring them back, okay? I need to distract Momma for a bit. She's driving everyone crazy."

"Fair enough. Limeade, tater tots. What do you want, honey?" He was starting to fade a little.

"Nothing for me, thanks, Rachel."

"Oh, shut up. You're getting tater tots too." She winked and left the room.

"Quiet house. Let's get you to bed, huh?" Tyler shifted but then froze. "Or do you just want me to get you comfy right here?"

"Mmm...come to bed. The girls can find us." He hauled himself up, grateful for his core. He wasn't a bull rider, but he rode a lot, and his belly was solid.

"Wow. Those *are* good drugs. I don't think I even saw you

wince." Tyler took his hand as they headed for the bedroom. "You know your brother asked me if I was bored of ranch life yet."

"I'm surprised he didn't ask you if you were ready to leave." Jonas was his big brother, his protector (whether or not he needed it), and a giant turd.

"He got me out of bed to make him breakfast." Tyler laughed, stepping ahead of him to prop up the pillows on the bed. "And I actually did. How do you want these?"

"Oh, I'm going to kick his ass." He looked at the pillows, feeling a little overwhelmed. "Let me sit back against the headboard, and I'll get you to help me pad and prop. Sound good?"

"Sure. Whatever you need. Just leave some room on your good side for me." Tyler winked at him. "Sit."

"Yeah. Yeah. God, honey..." He shook his head and sat. He wasn't ready to talk about what had happened. Not even close.

Tyler helped him, putting pillows where he needed them for support, and stealing light kisses every time he had to lean over. Then Ty climbed up next to him so careful the bed hardly shifted. "Good?" There was that hand again, resting right on his abs.

"Yes. Jesus, it's good to be home." He kissed the top of Tyler's head. "You're okay?"

"Well. I wasn't. I've googled flights back to New York twice in as many days, but I think I'm over that now." Tyler leaned a little harder. "Your three-ring circus grows on a guy. But...this. This doesn't. This scared me, Matt. Really fucking scared me. I am not ready to add you to the list of people I've lost. No way."

"Trust me. I've never—no one's ever shot me before. No one's ever shot *at* me before." He still didn't believe it. How many people had he had to fire over the years? How many rustlers had they dealt with? And he got shot the first week Tyler was here?

His belly tightened, and for a second he thought for sure he was fixin' to puke.

Tyler rubbed his middle in slow, firm circles. "Shh. Sorry. Maybe that was too much honesty for...you're tired, you're hurting. I'm sorry. I'm fine now that you're home. That's all I wanted. I'm fine."

"I'm good. I got you. I'm sorry I wasn't here last night." He wished he could promise it wouldn't happen again, but he couldn't. It might. It probably wouldn't, but it might.

"I'm sorry you were in a shoot-out." Tyler sighed. "We don't owe each other apologies, babe. I mean, I've heard guns go off in the city a couple of times. Just never close enough that anyone I knew was involved. It's just crazy that's all. I'm glad I was here, though, for the girls. They kept me from losing my mind."

"He said—" Matthew clamped his lips shut. No. No, that would just scare Tyler and make things worse. "I'm so glad you were here. I could breathe knowing they were safe."

"He who, babe?" Tyler tilted his head back and caught his eyes. "Who said what?"

"I—Jesus, Tyler. I fired the guy for stealing. Vernon Freid. He said he was gonna tear my girls up." And he bolted from the bed, managing to make it to the commode. Pills, stress, pain—it was getting to him.

"Shit." Tyler chased after him. "Oh, Matt. I'm so sorry." He heard the water running and Tyler laid a cool damp cloth over his neck and rubbed his back. "Just breathe, babe."

"I was fucking scared," he whispered. "Krissy went down, and I thought the bastards would shoot Violet."

"They only spooked Krissy's horse. They didn't find even a scratch on him. And she'll be fine." Tyler was talking low and easy. "Your dad said all four of them are headed to jail. It's over and everyone is okay. You're going to be okay."

"I am." Cowboy up, dammit. "But damn. Y'all are my life. This is my world right here."

"We know. And we're all here." If Tyler was worried about more men coming or more trouble it sure didn't show. "We needed you home and you're here now. That's it. We're good."

"Yeah. Yeah, sorry. I'm not—I'm not all here, huh? I just need to calm the fuck down."

"We're both fried, baby. We need some sleep, that's all. Nobody can cope this...tired." The little break in Tyler's voice was telling.

"No. No, that's true." He got himself up and brushed his teeth. Lord, they needed a nap. Maybe ten. In a row.

Tyler fussed over him when he was done, got rid of the washcloth, and hustled him back to bed. "There are a dozen or more people out there, including your brother and your father, making sure things get done, and we're all safe. So you close your eyes and don't worry." Tyler sounded like he believed that, like he had faith in all those people.

"I love you." Three little words, and they didn't fix everything, but he meant them.

They fixed enough, though. Tyler's smile proved that. "I love you. That's enough for us, right? Close your eyes."

"Right. Rest." And he thought he could now. Finally. Please.

22

"Uncle Tyler." Emma whispered. Her little hand patted his cheek, and he thought about not opening his eyes because it was so cute.

He smiled, though, and blinked them open. "Hey, you. Oh, whoa." The room was dark, and the moon was up. "You okay?"

She nodded. "Uncle Jonas is going back to Mamaw's now, so he said to wake you up."

"He likes to do that." Hopefully it wasn't going to be a habit.

"We put y'all's drinks in the fridge and stuff. Mamaw said sleep was important. Is Daddy better?"

"Yeah. He's better, honey. He's just on medicine that makes him really tired." He swung his legs over the side of the bed. "Let's go say goodbye to Uncle Jonas."

"Mamaw says we can go to her house, but Sister and me want to hang out with y'all. Daddy said we could have a movie night." She took his hand. "That's going to be fun."

It would be fun, but he wondered if Matt would really be

awake long enough to enjoy a movie. "Let's talk with Mamaw and see."

He smiled and gave her hand a squeeze. All the chaos around the place was nerve-racking, but this sweet eight-year-old calling him Uncle and holding his hand was pretty awesome.

"Hey, guys." He tried to straighten his hair with the hand that wasn't holding Emma's and nodded to Jonas. "Thanks for hanging out a while. We crashed."

"No problem. How's Bubba doing?" Jonas smiled at Emma, and the expression transformed the man's face. He was still scary as fuck, but he loved his nieces.

"It's...a lot." He tilted his head at Emma. "Probably a conversation for later. But he's got some kick-ass meds that knocked him out. I don't know if he'll wake up for long, but he wants everyone home tonight. Maybe the girls could do a sleepover another night soon." He wasn't going to send Matt's girls away. They could at least have breakfast together tomorrow morning if the movie didn't work out as planned tonight.

"I would think he'd like to get his rest." Peg sounded doubtful.

"He just wants his family under one roof tonight, Peg. I'm sure you can understand that. It's been a...tough couple of days." A scary couple of days. Matt wanted his kids where he could see them. Tyler got it, surely Peg could too.

"Yeah, trust me. It's no easier when your baby is grown with kids of their own." Peg smiled and shook her head. "Y'all call if you need us. We're close."

Ouch. He sighed and nodded. "Yeah, okay. I hear you. I'll have him call you tomorrow."

"Excellent." She came and hugged him tight. "You get some rest, son. You need it too."

He hugged her back, maybe a bit too long but man, he really needed a hug. "I will. Thanks, Peg."

"I'll be back early, if he asks. Fences will be done tomorrow, and then Krissy has a whole...plan." Jonas took Peg's arm. "Come on, Momma."

"I'll bring brisket over tomorrow in the afternoon. Rolls. Maybe a cake."

Lord, in this family, food was love.

"Thanks, Peg. That would be great." He saw them out, then looked at Emma. "Where's Sophia?"

"She's upstairs singing." Emma rolled her eyes.

"Why don't you grab her, and we'll start a movie on the couch. Then if Daddy wakes up there will be room for him. Sound good?"

"Yep!" Emma trotted off.

He opened the fridge looking for that lemon pie he'd had a bite of earlier. He found it and set it on the counter. Dinner of champions. There was plenty of real food, but all he wanted was pie.

"Mmm...that looks good. Can I have something to drink, honey?" Matthew was standing there, blinking at him owlishly.

"Oh, hey, babe. Come sit. You want a Coke or water? Coffee?" Matt looked better. Still stiff, still tired, but better. "You got some color back. Did you sleep hard?"

"I did. Milk? I think I want a glass of milk." Matt smiled at him, and the expression in those gray eyes was more focused, more sure.

"I think I can handle that." He grabbed the milk and two glasses and set them on the table, then brought his pie over to sit. "The girls will be down in a minute. They're deciding what movie to make us watch."

"I thought I heard Sophia singing. So, you think *Moana* or *Frozen 2*?"

"She was singing. I haven't seen *Frozen 2* yet, let's hope for that one. We just watched *Moana* yesterday." *Was it...?* "Yesterday? The day before? God. What the hell day is it?" He laughed. "I feel like I've been here forever."

Matthew snorted, the sound bubbling in his milk, making Tyler crack up. "Me too, and I have been."

"Dork." He reached for Matt's hand and held on, giving it a squeeze. The fucking ranch had done its level best to scare him off over the last few days, and he'd thought about it. But he was still here, wasn't he? The man across the table from him was the reason why. Matt was his anchor, keeping him here, keeping him focused.

"You're still here, though. You're still hanging tight with me, dork or no."

"I'm here. I'm staying here."

There was a thundering on the stairs and Sophia and Emma ran into the kitchen, both of them coming to a sliding, clumsy halt in front of Matt instead of going right in for the hug.

Good girls.

"Morning, Daddy." They said together and then looked at each other and giggled.

"Uh-huh. Evenin', girls. How goes it?" Matthew opened his arm and offered the hug.

Sophia leaned in first. "Are you feeling better? Are you going to watch *Frozen 2* with us?"

"I am feeling better, and I said we were having a jammie night together, didn't I? I live for this stuff." Matthew hugged Sophia tight. "This is Tyler's first jammie night with us!"

"Uncle Tyler doesn't even have jammies. He wears

shorts." Sophia sounded stunned. "We have to get Uncle Tyler some jammies for next time."

"It's true. I don't own pajamas." Not since he was Emma's age.

"Olaf jammies!" Emma suggested.

"Yeah?" Tyler laughed happily. "I could rock some Olaf pa-jammies." Jammies. Pjs. Whatever.

"Olaf jammies would be cool. Or Cookie Monster. He looks good in blue."

Tyler loved that—that Matthew would compliment him in front of his kids.

"Cookie Monster is actually pretty accurate." He took a big bite of his pie, grinning. Then he got up. "Who wants popcorn?"

"Me!" Emma squealed. "Can I help? Can there be butter? Can we throw it at the TV?"

"Is there such a thing as popcorn without butter? That's called cardboard where I come from. No throwing it at the TV. Or Daddy. You find the popcorn. I'll get the pot."

He caught Matt watching him and smiled. "Are you feeling okay?"

Matt's smile was like the Texas sun. "I have my lover and my girls with me, and we're fixin' to have jammie night. I'm feeling amazing."

"All right. Let's get this party started." He pulled out a big pot and found the oil in the cabinet. Then he lifted Emma up so she could pour the popcorn in herself. "And...stop. Perfect."

He put her down and put the lid on the pot. "Sophia can you please put that carton of milk on the table back in the fridge for me?"

"Yes, sir." She bebopped over, bumping him gently. "Hey, goat-man."

"Hey, Princess Mud." He smiled at her. "I like your singing, you know. You sounded good."

Sophia turned a dark, deep red. "Y-yeah? Thank you. Daddy says I should try out for choir."

"Daddy knows what he's talking about. But you knew that already, right?"

"It's popping!" Emma tugged on him. "Uncle Tyler!"

"Try out." He gave Sophia a wink. "Okay, Em, I hear it. Popcorn soon!"

"Popcorn!" Emma's eyes were lit up as she bounced. "We're going to have a jammie night!"

"Em! Sophia! Go get your jammies on!" Oh, Matt was good at that making himself heard thing.

And the girls disappeared, just like that. "You're a pro." He gave the popcorn pot a shake and glanced over at Matt. "Do you know how beautiful you are, cowboy?"

Matt blinked over at him, obviously surprised. "Me? Now? Lord, I'm going to blow your mind when I'm dressed up fancy."

"It's not about how you dress. It's your eyes. Your smile. It's the way you look at me." A little wonder, a little heat, it was sexy as hell.

"Oh honey, there's nothing hotter on earth to me. You—you do it for me, all the way."

He gave the popcorn another shake and shut it off, leaving the lid on the counter. "I'm coming over there to kiss you. Can you handle it?" He squinted at Matt. "I'm not actually giving you a choice." He perched carefully on Matt's knees and rubbed Matt's beard with one hand.

"I'm glad you're here, honey. I—I know that it's been a fucked-up couple of days, but I swear to God, I will take care of you, love you."

He believed that. With his whole heart. "It has been a

fucked-up couple of days. That's true. But somehow, not as fucked up as my last couple of months in New York. If I had to pick, I'd redo these two days over those two months in a heartbeat. No question. So... I guess I'm gonna learn how to be a cowboy."

Maybe he should first learn how to drive.

EPILOGUE

"Come on, Daddy! We're fixin' to be late!" Emma tugged on his arm, and Matthew rolled his eyes.

"Girl, I am getting my boots on. If you want to go, go on with your Uncle Jonas." The bastard was napping in the front room, last he checked. Of course he was napping while the rest of the family was running around like chickens with their heads cut off.

She sighed and ran off. "Uncle Jonas!"

"She only thinks we're late because your parents are always early." Tyler's fingers trailed over his shoulder. "It's like your mom thinks she is going to miss something. Do I look okay? This button-down thing doesn't look weird on me?"

They'd been shopping, and Tyler had on his new jeans and boots too.

"You're the hottest motherfucker on earth." He tugged Tyler close and took a deep, hard kiss.

Tyler's squeak of surprise was gratifying, and so was the way Tyler molded right into him. "I'll take it." Tyler flushed, though it was getting harder to see now that his lover had started to tan. As it turned out, Tyler wasn't as permanently pale as he'd seemed. "You ready?"

"I can't wait, honey." He held Tyler for a minute, then headed out front. Folks were already starting to come from all over.

"I'm excited." Tyler tangled their fingers.

He'd seen bits of the restored folly, but it was Tyler's pet project, and he hadn't been allowed inside yet. School was starting up next week and the party they were hosting was sort of an end of summer celebration as well as an excuse to show off. And it wasn't small, even by his standards.

They'd laughed and swam, driven all over, gone to Austin for a long weekend, taken the girls to Houston for school clothes. No one had shot anyone.

"Here they are." Momma came right to them but stopped a few feet shy. "My goodness you both look so nice. Tyler, you clean up handsome."

Tyler blushed again. "Thanks, Peg."

"I want to thank you again, for fixing up the folly, Tyler. It's amazing. You're quite the restorer. Aunt Kathy wants you to dig through her big old storage building and see what you can make right again." Momma winked at him, her eyes dancing. "That thing is like a Tardis."

Tyler laughed. He loved how relaxed it sounded, more proof that he'd won the city mouse over. "Like a—I hadn't pegged you for a *Dr. Who* fan. We really need to have that tea you keep threatening me with."

"Maybe next week when we've got the girls in school, huh?" Of course they needed to unpack the rest of Tyler's things, make Tyler his own office and work space, have nooners like mad things.

"Next week. I'll make sure to call so I can get on your busy calendar." Momma rolled her eyes, playing.

"Daddy! Come see!" Emma was bouncing and waving.

"He really hasn't seen it?"

"Well, not officially." Tyler leaned closer to Momma. "I asked him to wait."

"My romantic boys. At least I have one set of romantics. Rachel and Jonas are just as practical as stone." Momma's eyes rolled like dice. "Come on, Emma. Let's party!"

"Another summer gone!" Emma's laugh filled the air.

Matthew leaned in, lips brushing Tyler's temple. "Our first summer."

Tyler leaned against him for a second, then tugged him toward Emma, who was waiting even more impatiently than he was. "I wonder what project I'll take on next summer?"

"Redoing my office? Learning to ride bulls? Champion goat herder?" Tyler had become the goat guy—milking, feeding, hell, even helping birth the kids.

"Me on a bull? I've only just learned to keep my ass on a horse. Can I get a belt for goats?" Tyler laughed. "Your office would be an indoor winter project. It does need a facelift." Tyler steered him over. "So you have the jail, the saloon, the little hotel...this part restored pretty well. Better than I thought it would. Sophia had to help me puzzle this one out. We made it a General Store."

"Oh, how clever. I love how y'all kept some age on it, but it looks loved." The old folly looked like a happy place now —somewhere to have a dance or a party, maybe a wedding. Somewhere his great-granny was beaming down. "I bet Texas Monthly sends someone to interview you about it."

Especially since he fully intended to make a couple of calls.

"What? Interview me? It's not even mine. They can talk to you." Tyler linked arms with him. "Come see inside. Soph says she wants to have her birthday party in here. It's pretty festive. All we'd need to do is rent this tent and some tables again."

There were already people milling about inside. There was a bar set up at one end, cocktail tables around the outside, and a hard floor in the center.

"It would make a great place for the Girl Scout Halloween party, or any of the dozens of get togethers these hooligans have." It was perfect, and Tyler seemed to just have a knack for it.

"You're a hooligan, Daddy." Emma stuck her tongue out at him.

"Uncle Tyler! You put rocking chairs on the saloon!" Sophia came running over. "For me?"

"For you, just like you asked. And the jail door works too, like you suggested." Tyler looked at him. "Soph was very helpful."

"Was she?" That didn't surprise him. Sophia had a little crush on Tyler, and that made her very careful, almost detail oriented. She was growing up, too, and this was like playing house, but with a budget.

Krissy and Lisa strolled over, arm in arm. Lisa was grinning and Krissy looked...perplexed. She pinned him with a strange look.

"I'm going to blame your Tyler for this."

Tyler blinked. "Me? Oh, man. What happened?"

Lisa beamed at him. "Wouldn't this be the *best* place for a wedding, Matt?"

Matthew stopped and blinked. "You're serious. You asked her?"

He wasn't sure who he was asking, but it didn't matter.

"She's asked me four times this week." Krissy sighed. "Four times."

Tyler laughed. "Jesus, Krissy. Answer her already."

Lisa poked Krissy in the arm. “She’s a pain in the ass. I know what the answer is. I just want her to say it.”

“Dammit, woman! Fine. *Yes*. Happy?”

“Yes!” Matthew hollered and whooped as Lisa grabbed Krissy up and spun her around. “Y’all! She said yes!”

He got a loud, cheering response for Lisa and Krissy, and as Lisa set Krissy back down, she looked right at him. “You should make it a double, cowboy.”

“Whenever Tyler’s ready. He’s already got a place at my side.” He knew he moved fast, and Tyler might never want to marry him, but the option was open.

Krissy snorted, admiring the new ring on her finger. “Whenever he’s ready? He hasn’t been ready for a single thing—not one goddamn thing—since he set foot on this ranch, and that hasn’t stopped you.”

Before Tyler could fuss, Matthew stepped in. “I don’t know. He was helping with the girls in a second, along with other things.”

Those other things were important, dammit. Vital.

Tyler laughed. “She’s right, you know. Stepping up doesn’t mean I was ready. Maybe I don’t know what ‘ready’ feels like.” His lover moved in close.

“So you’re going to wait for Tyler to tell you when to propose.” Lisa shook her head. “So romantic.”

“Leave him alone, ladies.” Tyler gave him a wink. “Go on. Go bask in your engagement glow.”

“Show me more of your project, love.” He didn’t want Tyler to feel pressured, that was all. The man’s life had changed a ton in a short period of time.

“Okay.” Tyler pulled him back outside, giving him a more detailed tour of the town. “Did you see the welcome sign?” Tyler pulled him over. The sign was painted to look weathered and bore his family name. “Welcome to the town of Whitehead. Also, you're the sheriff. Your name is on the sign at the jail."

He chuckled softly, then leaned down to whisper low. "Does that mean I get to come to you and say stick 'em up?"

He heard the soft inhale, and then Tyler replied playfully. "Of course, Sheriff."

"Mmm..." He liked that little breath, yessir. "I'll remember that."

"Doesn't seem like you forget much." Tyler took his hand. "Quit being naughty and come see Sophia's rockers." There were two of them on the hotel porch, with a little table between them. "Cute, right? She and Emma can have tea."

"That's adorable. Man, I'm going to have to watch this thing when they get a little older..." This was altogether too much alone area for frisky teenagers.

"Oh. I'll install one of those motion sensor floodlights. You'll be able to see them from the moon." Tyler grinned wide.

"You're a good man. Lights and cameras and a bullhorn." He loved that idea. "Have I mentioned I love having you here with me?"

"Once or twice." Tyler drew a circle on his chest, flirting. "You were convincing enough that I moved in."

"I'll keep convincing, keep making sure you stay." Because his heart had said, right from the get-go, that this was his man.

Tyler pulled him down and touched soft lips to his ear. "I'd say yes, you know. If you asked. I'd say yes, too."

"I have a ring for you at the house," he whispered back. "I want to marry you, Tyler. I want you to be mine, all legal and everything."

Tyler flushed, cheeks turning pink. "Well, you can ask

me later. I won't make you ask four times. I won't have to think very hard."

Feeling daring as hell, Matthew hummed softly. "Fair enough. You'll have me on my knee tonight, when we can lock the door."

"And close the windows," Tyler suggested, coyly. "So the whole ranch doesn't hear me screaming *yes!*"

Either that or they could send the girls with Momma and he could ask on their porch. It wasn't like Lisa and Krissy would be listening this time, and if they were?

Well then, the ladies would be the first to know.

Roped In
Lone Star Series, Book 2
By Jodi Payne and BA Tortuga

They say absence makes the heart grow fonder, but sometimes distance makes people drift apart.

Rope Canutt has announced his retirement from bull riding and is making the most of his final year on the circuit, riding the big shows and resting in between so he can finish the season on a high note. He isn't sure what's next for him. He has no plan yet and nowhere to go, especially since his family sold their ranch a few years back.

Jude Sharpe remembers Rope fondly from their younger days in Austin. Mostly he remembers how hot the rodeo cowboy was and how much fun they had hooking up every time their paths crossed. That was a long time ago, and Jude's been married and lost his husband to cancer in the years since they've seen each other. Now he's raising a son alone.

When bull riding comes to New York City, Jude's consulting firm uses their private box to entertain clients from Houston, and Jude brings his son Silas along to see the show. Rope is riding and Jude hopes to introduce Silas to a real bull rider. They've each lived a whole lifetime apart, and Jude and Rope aren't sure how much they have in common anymore. So will they be drawn to each other when their paths cross again?

The books in this duet are stand-alones and can be read in any order.

Buy Now!

Interested in learning more about BA's cowboys and Jodi's gentlemen? Want free fiction and news? Join our newsletters!

What's Up with Jodi

https://readerlinks.com/l/2317334

Spurs and Shifters

https://lp.constantcontact.com/su/A9CRUzp/baandjulia

Howdy, Y'all!

We want to thank you for giving Tending Tyler a try. We hope you enjoyed the story.

If you can spare a few minutes to post a review at the retail website where you made your purchase, we'd very much appreciate it!

Don't forget to "like" our Facebook pages and groups to keep up with all the news--new releases, sales announcements, giveaways, sneak peeks-- and of course the rodeo pictures, coffee memes and just general fun. We'd love to have all y'all!

Yeehaw and thanks for reading!

BA & Jodi

ABOUT JODI

JODI takes herself way too seriously and has been known to randomly break out in song. Her queer MCs are imperfect but genuine, stubborn but likable, often kinky, and frequently their own worst enemies. They are characters you can't help but fall in love with while they stumble along the path to their happily ever after. For those looking to get on her good side, Jodi's obsessions include nonfat lattes, basketball (go Celtics!), and tequila any way you pour it.

Website: jodipayne.net

Newsletter: https://readerlinks.com/l/2317334

All Jodi's Social Links: linktr.ee/jodipayne

ABOUT BA

Western to the bone and an unrepentant Daddy's Girl, BA Tortuga spends her days with her hounds and her beloved wife, having mother-daughter dates, and eating Mexican food. When she's not doing that, she's writing. She spends her days off watching rodeo, knitting, and surfing Pinterest in the name of research. Following their own personal joys, BA and Julia heard the call of the high desert and they now live in the New Mexico mountains. BA's personal saviors include her wife, her best friends, and coffee. Lots of coffee. Really good coffee.

Having written everything from fist-fighting cowboys to rural single dads to werewolves, BA does her damnedest to tell the stories of her heart, which is committed to giving everyone their happily ever after. With books ranging from heart-warming stories of found families, to rodeo cowboys that are fighting to make a mark, to fiery passionate love affairs, BA refuses to be pigeon-holed by anyone but the voices in her head.

BA loves to talk to her readers and can be found at http://batortuga.com/ and her newsletter signup link is http://bit.ly/BAJulianews

AVAILABLE FROM JODI & BA

East Meets Westerns

The On the Ranch Series

Tending Tyler

Roped In

Diamonds in the Rough

Outfoxed

The Wrecked Universe

Wrecked

Flying Blind

Special Delivery, A Wrecked Holiday Novel

Seeds and Sunshine

Pickup Man

Cowboy for Sale

The Merry Everything Series

Window Dressing

Cowboy Protection

Cowboys and Cupcakes

Thawed Out

A Present for Parker

The Higher Elevation Series

Heart of a Cowboy

Keeping Promises

Bigger Than Us

Home Free

BDSM/Kink

The Cowboy and the Dom Trilogy

First Rodeo, Book One

Razor's Edge, Book Two

No Ghosts, Book Three

The Soldier and the Angel, a Cowboy and Dom Novel

The Sin Deep Series

(set in The Cowboy and the Dom Universe)

Sin Deep

Trouble with Cowboys

The Triskelion Series

Breaking the Rules

Making a Mark

Making the Rules

Les's Bar Series

Just Dex

Hide Bound

Wholly Trinity

New Tricks

Lost Boy

The Barn Series

Zeke & Wesley

Other Titles

The Collaborations Series

Refraction

Syncopation

Puzzles Series

Cryptic

Single Titles

Temptation Ranch

Land of Enchantment

Summit Springs Sapphic (F/F) Romance

Christmas Bizarre

Honeymoon in the Cards

www.ingramcontent.com/pod-product-compliance
Lightning Source LLC
La Vergne TN
LVHW091042080826
845145LV00002B/588

* 9 7 8 1 9 5 1 0 1 1 4 7 5 *